Renascence

Bloodlines: Book One

J. Elle Ross

J.E.Ranch Publishing

ISBN (Paperback): 979-8-9914160-8-5

ISBN (Hardback): 979-8-1951938-2-9

ISBN (eBook): 979-8-9914160-9-2

Printed in the United States

J.E.Ranch Publishing

First edition June 2026

For every woman who has ever felt that life was asking her to start over,

to stand back up,

to reclaim herself,

or to become something new,

This story is for you.

Readers should be aware that this novel contains sensitive or difficult topics, especially for those who may have experienced similar trauma.

- Sexual Assault/ Drugging

- Implied Grooming

- Abduction/ Coercion

- Medical Trauma

- Psychological Trauma

- Scenes of suicidal ideology

- Violence/ Murder

These themes are included not for shock, but because they are real, and too often silenced. The heart of this book is not the violence, but the way mothers, daughters, and sisters fight to reclaim their voices and their power in the aftermath.

If any of these topics are difficult for you, please know that it is okay to step away. Take care of yourself first. And if you do choose to walk with these characters through their pain, my hope is that you also feel their strength, their fury, and their love.

Renascence: Bloodlines Book One

re·nas·cence

Noun; formal

The revival of something that has been dormant.

Renascence

"I saw and heard, and knew at last,

The How and Why of all things, past,

And present, and forevermore.

The Universe, cleft to the core,"

-Edna St. Vincent Millay (1892-1950)

Cataleya "Cat" Ortega-Reynolds

I'VE ALWAYS FELT THE pull toward magic.

Not the glam and glitter of fairy tales, but the hushed pulse of life woven into every natural thing. The subtle electricity that makes your skin tingle in empty rooms and whispers in the pause between heartbeats.

My early teens belonged to the '90s, when being a witch bloomed into something coveted and suddenly *chic*. Girls like me finally saw ourselves in the moonlit gardens of *Practical Magic*, in the quirky spells of *Sabrina*, even in the black-lipstick grins of *The Craft*. We lit candles. We cast circles. We *believed*.

And then, life happened.

Now the mirror reflected a middle-aged woman with a stretch-marked body, bills, and the kind of quiet rage that built over years of countless compromises. I blinked, and the wide-eyed girl who dreamed of magic was gone. The one who believed becoming a witch only happened to girls in coming-of-age movies, not women who'd already lived too much life.

I was wrong.

We were all wrong.

It has nothing to do with youth. It isn't about chanting the right words or burning the right herbs.

Magic is the waking of power within, the connection to the energy that hums beneath the surface. Magic reveals the secrets of nature we already feel but can't explain. Magic is healing. Magic is blessing. If you're not careful, magic can be a curse.

If you're the right person. In the right place at the right time. It doesn't knock. It *shatters* the door. What follows depends entirely on what's inside you.

Your heart. Your choices.

Magic doesn't make you who you are.

It reveals you.

ONE

Cataleya

OUR TEAM OF NURSES and doctors moved around the two-pound baby splayed out in front of us with urgent efficiency.

"FiO2 is at one hundred percent. Pressures are maxed out," the respiratory therapist called out.

We watched for any flutter of movement, any change in the monitors that continued shrieking a discordant symphony of alarms, their urgency a counterpoint to our focused calm in the chaos.

"Heart rate not responding. Continuing compressions," I said between breaths. My hands, guided by muscle memory, pumped while my mind raced, tallying the agonizing minutes. Twenty-five. An eternity in this realm between worlds.

Too long.

"Give another round of Epi," the doctor ordered.

Another nurse stepped in beside me, pushed the medication into the baby's IV line, then followed it with a saline flush. "Epi's in."

Still no change.

"Continuing compressions." I wrapped my gloved hands around the baby again, not missing the tremble in my fingers as the adrenaline coursed through them. The baby's nearly translucent skin was already a color none of us wanted to see. And way too cool to the touch.

"Hold compressions." The doctor touched my wrist. He pressed the small bell of the stethoscope to the tiny chest. Silence stretched for an aching second. Then, with a slight shake of his head, he asked for the last blood gas numbers again, though he didn't really need to. A formality, or a last plea to the universe.

"Any objections to stopping CPR?"

A room full of trained professionals and no one spoke. We all simply *exhaled,* crushed under the quiet finality of the moment with the barest of head shakes, our surrender to the inevitable.

As the alarms were silenced, the hum of the fluorescent lights and the soft whir of machines filled the void, a stark reminder of the world outside. Discarded packaging, gloves, gauze, and wrappers littered the floor, the debris of our desperate fight.

Unfortunately, we were used to emergencies here, that thin line between stability and disaster. Loss, however, was always an unwelcome and un-bearable trespasser.

"Cat," a nurse's voice, soft and tentative, broke through the stillness. "The parents of your other patient are on the phone asking for an update."

"I'll be right there." I swallowed the lump in my throat, swiping away a stray tear that had slipped free. Mourning would have to wait.

Such was the job of a nurse. We were required to go between life and death, often in the span of a heartbeat, and ideally, with a smile.

However, another pair of parents waited on the phone, their hope still burning bright, eager to bring their living child home.

I took a deep breath, then another. When I was sure my voice wouldn't shake, I picked up the handset.

"Hey, I've got good news for you."

The baseball game blared from the living room as I stepped into the house through the garage. Normally, those sounds meant home. Tonight, it was sandpaper scraping against my skin. I craved silence, a quiet moment to unburden the weight of the day.

I dropped my keys into the bowl on the entry table, kicked off my shoes, and emptied my scrub pockets.

"Hey babe, you just missed a killer play. They'll probably show another replay," Nick's voice, cheerful and distant, drifted from the couch, his eyes never leaving the screen.

I didn't answer. He didn't notice.

Barefoot, as I preferred to be, I made my way to the kitchen, where I poured a generous glass of my favorite white wine. I took two long swallows, then a third of the tart liquid, before finally greeting my husband.

"I'm going to take a bath," I uttered, pressing a quick kiss to Nick's cheek.

"Okay... Bullshit! He was out!"

I inhaled slowly, fighting the urge to lash out at the man in front of me for being clueless and insensitive. He had no idea what kind of day I'd just been through. If I wanted him to know, I'd have to articulate it, translate the unspeakable into words. But the thought of having to explain anything to anyone was far beyond my capabilities. Not tonight. Tonight, I needed to escape my reality. Even if only for an hour.

Thankfully, Jenna was out. If she'd been home, I would've had to pull it together. Slip into Mom Mode. I'd done it so many times in the past. Bury the day's sorrow and pick it up again later, if ever. Though Mom Mode wasn't the same as in years past. Jenna was grown, though she still lived at home as she made her way through what would eventually be eight years of school.

Why *did* it take as long to become an animal doctor as it did to become a people doctor?

These were the comfortable ruts we'd carved over twenty-four years together, twenty-two of them married. There was a time I found comfort in the predictability. Until that predictability ghosted what was once a bright and fierce relationship. We still slept in the same room, shared a bed. Sleeping being the only thing that happened there anymore.

I slipped into our bathroom, lit candles, and filled the tub, adding a few drops of lavender essential oil for peace and Epsom salt for protection. Things I'd learned from watching my father. Though he probably never realized he did them.

The scent rising with the steam as the tub filled did nothing to ease my weariness. I stood there, watching the swirling water, lost in impossible wishes. I wished for someone who truly understood the weight I carried, the silent screams that echoed in my soul. Which only made the ache widen, because I'd had that someone.

Salvia, my big sister, used to be the one person who could hear the pain in my voice by the way I said hello. Growing up without a mother had forged our bond, despite the four-year gap between us. Her passion was art, her days filled with beauty and creation, yet she possessed an uncanny ability to hold space for all the heaviness that I saw day to day in the medical world.

Any time of day or night, Sal would drop everything to answer my call, to offer a listening ear and a comforting presence. Usually with a bottle of wine in hand.

We still spoke practically daily. Celebrated birthdays and holidays together. Maybe we clung to those rituals for the sake of our daughters, who weren't only cousins but best friends, like we used to be.

Nick did his best to offer a focused gaze and occasional questions when I poured out my feelings about a particularly hard day at work. Mostly, he gave logical solutions and practical advice, a response that was anything but comforting, even infuriating. He worked with computers that had no living heartbeat, no breath to take. No one died in his day-to-day in the IT department. How could he ever truly grasp the weight of what we did as nurses, the constant dance with life and death?

I lowered myself into the hot bath and finally surrendered to the tears that had been threatening to spill all day. For the life that I felt slip through my fingers. For the parents who would walk out with empty arms, the nursery that would remain empty.

Inevitably, guilt crept in, a suffocating fog that would linger for days, weeks even. The same questions resurfacing, daggers to my heart and confidence. What signs could I have seen sooner? What could I have done differently?

It was a familiar script, one that would beat my mind into a pulp of insecurity and self-doubt. It always did.

By the time Nick walked into the room, I had cried myself dry, my body depleted.

"You wouldn't believe the level of stupidity I had to deal with today," he said as he readied himself for bed, oblivious. "If people just used their brains once in a while..."

"At least no one died," I whispered.

He paused. "Uh-oh. Bad day?"

A bitter laugh escaped me. "The worst."

Nick pulled a T-shirt over his head. "Babe, you knew this job would be hard sometimes."

And there it was. The sentence that tripped too easily from his lips, the type of phrase I had come to loathe.

I set my wine glass down with more force than intended. The clang of glass echoed in the sudden silence. "That doesn't make it any easier."

He blinked, confused. "No. I get that. And it shouldn't. I'm just saying—"

"You should say less and listen more," I snapped, the words sharp, laced with bitterness. I hadn't meant to say it out loud. The thought had simply burst free. "For once, just stop trying to logic your way through my pain."

"So what? You want me to just sit here and say nothing?"

"No. I want you to *feel* something, Nick. I want you to stop acting like this is just an inconvenience I'll bounce right back from."

His brow furrowed, his eyes searching mine. "I never said that."

"You didn't have to!" I shouted, rising from the tub, my skin flushed with anger. "You never *have* to say anything. Forget it. I don't know why I'm trying to explain. It's not like you actually *see* me. Not anymore."

"That's not fair," he said, his tone wounded. "I'm here, Cat. I've *always* been here."

I snapped, fueled by years of unspoken resentment. I couldn't stop it now. "Physically, sure. Emotionally? Not for years."

That landed. He took a step back as if I'd slapped him. My husband's hazel eyes stared at me, a mixture of hurt and confusion clouding them.

"I come home soaked in other people's sorrow. I carry death like a second skin. I lose babies, Nick. I hold mothers while their worlds end. And you think I can sweep it away so easily. Compartmentalize it like one of your goddamn spreadsheets."

"What do you want from me?" he shot back, his own frustration rising to the surface. "You want me to cry with you, is that it?"

"I want you to *try*. I want you to show up. I want to stop feeling like I'm married to a fucking robot!"

Silence slammed between us, thick and smothering.

Nick looked like he was teetering on the edge, unsure whether to unleash his anger or retreat into his shell.

"You don't think I feel it? This drift between us?" he said finally, his voice raw and deep. "You think it's easy to watch you pull farther away from me and not be able to reach you? I *miss you*, Cataleya."

His words struck a tender chord. Still, the part of me that had spent years swallowing loneliness remained guarded, unwilling to soften. Too many times, he would find the right words at the very end. One day, it was going to be too late. If only he could find them *before* it came down to wanting to leave.

"Then why haven't you noticed I stopped kissing you goodnight, or that I cry in the shower? Or that I pull away when you touch me?" My voice trembled. "Why haven't you tried?"

He stared at me, his face paling.

A beat passed, saturated with hard truths.

He turned away, rubbing his jaw. "I'm trying, Cat. I really am. But I'm not a mind reader."

"I don't need a mind reader, Nick. I need a partner. Someone who will walk into the fire with me. Not stand at the edge and tell me I'll be okay."

When he looked at me, really looked, for the first time in months, I saw a glimpse of the man I'd married. The one who used to pull me into his arms and kiss my forehead as if it meant something, like I was precious to him.

"I don't know how to fix this," he admitted.

"I don't know if it *can* be fixed." It was more of a confession than a statement.

Silence settled again. I stepped out of the tub, grabbing a towel to dry my shivering skin.

"Scotland. We've been talking about going for years. You've always said you wanted to see where your mom came from. Scotland would be perfect this time of year. And your fortieth birthday's coming up." He stepped closer to me, gently taking my hand, his touch tentative. "Let's go. Not because it'll fix us, but because we need a reminder of who we were. Who we can still be."

"My dad is Costa Rican. Why not Costa Rica?"

The dimple in his cheek flashed. "Because it's the middle of summer and we're already melting in this miserable Charleston humidity. It'd be nice to go somewhere for some relief. Somewhere we can breathe."

My mouth tugged into the slightest smile. My parents had gone to Scotland once, a trip shrouded in the mists of my memory. I shouldn't remember. I was only two years old. Yet, I did. Just a fragment of their return, their love even stronger than before.

My own marriage, with its dwindling passion, could use a little of that Scottish magic. More than ever. And my heart could use some rest, some time to recover from the onslaught of sorrow.

Right now, Nick looked serious enough. Though he always did. No matter the situation. Maybe this time...

"Okay," I said. "Scotland."

"Great." He kissed my cheek. "Let's go to bed. You'll feel better in the morning."

A wave of resignation washed over me. He didn't get it. Still. Nor would he *ever* truly understand.

It wouldn't *go away* in the morning. It cut out a piece of you forever. And piece by piece, you're never whole again.

Two

Jenna Reynolds

THE BLESSED AROMA OF coffee was the only thing that coaxed me from the depths of sleep, dragging me downstairs. As I descended, burnt toast, acrid and sharp, betrayed the promised bliss of that sweet, sweet coffee.

My dad, bless his heart, stood at the stove, humming way off-key, trying his best to assemble some version of breakfast.

"You're lucky Mom's not here. She'd stage a kitchen intervention." I kissed his cheek, popping the burning toast up from the toaster before I grabbed a mug and started filling it with coffee, the only unburnt survivor.

"Hey now," Dad defended, flipping what was supposed to be a pancake that more closely resembled something regurgitated. "Your mother fails to appreciate the chaos of my culinary genius."

I rolled my eyes and smiled as I took a sip of my lifeline.

"Big test today."

It was uncanny, the radar he possessed. I almost believed he really *did* know everything, as he'd claimed so many times growing up. "Yup. The big final. Then I can actually get a break before fall classes. Thrive and not just survive."

"I still don't know where you get all this grit from. You're killing it. Makes a dad proud." He turned, gifting me with one of his rare, genuine smiles.

My *grit*, my relentless determination, came from them. From watching them carve out the life they'd dreamed of through hard work and sheer force of will. Especially knowing that they'd been together since they were basically children and I had arrived early in their story. Since I had no such distractions or detours, I had no excuse to aim for anything less than gold.

"Well, kid," he said, sliding a mangled pancake onto a plate and placing it in front of me with an exaggerated bow, "here's your armor. Eat up."

⚜

When most girls turned twenty-one, they threw on something tight and sparkly, hit the clubs, and downed enough shots to forget how bad the music was. That usually meant Charleston's trendiest club, *Shadow & Silk*.

I'd never been like most girls.

Where their dressers were littered with makeup and sparkly jewelry, mine was inundated with schedules and books, my all-consuming focus.

No one landed early acceptance to one of the best veterinary programs in the country by throwing weekends away on hangovers and hookup culture. A year from now, I will have my double major in hand and be ready to storm the gates of vet school. Partying could wait until I'd made something of myself.

And bonus, because I'd never been a partier, my parents didn't worry when they left me at home. Mom's fortieth birthday was in a couple weeks, and they were planning a romantic trip to Scotland to celebrate. Though *romantic* wasn't a word I would've used to describe my parents lately. They were still together, still solid. But affectionate? It had been a minute.

Not that I planned to rattle around our empty house alone. Most likely, I'd take refuge at Tía Sal and Uncle Z's beach house, hanging out with Dahlia. Dahlia felt more like my other half than a cousin. Even our names were kindred spirits. Jenna was a bright pink dahlia, after all.

Still a few weeks shy of eighteen, clubbing was off-limits for her. If we couldn't storm the gates together, there was no point in going at all.

My twenty-first came up last month, and all I'd wanted was a low-key hangout with Dahlia. However, celebrating had to wait since she was still at Brevard in North Carolina. Same as every summer, she was studying with the best of the best. That place was practically sacred to her, a temple for prodigies like her.

When she finally came home, excited and radiant, her face lit up as she talked about her time at Brevard.

"They said my phrasing's getting more instinctive," she told me, still wide-eyed.

She made it sound easy, as if talent was just something that could be practiced into existence. I might have rolled my eyes, but there was no denying the palpable intensity that surged through her as she played. The way her voice could still a room. The way every song she touched became a living thing.

When we finally got to ring in my twenty-first year, we made a pilgrimage to the liquor store, where I legally purchased my first six-pack. White Claws, because apparently, that was what all the girls raved about, and of course, lots of snacks. We took the longer scenic route back down the coastal roads. Windows down, Dahlia drumming her fingers on the dashboard like the world itself was her metronome. She never could sit in silence. It was in the tap of her heel, the hum under her breath, the rhythm of her laugh.

We shared the snacks and White Claws as we lost ourselves in the Marvel Universe. Which proved to be a treacherous decision. Nothing like a sugar-fueled hangover to remind me that the party life and I were not allies.

Another reminder of what I wasn't missing out on was some of the pricks that lived and died in those clubs. Specifically, people like Jared Allon, who was currently assaulting my vision.

He leaned against a wall at the front of the classroom, talking to a girl who clearly didn't realize she was being played.

It was bad enough that I'd needed to take Organic Chem, the bane of my existence, as an accelerated summer course to stay on my strict, self-imposed schedule. And then *he* showed up.

Why the hell did he have to take *this* accelerated summer course? Wasn't he pre-law? Surely pre-law didn't require organic chem. Did it?

At least today was our last day. The final exam. If the universe possessed even a shred of mercy, soon I'd be free from his orbit forever.

Bile was actually frothing up, the bitter taste building at the back of my throat. My eyes ached from the constant rolling, a physical manifestation caused by the obnoxious performance I was witnessing.

Parents with money and influence. A flashy smile. Zero soul behind the eyes. There was usually a foundation on which stereotypes were built. Jared was a prime example of one of them. He thrived on validation and manipulation, dropping names and pickup lines with equal skill. And somehow, girls ate it up. He possessed that cocky, frat-boy charm, a smoke-screen that hid his desperate overcompensation for a lack of genuine depth.

He wasn't repulsive. Unfortunately, he was unfairly attractive, at least until the massive ego erased it.

My way of giving him the benefit of the doubt was assuming he had some tragic, twisted origin story that would explain his vileness. In fact, I'd once stumbled upon a glimpse of that theory.

"Dad, it was a C, not exactly flunking. Stanton & Royce still want me for their summer program."

Jared had burrowed into a hidden alcove, shielded from prying eyes. His face was a mask of controlled fury, his jaw clenched. One hand gripped the phone, the other pinched the bridge of his nose.

"I know it's important..."

Another pause.

"My grade in some obscure class is not going to affect your position with them... I don't think I need to worry. I bring in plenty of product... It won't... well, if it did, maybe that wouldn't be such a horrible thing... I do appreciate... I'm not being ungrateful. Look, I have to go."

I hurried past, quickening my steps when I overheard what was clearly a private unraveling. Usually, Jared was the embodiment of confidence and swagger. Yet here he was, groveling to someone higher on the food chain.

He ended the call, shoving the phone into his pocket. His posture snapped back into place when he saw me, his smile sliding back on.

"Hey... you," he said, feigning nonchalance. "Rough night?"

A scoff and an eye roll escaped me. "Gee, thanks." I kept walking, not bothering to engage further.

Only once had he offered a morsel of humanity behind the carefully constructed facade.

I'd stopped at the campus café for my usual Americano only to find the line snaking out the door. Five minutes stood between me and the class run by a professor with a zero-tolerance policy for tardiness. Coffee was nonnegotiable. There was no way I'd get through his monotone drone without it. Ahead of me, Jared's eyes met mine. I looked away immediately, desperate to avoid any interaction. He turned back.

By the time he had ordered, tapped his card, and collected his two drinks, I was still trapped, at least five people behind in line. As he passed, he handed me an Americano, my exact order, and kept walking. No flirting, no pickup lines, insults, or expectations of gratitude. He'd simply handed it to me and left.

Still. It wasn't enough to change my mind. My intuition screamed warnings at the mere sight of him. Intuition triumphed over pretense every time.

By divine intervention, the professor finally released us. I packed up my notes quickly, shoving them haphazardly into my backpack, and bolted for the door, only to find Jared blocking the escape, still engrossed in his attempt to get into this girl's pants.

I stood there. Waiting. Glowering. My expression screamed annoyance.

"It would be great if you could continue your conversation elsewhere and let the rest of us leave."

He glanced at me sideways, that smug smirk twisting. "My apologies." His eyes trailed up my body with a casual leer that made my skin crawl before finally meeting mine. He slowly moved aside.

I prided myself on being the anti-violence type. Yet my first instinct was to punch that arrogant face. I shoved past him, the weight of his stare following me out.

THREE

Nick Reynolds

T HE DIGITAL GRIND OF the day had sanded my nerves raw, each line of code a tiny abrasion. Ten hours staring into the abyss of debugging left a man questioning not just his choices, but the very architecture of his life.

By the time the truck shuddered to a stop in the driveway, my brain was a motherboard fried beyond repair. All I looked forward to was the Chinese food I'd picked up and a couch that didn't silently judge me.

I killed the engine and lingered in the truck a second longer, suspended between worlds, listening to the rhythmic hum of cicadas and the faint thump of music leaking from Jenna's bedroom window upstairs. Probably some sad indie artist named after an obscure spice.

God, I was getting old.

Inside, I dropped my keys into the ceramic bowl by the door. "Anyone still alive in here?"

"You got the dumplings, right?" Jenna's voice floated down from the staircase.

I held up the white paper bag as if it were sacred treasure. "Your savior has arrived."

She padded down in her usual college-girl uniform. A giant hoodie—how in this southern summer heat?—bike shorts, and bare feet. Like mother, like daughter.

"Did you get veggie ones this time, or am I going to be disappointed? Again?"

"Mock me all you want, kid. I'm the reason the fridge isn't a wasteland of protein bars and expired oat milk."

A grin flashed as she stole the bag, peeking inside. "Okay, fine. You get one gold star."

"Just one?"

"Don't push it."

We stood shoulder to shoulder at the kitchen island, passing the boxes back and forth, half-arguing over who got the last dumpling. Her phone buzzed. She ignored it.

"Dahlia?" I asked, mouth half full of lo mein.

"No, it's just this girl from Org Chem. She also got into NCSU. You think I'm driven? This girl is already halfway through the syllabus. Her last text was about parasitic infections in goats. Riveting stuff."

"I can't believe I spawned a future goat doctor."

"Veterinarian," she corrected, raising a brow. "Also, yeah, goats are cooler than people most days."

I smiled. Truth was, these quiet moments with her, casual skirmishes of words and shared food, were some of the only parts of my life that were still normal. Solid.

Cataleya walked in, her hair wet from a shower, barefaced, her skin flushed from the steam. She still stole the air from my lungs. Though apparently she needed a lot more convincing than just my word.

"Hey," she said, her tone flat.

"Hey," I echoed.

She pecked my cheek, a gesture of habit more than intention, then poured a glass of wine, the clink of glass a sharp note in the quiet. No inquiry about dinner. No meeting of eyes.

Jenna's gaze flickered between us, then cleared her throat. "I'm gonna, uh, take this upstairs."

She vanished, a swift and strategic retreat. Smart kid.

I leaned against the counter, watching my wife sip her wine. The shadows beneath her dark eyes looked like bruises, worry lines etched into her forehead.

"Rough shift?"

"Yeah." She massaged her temples. "Twenty-eight-week twins came early. They're fighting."

"You okay?"

A too-quick nod. "Just tired."

Always tired. Her mantra to shut me out.

"You all packed yet?" The question was clumsy, desperate even, for connection.

She blinked. A flicker of confusion passed across her face. "Packed?"

"For Scotland?" I forced a chuckle. "You know, Highland cows, castles, marital rekindling?"

Recognition dawned. "Oh. Right. I'll do it tomorrow."

I offered her a tepid grin. "Just making sure you're still coming with me."

Her lips twitched. Almost a smile. Almost. "I'm coming, Nick."

We stood there a beat too long in that weird, brittle silence. I hated it. Hated the ache of missing her when she stood within arm's reach.

"I was thinking," I began, grasping for anything lighter, "we rent a car. Get lost in the Highlands. No plans. Just us and a tragically outdated GPS."

Cataleya hesitated, then nodded. "Yeah. That sounds nice."

It wasn't exactly enthusiasm. I'd take what I could get.

Later, when the house had gone quiet, I sat hunched over my desk, trying to finish a script for work. My fingers hovered uselessly over the keyboard. The cursor blinked, the code blurred, and all I could think about was how I no longer understood the woman I used to know better than myself.

It wasn't that I feared she no longer loved me.

It was the terrifying possibility that *she* didn't know if she did anymore.

FOUR

Cataleya

I WAS STANDING AT *a window, forehead pressed to the cold glass. My breath fogged the pane, blurring the gray morning beyond. Through the mist, something moved, swift and desperate.*

A woman burst from the treeline, *barefoot in the bracken, her long brown hair whipping behind her like smoke. She ran as though something unseen was chasing her, her dress torn and streaked with red. Blood or earth, I couldn't tell.*

Behind her, another figure emerged from the fog. Her golden hair caught the pale light like flame from under the dark hood. Her posture calm, almost graceful. In her hand, she carried a torch. And power. It shimmered faintly, bleeding light through her fingers.

The fleeing woman stumbled, gasping, turning toward her pursuer. Her face came into focus through the veil of mist. Tear-streaked, fierce with fear and disbelief. Eyes gray-blue as stormwater, wide and searching. Eyes I recognized. My mother's eyes. Eyes she'd inherited from her mother.

My breath caught. I didn't know her, but she felt familiar.

The other woman slowed, closing the distance with an almost tender smile. The fog bent around her, drawn to her like worship. Her voice carried through it, soft yet cutting.

"You can't hide from what you are, Ivy."

Ivy. My grandmother's name struck an echo inside my bones.

Ivy backed away, shaking her head. "You don't have to do this."

"Oh, but I do," the golden-haired woman whispered, and lifted her hand. The air rippled. The trees shuddered. The ground between them glowed a deep, pulsing red.

The world went still. The fog rolled forward like a tide, swallowing them both. A vibration pulsed beneath my fingertips, the glass humming softly against my skin. Then everything fell away.

I woke with a sharp inhale, tangled in the hotel sheets, my heart thudding hard enough to make my ribs ache. The Glasgow morning seeped in, pale and thin around the curtains, as the tingle from the dream still echoed.

"Just a dream," I whispered to no one. Beside me, Nick shifted in his sleep, then slipped back into a soft snore.

The clock on the bedside table blinked 7:04 a.m. The day before my birthday. Forty.

I let out a shaky laugh and rubbed my face. Great. Leave it to my brain to decide that forty required fog, blood, and reminders of maternal abandonment. The mother who left, the grandmother I never got to know, and apparently, some blonde stranger thrown in for good measure.

Still, I couldn't shake the image of her, the calm one with that halo of golden hair, who looked like she already knew how the story would end.

I got up, shaking off the strange dream, determined not to start my fortieth year already losing my mind.

***

Fog veiled the rooftops of Glasgow. The city, ancient and proud, blurred into a watercolor of gray stone and verdant hills. Even in August, the Scottish summer was a stark contrast to the Charleston heat we'd left behind.

"We've been in Scotland for eight days," I said, pulling an extra blanket around my shoulders, "and we've only gone to battle sites and lots of pubs, which have been amazing, don't get me wrong. Let's expand our horizons and tour some of these castles we keep passing everywhere. Do some hiking, or something that feels historical. This place has some of the most majestic trails and waterfalls in the world." I stared out the window of our new hotel room, where the towers of the relics disappeared into the mist.

Nick didn't look up from his phone. "We're on vacation. Why would we want to go do extraneous activities that are mostly exercise? Besides, preseason starts tonight. We can hit up the pub and see if they'll turn it on for us."

I tried not to gape at my husband. He had never balked at physical activity before. Usually, I could barely get him to relax.

"Seriously, Nick?"

"What?"

I rolled my eyes and shook my head with a sigh. "I grabbed these brochures from the lobby. They have a bunch of day tours that leave from here."

"We can do that. I was just messing with you."

"Mhm."

"I was. Besides, it's your birthday tomorrow. You get to pick our agenda."

"Well, this one looks interesting," I murmured, thumbing through the glossy brochure. The brochure pictured a deep, narrow gorge with lush green moss covering the rocks, and a small waterfall cascading into a dark red pool. It looked like something out of a fairy tale, or maybe a horror movie. "The Devil's Pulpit. Beautiful." The words were mostly for myself, but the truth was, something about the image snagged on my soul, tugging me forward with irresistible force.

"Come on, let's head to the pub. Catch the game, get some food."

"Yeah, sure."

Sitting in a pub older than our entire country, I sipped my wine and watched Nick. My husband, my high school sweetheart. It was a staggering thought that by this time tomorrow, I would be forty. Time had a way of vanishing when I wasn't looking, and somehow, I'd arrived at middle age.

How did we get here so fast?

We'd both worked our asses off to reach our version of making it. I saw my father, Diego, in the way Nick leaned over his glass. That same relentless, rinse-and-repeat work ethic forged in grease and car engines. My family had come a long way from the quiet Appalachian town we'd fled for a fresh start in Charleston. Salvia had practically raised me during that transition, acting as the mother we didn't have while I was still too young to even remember the mountains we'd left behind.

Then came Nick. The tech-obsessed rebel, a grade above me, who'd stolen my heart. We'd traded vows the second the law allowed, and by nineteen, my world was defined by the weight of a baby girl in my arms.

And not long after that, the crushing stack of student loans for a nursing degree. I loved my career in the NICU. Those fragile babies were my life. But tonight, my heart was restless.

I studied my handsome husband, the way a bit more salt was creeping into his pepper these days. The hazel depths of his eyes reflected the emotions he otherwise maddeningly concealed. The mischievous curve of his lips, hinting at a playful nature. I loved my husband. Truly, I did.

But I wanted more. Not a different life, just more *within* the one I had. I wanted to feel that mind-blowing, all-consuming passion. The kind that burned my skin, leaving my body desperate for his touch.

"What's up?" Nick was looking at me, that lopsided smile stretching across his face.

"Just thinking about how old we got all of a sudden."

"*We*? Speak for yourself. I'm just getting started, baby."

"Really?" I teased in my most seductive voice, looking at him over the rim of my glass as I took a sip. "Well, why don't you show me back in our room?"

"Are you flirting with me, Mrs. Reynolds?"

"Perhaps, Mr. Reynolds."

"All right." He grinned, taking a long swallow of his beer before glancing back at the TV. "Ten minutes left in the half. We'll head out then."

So much for hot, passionate, and spontaneous.

The drive from Glasgow to Finnich Glen, also known as the Devil's Pulpit, was supposed to take forty minutes. From my window seat on the bus, I watched the Scottish countryside stretch wide, rolling hills wrapped in green patchwork, wild heather, and stone walls winding across a land unchanged by time.

I pressed my fingers against the glass, longing to touch it, to become one with a land that was both foreign and strangely familiar. The need so visceral, my chest tightened with yearning. The land whispered to me, calling me home. I took it all in, not wanting to miss anything, while Nick napped next to me.

Finally, we pulled into the car park of a charming little shop. I elbowed Nick. "Wake up, Sleeping Beauty."

"That was quick," he said, wiping his face and looking around.

"I bet." I shook my head and nudged him.

We followed the small group into the cutest village store I'd ever seen. Straight out of a storybook. The bright white walls and black roof contrasted with a bold red door welcoming us. Inside, lavender florals and sandalwood incense filled the air. Dried herbs hung from the ceiling. Jars, bottles, and crystals glittered on dark oak shelves. I drifted toward the back, past the touristy souvenir gifts adorning the front windows.

Then I saw the book.

It sat on a pedestal carved with a massive Tree of Life. Its weathered leather cover was embossed with intricate knots. It looked centuries old and was thicker than any book I'd ever seen. My fingers hovered above it, trembling with the need to touch it.

As I reached out, a woman stepped out from behind a curtain.

A bolt of awareness froze my hand in midair. A recognition clicked into place inside me.

The woman stopped as well, her warm brown eyes looking at me with the same cognizance. The air was vibrant around her, pulsating. Her mass of curly light-brown strands escaped taming, flowing freely past her shoulders, more whimsical than unkempt. Like her.

Seconds passed as we looked eye to eye with each other. Finally, the woman smiled, wiped her hands down the front of her puffer vest, then stumbled over nothing as she approached me with her hand stretched out.

"Sheesh. Here I am, tripping over my own feet. Again. Hello there. I'm Kelly. Is there anything I can help you find?"

The sweetest Scottish brogue came from Kelly as she smiled at me. Though I'd never seen this woman in my life, the feeling that she'd been a lifelong friend warmed me. *So strange.*

I blinked, still stunned. My mouth refused to form words, all thoughts vanishing from my head.

What the hell was wrong with me?

I had to clear my throat to find my voice as I shook Kelly's hand. "Sorry. For a second, I thought I knew you," I told her and laughed. "I'm Cataleya. Cat. I was just poking around. My husband and I are with the group for the Devil's Pulpit tour."

"Fantastic. I'm your guide. Come, I was just about to give you all the history of the pulpit, and then we'll head out," Kelly said, her brogue lilting like music.

I watched her walk to the others gathered near the front, that familiarity still holding me in its grip. I followed a magnetic pulse pulling me toward her.

So strange.

FIVE

Cataleya

THE STEPS DESCENDING INTO the glen, if you could call them that, were steep and slick with wetness. Rich green of the cavern walls contrasted against the rushing water, so red it looked as though rubies sparkled beneath the surface. The hum in my chest, the way the canyon was alive underfoot, pulled at me, *called* to me.

Nick had already started making his way through the water, around the rock walls to the other side. I stood in place with my eyes closed, feeling the energy pulsing around me. My breathing quickened, coming faster than before, and it wasn't because of the climb down.

I opened my eyes and took off my shoes so that I could wade through the water to the mushroom-shaped boulder on the other side. The need to put my hands on its smooth, moss-covered surface yanked me toward it.

The red water chilled my ankles and calves, numbing my toes even in the warmth of August. I trudged through, the coldness of the water evaporating as electrical currents licked at my skin. The sound of the others faded. Their voices, laughter, and conversations disappeared. All that remained was the hum of energy, ancient and wild.

Finally, I made it to the shoreline next to the massive boulder, its energy vibrating beneath my skin. Not imagined. Not metaphorical. Real. My heart thundered with it.

I rubbed my hands together, gathering the courage to touch it, to feel it under my palms. I reached out and placed my hands flat on the red boulder. My pulse pounded, a raging river in my ears. The vibration strengthened, quivering through my hands and into my body.

I know this place.

I've always known it.

The thought repeated itself over and over.

"Cat?"

A faraway voice pushed into my thoughts.

"Cat," it said again, adamantly this time.

The vibration diminished as the voices of the group came back over my roaring pulse. I opened my eyes to see Nick staring at me, a bewildered eyebrow cocked.

"You good?" he asked, moving toward me.

"Huh? Yeah. I'm fine. I was just listening to the stone."

Listening to the stone? What was I saying? A pleasant buzz bubbled through me, loose-limbed and warm despite the cold. I managed to give Nick a reassuring grin as I took my hands off the boulder.

Just behind him, I caught a glimpse of Kelly. She was watching me, too, with an understanding expression on her face.

After the tour of the pulpit, our group hiked back to the shop for some shopping time before we were supposed to pile back onto the bus. I wasn't ready to return. I wanted to stay longer, see this place, this town. *Needed* to.

After the last purchases had been made and the other couples waited at the bus, Nick found me loitering around the back of the shop, looking toward that book again.

"We have to go. They're waiting for us."

"Can we stay? Just one night. I'm sure we can catch a taxi back tomorrow. We can go to that cute little pub across the way, explore the village."

Nick looked skeptical. "All our stuff's at the hotel."

"C'mon. What happened to getting lost in the countryside? Remember when we used to fly by the seat of our pants, go where the wind carried us? We used to be fun. Besides, *you* said I could pick what we do today since it's my birthday." I must have been going out of my mind. I didn't do this type of thing, at least not for a long time. And he was looking at me like I was as crazy as I felt. "Please?"

"Is there even a place to stay around here?" Nick looked out the front windows of the shop as if he'd be able to see some kind of hotel from here.

"Actually, there is," Kelly said as she stepped out from behind the register. "I have a friend who runs a B&B just up the road. Quiet. Cozy. Great breakfast."

"Will they let us just ditch the bus?" Nick looked apprehensive, yet also like he was bending.

"Sure, why not? I'm sure people do it all the time. Go tell the driver we're staying for the night." For the first time in far too long, genuine excitement rose. It took everything in me not to jump up and down and clap my hands like a child.

Nick glanced between us. "Okay. I promised you would run the show today. Happy birthday." Nick kissed my cheek and walked out to talk to the driver.

"This little town may change your life," Kelly said, smiling in that knowing way she'd had at the pulpit. "I'll give my friend a call and tell her to ready a room for the two of you."

"Thank you. Before you go, can I ask what that book is back there? It's so mysterious," I asked, pointing to the giant book on the pedestal.

"*Leabhar de Bristeadh-Cridhe*. The Book of Heartbreak. It is a record of those accused of witchcraft from the 1500s and beyond." Her eyes clouded with sadness as she walked over to the book, carefully opening it. "Each name diligently recorded. A tribute to remember the shameful evil that once shook our homeland."

There were lists of names, three columns wide on each page. Thousands of names. All of them whispering to me.

"May I look through it? My mother was Scottish. From what I know of her, she had hippie tendencies. One could say she was witchy." The spark of a memory flickered, then was gone again before I could grasp it.

"What was your mother's maiden name?"

"Auchter."

Kelly raised an eyebrow. "Auchter? Interesting. That's not a name I hear often anymore." Her mysterious, all-knowing smile returned. "Here. Look through these. They're listed alphabetically. I'll be around if you have questions." She left to attend to someone who had just walked in.

Finally alone, my mouth went dry, and my palms worried the hem of my sleeve. A thin line of sweat dampened my hairline as my half-formed thoughts scattered. What if what happened at the pulpit happened when I touched the book? What that was exactly, I had no clue.

Nerves had my fingertips tingling as I reached for it. I placed my palm on the page, like I'd done with the stone in the pulpit.

Nothing happened.

No humming, no zaps of energy. I laughed at myself as I read through the names, the handwriting sometimes difficult to decipher.

"I'm kind of bummed. I don't see any relation here. It looks like I'm not a descendant of any witches after all. I was so hoping, too," I said to Kelly when she returned a few minutes later.

"You're looking in the wrong place if you're trying to find true bloodlines. That book is filled with the names of innocent women accused."

"True bloodlines? As in *real* witches?" I asked, intrigued.

"I'm always talking about real witches." She walked over to a shelf of books, scanned the titles, and pulled out a slim book.

I trailed my fingers over the slim volume Kelly handed me. It felt lighter than the heavy Book of Heartbreak, but the air around it seemed to hum.

"We call ourselves the Awoken," Kelly said, her voice dropping to a conspiratorial level that made the hair on my arms stand up. "Hollywood loves the flick of a wrist and flying chairs. Though that would be fun, the truth is much quieter. Really, it's just basic science."

"Science?" I let out a dry laugh, thumbing through pages filled with sketches of herbs and geometric patterns. "I'm a nurse, Kelly. This doesn't look like any of the science I know."

"Then you know everything is made up of energy," she countered, leaning closer. "Energy makes up atoms. Atoms make up matter. And matter makes up all living things. Women who are Awakened can manipulate that energy. We learn to catch it in ways that others can't."

I looked at the book, then at her. "And men? They don't... catch it?"

"They carry the spark, but they don't light the fire." She shrugged, a small smile playing on her lips. "Men cannot be Awakened themselves. They're more like the bridge between generations. The longer a bloodline goes without a daughter, the more concentrated the lineage. It stays dormant, waiting for a female heir to claim it. The same goes for an Awoken who never finds her power source in her lifetime. She will carry it to the next generation."

A sudden, sharp image of Salvia flashed in my mind. Her white-hot temper, the way she could command a room just by walking into it.

"What about sisters? Would both be able to become Awoken, or could only one of them be the lucky one? And if this is about bloodlines, if those sisters were of mixed heritage, which wins out?"

"Like *you* and *your* sister?"

I chuckled. "Sure. We are Scottish and Costa Rican. And my sister has always been a force of nature. She is all fire bottled up."

Kelly laughed, a bright sound that broke the tension. "Scottish and Costa Rican? Lord help the man who crosses the Ortega sisters."

"I'll say," Nick said behind me as he looped an arm around my waist. He planted a kiss on my temple, oblivious to the talk of energy manipulation. "Cat is the calm one, but Sal? She's a hothead."

"This has been such a great experience. Definitely my favorite part of this trip so far. Thank you for the fun story. It was actually really beautiful," I said, handing the book to her.

"Yes, well, every story starts with truth. Keep it. Read it. A birthday gift." Kelly pushed the book back. "Go on, explore some more. I'll call my friend Kait about your room. By the way, tonight is not only a full moon, but a supermoon and a seasonal blue moon. Since it's your birthday, going to the pulpit for a night swim might prove... interesting," Kelly added, her eyes twinkling.

Six

Jenna

Most Friday nights, I went with Dahlia to Joe's. A bar that, from the street, looked like a forgettable hole-in-the-wall. On the inside, it pulsed with soul.

Joe's was a local legend, a haven for Charleston's best hidden talents. And none shone brighter than Dahlia.

As beautiful as Dahlia was, she was downright hypnotizing when she played, her voice nothing short of spellbinding. I'd teased Dahlia that she came out of the womb singing instead of crying.

Dahlia wasn't even close to drinking age, but she was so ridiculously gifted that Joe Jr., the current owner, looked the other way.

We loaded her special, aka very expensive, keyboard and her favorite acoustic guitar into the backseat of my car. Both of which she played effortlessly. Not that I was biased. Juilliard hadn't hesitated in snatching her up, knowing what kind of talent she possessed.

"You ever wonder what your parents think you're doing hauling off your big-ass keyboard every Friday night?"

"I just tell them I'm with you. They don't question it." Dahlia shrugged as she tossed sheet music into her bag.

"Gee, spoiled much? My parents would hound me for every detail."

"What you call spoiled, I call trusted. It's not like I'm a storm stirrer."

"You mean shit stirrer."

"No, I meant storm."

I just looked at her. The eye-roll I'd held back probably didn't disguise the annoyance on my face.

"Hey, don't blame me if your parents know you're a troublemaker at heart."

"Oh. My. God. I am not. When have I ever done anything *bad*?"

"Well, then I guess we're both saints," she teased. "Let's go. I'm gonna be late for sign-ups."

"Joe would save you a spot if you were two hours late. He practically drools at the crowd you pull." I got into the driver's seat, pausing as Dahlia buckled her seatbelt. "Here's a crazy thought. You could always tell your mom what you do on Friday nights. Your parents would probably be in the front seats."

"We've talked about this." As usual, Dahlia wouldn't look at me when I brought the subject up.

"You're crazy good. Why can't you just talk to her, let her see how incredible you are?"

"Jenna, you already know why." Dahlia's gaze veered up at a light on the second floor, her mother's home studio.

"As I've said before, and I'll keep saying, I think you should give her a chance. If she dogs on you, then we both have our answer. I really don't think she will."

"My mother chases perfection all day, every day, for the galleries. She's known for her impeccable taste. Her own paintings are flawless, yet she says they're trash. If that's how she sees her work, imagine what she would think of me." Dahlia's voice got low, a familiar sadness etching her words, as her shoulders curled in.

"You're both cracked as far as I'm concerned. Both of you are talented beyond measure. But fine. We'll keep doing this your way. Until you're discovered and become this stupid famous singer-songwriter, and the world finds out what I've known all along."

"To become one of those, I have to actually *get* to the venue and perform."

"We're going. We're going."

⁂

Joe's was packed, standing room only. People even braved the heavy, damp air out on the patio just to listen through the speakers.

Coming with the talent had perks. Our same bar-top table was reserved for us each week, where we'd sit and watch those who braved open mic nights. Some good. Some not so much.

I usually ordered a soda, and Dahlia would sip on her water. No bubbly anything before performing. She said it made her *burpy* and *phlegmy*, whatever that meant. Dahlia always closed. Joe made sure of that.

When she finally stepped onto the stage, her keyboard already in place, her guitar sitting next to it, the room shifted. The lights dimmed until only the string of Edison bulbs glowed above her, a halo of warm starlight. The crowd hushed. Even the clinking of glasses quieted.

Then she played the first haunting notes of "Creep," her own arrangement. Just her voice and the piano, all heartbreak and longing. My favorite thing to do was to glance around, watching people fall under her spell. A few even wiped away tears.

She was magic.

Then I saw him.

Jared Allon stood in the shadows near the stage, watching Dahlia. The *hunger* in his stare, the way he never took his eyes from her, froze the blood flowing through my veins.

While everyone else swayed and sighed, caught up in Dahlia's voice, Jared was leering, as if she were a prize to possess, a challenge to achieve.

Dahlia sang four songs, two revamped covers and two originals. She picked up her guitar and closed with her acoustic rendition of "Sweet Child o' Mine." Still, I couldn't tear my eyes away from Jared, waiting. Bracing for what he might do.

As she thanked the crowd, he was already moving in. I pushed past clusters of people, trying to reach her before he did. He got to her first.

I expected to see fear on her face. Unease.

Dahlia was smiling.

Jared leaned in, saying something I couldn't hear. It was obvious from the look on his face that he was working his usual charm.

She laughed. *Laughed*. Sweet, naïve Dahlia had no clue.

I slipped my arm through hers, becoming her human shield, cutting her off as she turned to answer him.

"Sorry. Didn't mean to leave you alone. It's crazy in here tonight." I turned to Jared, locking eyes. I did my best to give him the look that told him with no uncertainty that Dahlia was not, in fact, alone, nor would she be for the rest of the night. He glanced at me, recognition flashing in his eyes.

"Long time no see. Org Chem, right?"

"That's right," I spat, not bothering to hide my contempt. I turned my attention to Dahlia, who was looking at me like I'd completely lost it, embarrassing her beyond measure. "Ready?"

"Um, no, I wasn't." Her eyebrows furrowed at me. To prove her point, she slowly turned back to Jared.

"Before you go, how about an encore just for me? 'Sympathy for the Devil.' is one of my favorites."

"Fitting." I scoffed, not quietly. This earned another hard look from Dahlia over her shoulder.

"No can do. I'm not a jukebox." Dahlia patted Jared's arm and gave him one of her sweetest smiles as she went to move past him to pack up her equipment. Jared slid in front of her, blocking her path. Apparently, his signature move. I rolled my eyes, heat climbing up my neck. Before I could unleash on him, letting him know exactly how and where he could move his ass, Jared started talking again.

"Those things are heavy. Don't want those pretty arms getting sore. Let me be the muscle."

"These pretty arms are stronger than they look. They can haul those instruments while carrying a tote full of sheet music and still manage to throw a decent right hook if needed. Thanks for the offer, though."

I bit my bottom lip not only to hide a proud smile but to stop the rest of my face from contorting into full-blown amusement. There it was, the backbone of steel that lived under all of Dahlia's soft edges. Even Jared blinked in surprise for a second before his smirk slid back into place.

"All right. Then let me buy you a drink at *Shadows*. The night is still young. Just a few friends hanging out."

"That's not gonna happen. She's seventeen. Hence underage, and I do believe, jailbait. She's definitely *not* going anywhere with you or your friends. Have fun, though. Ta-ta."

Dahlia's mouth gaped open, her face set in an unspoken *What the hell is wrong with you* look. What can I say? Subtlety was never my strong suit.

"No worries," Jared said smoothly. "Next time."

"Wow. Dense, are we? The answer is no, now and always. Now go away." The glass on a nearby table started clanking against the wood, the liquid remnants rippling. I was too angry to look for the source of the vibration. My fist clenched, itching to rearrange the punk's smug grin after he laughed, truly *amused* by the whole interaction. To my credit, I refrained.

I grabbed Dahlia's arm, leading her away from the fuckboy, her whole body stiff with her own rage I'd have to face.

"What the hell, Jenna?" Dahlia snapped, yanking her arm away from my grip once we were in the parking lot.

"That guy is bad news."

"That doesn't mean you had a right to be straight rude. Besides, Jared seemed nice enough to me. He goes to school with you, so he's only a couple of years older than I am, which makes that scene you made totally uncalled for."

"*Jared*," I scoffed. Just saying his name burned putrid acid on my tongue.

"I *can* take care of myself." Dahlia huffed, rolling her eyes as she crossed her arms over her chest, staring out the window. She'd refused to look at me since we left the bar.

"Please trust me when I say that guy is beyond toxic. And the way he was looking at you was not okay."

"I'm not a child, Jenna."

"I'm not treating you like one, Dahlia. I'm trying to protect you. I just... I don't like him. He's..." I couldn't put into words why I was so insanely sure.

"I'll never be able to live any kind of life if all of you keep me locked up in a protective little bubble forever."

We said nothing else during the entire drive back to her house, nor did she speak to me as we unloaded her instruments.

"Okay, how about this?" I offered. "I'll take you to *Shadow & Silk* for your birthday. Eighteen-and-over night. We'll pregame, take an Uber, let loose. The whole shebang."

She eyed me skeptically. "Pregame, eh?"

"Oh yeah. I'll even hold your hair at the end of the night."

"Gee, sounds fun."

"I'm telling you, it'll be a blast." I pulled her into a hug. "I'd say I'm sorry for being a little crazy tonight, but I'm not. Trust me on this one."

"Fine. You owe me a hair-holding birthday night."

"So done." I released her, turning to leave. But it struck me. "Hey, you do a great cover of 'Sympathy for the Devil.'"

"I know I do."

I still didn't get it, which my expression must have shouted. She sighed, shaking her head.

"You lose respect as an artist when you start taking random requests."

I raised an eyebrow.

She smirked. "What's next, 'Sweet Caroline' at a frat party? Please. I have standards."

A snort of laughter rang out into the otherwise quiet night. "I love you, Dahl."

"Back at you, Jen."

SEVEN

Cataleya

WALKING ALONE AT NIGHT down a foreign road flanked by thick black forest on either side *should* have been terrifying. I should've been out of my mind with nerves. I wasn't. Instead, the moon led the way, urging me to follow her into the darkness to play.

The rest of my birthday evening consisted of takeout in our room at the B&B, a glass of wine, and Nick falling asleep halfway through the movie I'd picked. I tried to talk him into going back to the pulpit for an evening swim in the moonlight. It was this romantic notion I'd conjured in my mind, even though I could have predicted his response, down to the syllable.

"Why would we do that? We already went there."

I knew Nick wouldn't want to go. Still, I'd hoped.

Even after he fell asleep, the thought hadn't stopped lurking in my mind. So, I left a note in case he woke up, and filled the daypack with a towel, a bottle of water, and my phone. Then, quietly, I headed out, not the least bit guilty for basically sneaking out.

A wave of anxiety washed over me as I approached the slick, carved steps of the canyon. A fall here meant waiting until morning for Nick to realize I was missing.

I checked the time on my phone. Just before midnight.

I'd gone too far to turn back now. I blew out a nervous breath, steadying myself, and began the descent, the moon shining down, my only source of light.

My hand traced the cool rock wall for balance, its surface thrumming with an energy that nipped at my fingers. The closer I got to the canyon floor, the louder the hum became.

By the time my feet touched the ground, dizziness engulfed me.

The rock walls sang, whispering things I couldn't understand. The gorge *breathed* around me. The rolling water shimmered in the moonlight, giving it an unsettling hue reminiscent of freshly spilled blood.

The closer I got to the water, the more suffocating my clothes became. A sudden, desperate need to shed them overwhelmed me.

Alone, I wasn't a mother, or a wife, or a woman whose body had stretched and softened. I was just *me*.

I stripped off my shoes and socks first, then peeled away my leggings, my sweatshirt, and my T-shirt. In my undergarments, I stepped into the water.

The iciness of the water cut through, sending little pulses that caressed my skin, beckoning me in. I slipped deeper into the water, past my waist and past the boulder that sang loudest.

Keep going.

The ground dropped away as I swam toward the falls, suspended in crimson water under silver light. The water started swirling around me, the moon's reflection dancing across its ripples, hotter than the sun, warming the water.

It *welcomed* me.

I drew a breath, surrendering to the water's embrace, sinking beneath the glassy plane.

The current tugged me down, a gentle yet unyielding force. Around me, the water quickened its dance, swirling with increasing fervor. A fire bloomed within, not one that burned, but a pure sensation searing across my skin. Warmth tingled through my body, carrying with it a scent I couldn't place at first.

Sandalwood, rich and steady, threaded with something wilder. Clove. It shouldn't have been there in the water, yet it wrapped around me as surely as the current.

The hum of the gorge resonated deep, a forgotten pulse of the earth's heart, its symphony vibrating within my core.

Shadows flickered in the red-silver current, bending into shapes, then faces, familiar and impossible. First, my mother, Bloom, her light brown hair unfurling like liquid, eyes fierce with love and sorrow. Her lips never moved, but her voice echoed in the depths of my mind.

You carry what I could not keep.

Behind her, a taller figure emerged, cloaked in mist and moss. My grandmother, a woman I didn't remember but recognized from pictures. The same woman I'd seen in my dream. Ivy. Her hands lifted, palms glowing faintly, as threads of light leapt from her veins to mine. Her voice was older than words, yet I recognized its meaning.

Power finds its blood. You are never alone.

The water thickened, swirling around us, and I felt them pour into me. Their strength, their grief, their unfinished stories. For a breathless instant, I wasn't drowning.

I lingered in the depths until my lungs pleaded with a silent scream, urging me to get to the surface.

Not yet.

Only when the last remnants of air had fled my lungs did the water let me go. I broke the surface with a long gasp, dragging crisp, life-giving air into my starved lungs. A rebirth in the heart of the gorge.

Droplets cascaded down my skin, shimmering curtains of liquid rubies, each splash a spark igniting a thousand tingling sensations, electric pulses surging through my veins, transforming the unsettling chill into a vibrant, exhilarating rush, as if a thousand suns had ignited within my soul.

My muscles, once sluggish and weighed down, now hummed with newfound energy, each heartbeat resonating with a drumbeat of power. The world sharpened into vivid focus, colors brightening and sounds amplifying. I emerged from a cocoon into a realm of exhilarating possibilities.

The boulder sang, its magnetic pull beckoning me closer. I climbed onto it, stretching out against its rough texture. An unexpected warmth radiated from it, wrapping me in a gentle embrace. Cool night air contrasted with the boulder's heat, each breath filled with the scent of damp earth and pine.

The world looked different. The moon blazed down warm as a night sun, casting a silvery glow, illuminating the trees above, painting the landscape in hues of blue and green while the soft rustle of leaves and the distant call of night creatures harmonized into a lullaby that soothed my senses into its peaceful sanctuary.

I could have stayed there for hours, attuned to the symphony of the wild, but the energy within me surged and swelled, begging for release.

I dressed quickly and scrambled out of the glen, practically sprinting back through the forest, my feet barely touching the road.

Bursting into our room, breathless, frantic, I abandoned all pretense of quiet. The door slammed shut behind me, and my daypack hit the floor with a thud.

Nick stirred in the bed, still in the same position he'd been in when I left. Blissfully unaware of my brewing hurricane. The air crackled with tension as I turned off the television, then stripped off my damp clothes, letting my wet hair fall against my skin, red droplets tracing paths down my chilled body.

He blinked at me, his eyes clouded with sleep. "What's wrong? Are you all right?"

I didn't speak. Words would only shatter the moment. I needed to work off the raw energy burning inside. Calm it before I burst into flames.

The confused look in Nick's eyes faded away as I tugged off his boxers, then crawled on top of him, straddling him. His intense gaze never left mine, each breath coming faster. My hands worked feverishly, tearing at his shirt. I would have ripped it off if he hadn't assisted, struggling to keep pace with my urgency.

His hands caressed my back as I arched against him, feeling his body respond under me. My fingers tangled in his hair, pulling his face to mine so I could run my tongue along the rugged line of his jaw. My teeth nipped at his neck with newfound boldness. The sharp intake of breath that escaped him ignited a deeper hunger.

Control slipped out of reach. I couldn't hold back any longer. There was no slow build, no gentle intimacy. It was a collision of primal needs that unleashed everything pent up, devouring us both. I flicked my tongue along the bite, then consumed his mouth, pushing my tongue inside, staking claim with wildness racing through my blood.

Nick angled his face, taking the kiss deeper. His hands found my hair, pulling in a way he hadn't in such a long time.

My body rocked along his, a restless tide against a solid shore, as I raked my fingers down his wide chest, the chest that was still my favorite part of him, down his abdomen until I gripped the length of him in my hand. I sank myself onto him, barely giving him time to groan in surprised pleasure before I began riding him with the rhythm of the pulpit's song still echoing in my bones.

"Jesus. What's gotten into you?" Nick growled with that sly smile of his, the gravelly rasp of unmistakable desire in his deep voice.

I silenced him with a finger to his lips. "Touch me." Taking his hands, I pressed them to my breasts.

He obeyed, his large hand covering one breast, thumb and forefinger finding my nipple, tugging, teasing, igniting a cascade of pleasure that spiraled through my core, while his mouth took my other breast in a hot, insistent pull, his free hand sliding lower, kneading circles against the gateway to oblivion.

I gasped, arching into his touch, the pleasure building with each pass of his thumb. A low moan escaped my lips as I felt a surge of heat rush through me. My hips moved faster, instinctively seeking more of his touch, begging for release. His fingers danced against my skin, teasing and tantalizing, until I thought I might shatter from the exquisite torment.

Pleasure escalated into a tidal wave, our bodies slick with sweat, every nerve ending singing with ecstatic fervor. I could feel Nick teetering on the precipice, his moans a deep counterpoint to my own. Riding faster, harder, I chased the peak, pulling him with me into the abyss. When we shattered together, another awakening happened. One of my soul, of my power, of my heart.

I collapsed on top of him. Only the sound of our panting and the intoxicating scent of spent passion filled the air. The all-consuming energy finally ebbed, leaving my body trembling.

"Damn, woman," Nick chuckled, still dazed, as I shifted off him.

I smiled, curling against him, laying my head on his chest. I wanted to tell him everything I had experienced. About the pulpit. The hum of energy that vibrated through the stone. I wanted to tell him I'd been reborn.

The words remained trapped in my throat. This was my secret, not meant to be shared.

Not yet.

Nick pulled me closer, his body a warm anchor beside mine. I listened to his breathing deepen, the steady rhythm of his heart thumping against my cheek.

And finally, I let sleep take me. Dreamless and deep.

EIGHT

Nick

I DIDN'T KNOW WHAT time it was when I woke up, only that her silky skin was warm against mine and the light in the room had shifted to a golden hue. Her breath was soft, steady. My arm lay between her breasts, laying claim to her in my sleep. After last night, I didn't want to let her go.

She rolled toward me, her dark waves spilling across the pillow, her chocolate eyes heavy-lidded as her lips curled into that slow, sultry smile that had always been my undoing. For a second, I forgot how to breathe. We hadn't been like that for years. The way she *looked* at me. As if after all this time she still wanted me.

"Hey," I whispered with a lazy grin as I brushed my lips against the delicate bridge of her nose.

She purred as she pressed against me. I didn't need another invitation. There was no frenzy this time, no urgent need or desperate grasp. This was our dance, a slow, deliberate rhythm that only belonged to us. A knowing of each other that transcended words.

I draped her leg over my hip and slid inside her slowly. Her eyes never left mine. We moved as one, a seamless flow, the intervening years dissolving into nothingness. Her fingers in my hair. The soft hitch of her breath, a symphony of sensation, as I sank deeper. Our kisses were unhurried, each one a testament to a love that defied the boundaries of time.

Afterward, we showered together, laughing quietly like teenagers caught in a stolen moment. I soaped her shoulders, my hands roaming a slow, deliberate path downward, savoring the soft gasp of pleasure that escaped her lips. I couldn't stop touching her, consumed by the need to feel every inch of her, to lose myself in her intoxicating presence. An insatiable hunger that I never wanted to quell.

Even as she dressed, I was a fixture leaning against the bathroom door-frame, arms crossed, a silent observer to the goddess who was mine. She moved with languid grace, confident and unhurried. Her gaze met mine as she fastened her bra, her hands tracing the contours of her skin, knowing I was watching every aching movement.

I didn't just want her. I wanted the way she looked at me, like the cracks between us had finally started to seal.

"You trying to kill me?" I muttered.

A smirk played on her lips as she tossed me a pair of socks. "You'll live."

Barely.

The aroma of baking bread and rich coffee met us as we reached the dining room. Kait, our B&B hostess, looked up at us with a knowing smile.

"Well, good morning, lovebirds. Barely, but morning still."

Cataleya stiffened beside me, a blush blooming across her freckled cheeks. A grin stretched across my own face, unbidden and impossible to suppress.

I drew out her chair and pressed a kiss to the crown of her head before settling beside her. While she tried to disappear behind her coffee mug, I sat tall, my pride radiating, bordering on obnoxious. Definitely a little cocky. I couldn't help it.

"It warms the heart," Kait said as she filled our mugs with steaming coffee. "Inspirational to see love like that doesn't fade."

Another couple entered, their smirks mirroring Kait's expression. I choked back a chuckle, the sound thankfully muffled by my mug. Cataleya's glare only fueled my amusement.

Leaning close, I whispered, "Let's get out of here."

She tried to suppress a laugh. "Please."

We made our getaway, two steaming mugs in hand, slipping through the back door into the crisp morning.

We didn't get far.

Around the side of the cottage, a primal urge seized me. I stopped her, set my mug down on the weathered stone ledge, and pressed her against the ivy-covered cottage. I couldn't help it. I needed more. Of her. Of this.

"Why, Mrs. Reynolds," I breathed, my voice a husky murmur as I kissed her, slow and deep, "you've gotten us into some trouble. I guess there's no stopping us now."

A throaty laugh escaped her lips as she wrapped her arms around me. I hoisted her effortlessly, her legs instinctively locking around my waist. Ceramic shattered against the stone path when her mug tumbled from her grasp. Still, she was unfazed, her focus solely on me.

"Oops. Now we're really in for it," I said against the heat of her neck, already sliding my hands beneath her shirt.

She moaned, quiet and hungry, as she reached between us, into my pants, her fingers wrapping around me with a possessive grip that nearly shattered my resolve.

"I say again, damn woman," I groaned. "Whatever's gotten into you, I like it."

"Take me. Now," she demanded, her voice a mere breath against my ear.

"Here?" I breathed, already pulling her panties aside, guiding myself into her.

She pulled me closer until I was completely buried inside her. Her breath hitched, her head tilted back, and then the world didn't just blur. It snapped.

A static charge ignited where our skin met, a white-hot hum that by-passed my ears and vibrated straight into my marrow. I gasped, but the air I drew in tasted like hers. Suddenly, I couldn't tell where my heartbeat ended and hers began. When her fingers curled into my shoulders, I felt the pressure from both sides. Her nails in my skin and my skin beneath her fingertips.

Every peak she climbed, my own pulsed in the same rhythm, a mirror image of a sensation I wasn't supposed to own. Our bodies, minds, and souls synchronizing in a strange, impossible way. Both miraculous and unsettling, defying all logic and reason.

I dared not question it. Instead, I surrendered to the moment, moving with her, matching her rhythm, letting the intensity build. Her moans grew more fervent, her nails digging into my back as we ascended together, the cadence of our bodies crashing into the otherworldly.

Her body trembled when she came, and I had to kiss her hard to keep her from screaming out, giving our secret away. I followed her into ecstasy a moment later, my soul emptying into her.

I held her there, our bodies still joined. With a gentle hand, I caressed her cheek, softening the kiss into something unhurried, filling it with every word I knew she needed but didn't know how to say. I wanted her, but more than that, I chose her. Now and always.

Her breath was still shaky when she pulled back, her arms entwined around my neck, her legs still locked around my waist. We were both flushed and trembling, her forehead resting against mine, her lips parted as if she might say more and wasn't sure if she should.

Then she whispered, "I've missed this. I've missed you."

Such simple words.

And damn if they didn't knock the wind out of me.

Closing my eyes, I pulled her in until the steady thrum of her pulse against my neck was the only thing I could hear. My hands memorized the dip of her waist, anchoring her there as if the morning mist might actually dissolve her.

"I'm right here," I whispered into her hair.

It wasn't the heat left over from the rush in my blood, or the sex, though damn, that was something. It was how she didn't pull away. For the first time in years, the jagged silence between us felt less like a canyon and more like a seam, waiting for the right thread to pull it shut.

Maybe we weren't broken beyond repair. Maybe a path back to each other still existed after all.

She looked at me, and for a split second I saw it flicker in her eyes. A fierceness, tender and wild. A flicker that defied definition. I didn't push. I simply held her, clinging to that sliver of peace for as long as it would last.

"I know you are," she replied, her voice laced with a hint of doubt, as though she were trying to make herself believe it.

NINE

Cataleya

ONCE WE ESCAPED THE stares and smirks of the other B&B guests, we didn't get far.

Around the back of the house, Nick stopped me, his lips crashing against mine. "Why, Mrs. Reynolds, you've gotten us into some trouble. I guess there's no stopping us now." He backed me up against the house, his body pressed against mine. I lost grip of my mug, sending it shattering on the stone path.

"Oops. Now we're really in for it," Nick murmured against my lips, his hands already under my shirt, over my breasts and between my legs.

My breath hitched as I reached for him, my fingers wrapping around his length. He groaned in my ear.

"I say again, damn woman. Whatever's gotten into you, I like it."

"Take me. Now."

"Here?" he panted as he maneuvered me into position, lifting me to wrap my legs around his waist as he pulled my panties aside and thrust into me.

My heart hammered a frantic rhythm against my ribs, a wild drumbeat accompanying the symphony of our bodies. A subtle electricity sparked within me, a thousand tiny currents converging into a tidal wave. The world dissolved, leaving only the unfiltered sensation of him inside me, his girth stretching me, the exquisite pressure that stole my breath.

Sandalwood and clove enveloped me as a tingling fire danced across my skin, ignited by each thrust, each intimate exploration.

A shockwave zapped between us, painless but all-consuming. His pleasure became mine, a shared ecstasy as if a conduit had opened, merging our bodies and allowing sensations to flow freely. I felt the intensity of his experience as if it were my own. Each movement, each touch, each thrust of passion amplified the pleasure.

I pushed the logic from my mind, abandoned reason, and, for once, just let myself feel it all and be consumed by the all-encompassing tide of sensation.

The quickening of his breath against my ear, the shared sensation of him sliding in and out of me drove me up quickly. I moaned a primal sound of surrender as control slipped, barely able to hold myself together as the tsunami of untamed pleasure crashed through me.

I cried out, the rippling waves so strong. Nick crushed his mouth against mine.

"Shhh," he growled, smiling as he swallowed my scream with his mouth and let himself go with me. As our peaks faded, his crushing lips softened against mine, kissing me so sweetly, it brought tears to my eyes.

"I've missed this. I've missed you."

"I'm right here," he said and kissed the tip of my nose.

If only it would last.

"I know you are."

By the time we emerged from our bliss bubble, the sun had dipped low behind the hills. Our hunger for each other had been the deciding factor in staying in town another night. A more primitive hunger for actual food drew us to the pub across the street.

The jewel of a pub exceeded all expectations. A haven of warmth and cheer, alive with the vibrant pulse of music and laughter. A band tucked in the corner spun a tapestry of lilting folk melodies, while a little girl danced near her parents' table, twirling like a leaf caught in a playful breeze.

I watched her as I took bite after delicious bite of Guinness stew. Jenna used to do that, twirl to any song, arms stretched out like wings. That free, fearless wonder of childhood. She still loved music, but she'd stopped twirling long ago.

My gaze drifted to the baby peacefully snoozing in the stroller beside the dancing girl. A bittersweet ache bloomed with the tender pang of disappointment. I'd always imagined giving Jenna a sibling to share her world. We tried, we hoped, but ultimately we moved on. Though some days, the ghost of that unfulfilled dream still stung.

As I watched the young family, a different sensation stirred. An unsettling awareness. The strange, sudden scent of sandalwood and clove surrounded me again as tingling erupted on my skin, starting at my fingertips, racing up my arm and straight to my heart.

My eyes were drawn to the baby, though the stroller mostly obscured him from view. My focus narrowed until the rest of the pub was just a dull roar.

I set down my fork, the stew gone tasteless, dabbed my mouth with a napkin, and rose from the chair.

"Cat?" Nick looked up, concerned.

"Hold on, I need to check on the baby."

I approached their table with hesitant steps. "This might seem a little strange, but is your baby okay?" I asked, my voice trembling slightly as my eyes locked on the stroller.

The mother paused mid-bite, a frown etching itself onto her face. Her hand instinctively moved toward her child, a protective gesture.

"I'm sorry. My name is Cataleya. I'm a NICU nurse. I..." My words faltered, caught in my throat. What was I even saying? "I thought I saw something, and I just wanted to make sure..." My words trailed off, dissolving into the ambient noise of the pub. I hadn't *seen* anything. At least not in the conventional sense.

The word *nurse* unlocked urgency within the mother. Her eyes widened as she swiftly yanked the blanket off the baby.

The moment I put my hand on the baby, a surge of heat coursed through me, and a vision, vivid and overwhelming, slammed into my mind.

I saw the intricate architecture of the baby's airway from the *inside*. Descending from his mouth, to the back of his throat, past his little uvula. And there it was, a french fry his big sister shared with him, lodged in his trachea, a silent obstruction stealing his breath.

Without hesitation, driven by instinct honed by years of training, I scooped him from the stroller, cradling him face down over my forearm, angling his head toward the floor. I struck the heel of my palm between his shoulder blades, once, twice, three times, until the piece of potato dislodged and launched from his mouth, landing on the floor with a wet splat.

Then the baby wailed. Loud, beautiful, gut-wrenching. Screaming meant breathing.

I flipped him back over, checking the delicate landscape of his mouth. My eyes confirmed what my hands already knew. His airway was clear.

"Oh my god," the mother sobbed, a prayer of disbelief, as she took her baby in her arms, cradling him, kissing his head through a steady stream of tears. "I didn't see... she must've given it to him. I didn't know... he would have..."

"Thank you, miss. Thank you so much." The young father's hand moved in soothing circles on his wife's back, a silent promise of protection. I hadn't noticed him, or Nick, who had made his way over to the table, or that the band had stopped playing. The pub hushed, all eyes on the aftermath of a near tragedy.

Then, applause, a wave of sound that crashed over me. My face flushed hot under the weight of a dozen staring eyes.

"No need to thank me. I just... I saw..." The words crumbled. I didn't know *how* I'd known. Or what I had actually seen. "I'm sorry. I didn't mean to scare you."

I backed away until the young mother's arms wrapped around me, taking me into a fierce, shaky hug.

"Thank you," she cried in my ear.

"Of course. You're welcome," I replied, patting her back awkwardly before pulling away, trying not to recoil at the thought of touching the baby again, afraid I might see more of the strange and impossible.

Nick's hand found the small of my back, a grounding presence guiding me back to our table.

"How did you even see that the baby was choking? I can barely see the inside of the stroller from here." His eyes reflected a mixture of awe and disbelief.

"I don't know, I just..." The words tangled up in my mouth, in my thoughts. How *did* I see the baby? How had I just *known* something was wrong?

A wave of exhaustion washed over me, leaving my eyelids heavy, my body drained, and suddenly weak.

"You know, I'm really tired. Do you mind if we take the rest of this to go?" I focused my attention on cleaning up the table, fighting the urge to run out of the pub like I desperately wanted.

"Sure. Are you okay?" Nick put his large hand over my busy ones, his concern radiating.

I smiled at his sweet face. "Yeah. I'm okay."

As we gathered our things, I couldn't stop thinking about the baby. About how I'd *seen* inside him, not with my eyes. With something else entirely.

Ten

Jenna

THERE WAS PEACE AT Tía Sal and Uncle Z's breathtaking beach house. Being oceanfront was definitely a perk I enjoyed when I stayed over. The way afternoon rays reflected golden off the waves, the seagrass bending in an invisible breeze, and the wind chimes made of seashells tinkling on the deck.

The house wasn't built on the beach. It belonged to it. The way stone was part of the cliff, or roots were part of the forest floor. It was an extension of the earth itself, its frame humming with the same pulse as the ocean and sand beneath it.

Since my parents were still in Scotland, it was the perfect excuse to hang out at Casa de Eze. Especially out on the deck, where the world was quiet and peaceful.

Salvia walked in wearing sunglasses stylishly too big for her face, carrying iced coffees, a box of fancy pastries no one had asked for, and grocery bags piled up her arms.

"I've got caffeine and carbs. Come kiss your favorite aunt," she called, kicking off her sandals at the door before walking into the kitchen. "Where's Dahl?"

"Upstairs preening."

Sal chuckled, gesturing for me to kiss her cheek as payment for the iced coffee. "Are you picking your parents up from the airport, or are they getting an Uber?" she asked as I kissed her cheek. There was always a unique scent to her, some obscure indie perfume. Definitely expensive. No one else could pull it off.

"I'm picking them up in the morning."

"In that deathtrap of a car?" She grabbed my hand, eyeing my chipped nail polish with disapproval. I took my hand back and started helping put the groceries away.

"Yes, and I will until it dies a noble death in the middle of a CVS parking lot, thank you very much."

"Mm-hmm. Call me when it does. I'll come rescue you in my electric goddess of a sedan."

"Oh, please. That thing beeps at you if you breathe wrong."

She grinned. "Exactly. She's got boundaries. Unlike you."

I threw a wadded-up shopping bag at her.

Sal caught it midair, one-handed, like she was born to talk trash and deflect projectiles. "So," she said, changing the subject, "you ready for your mom's big birthday bash?"

"I mean, it's Mom's fortieth. Shouldn't we be burning sage and whispering over a fire pit or something?"

"She'd hate that," Salvia said. "Which is *exactly* why I might do it."

I laughed. "You are such a menace."

"I prefer *agent of chaos,* thank you."

"You're both."

She nudged me with her elbow. "That's why I'm your favorite aunt, right?"

"You're my *only* aunt."

"Semantics. At least tell me you love me more than beautiful Uncle Z."

I laughed. "Don't tell Uncle Z."

By the afternoon, the grill had been fired up, billowing a heavenly scent into the air to mix with sea salt and rosemary. Inside, music played. Stevie Ray Vaughan's smooth notes drifted through open windows as the breeze danced with the white, gauzy curtains. Dahlia was harassing her mother at the kitchen island, stealing strawberries out of a mixing bowl. Salvia slapped her hand playfully.

"Thief," Sal said, brushing flour from her hip. "Save some for the tart."

"You said you bought extra," Dahlia mumbled, mouth full.

"I lied. Take that tray out to the deck."

Z passed behind them, wineglass in one hand, a loop tool in the other, clay still dusting his fingers. "Don't fight in front of the art," he teased, nodding to the half-formed figure drying on its stand. "She's still finding her confidence."

He leaned into Salvia, kissing her. Not an absentminded kiss. A full-mouth kiss. If I hadn't been so used to seeing them this way, it might have been embarrassing.

Uncle Z, Mr. Zion Eze in the professional art gallery world, was Tía Salvia's adoring husband, Dahlia's dad, and my uncle by marriage, and always more than that. The man had a face that turned heads without trying.

Deep brown skin, high cheekbones, and a smile that could melt steel, all wrapped up in a swoon-worthy Creole French accent. And somehow, with all his international travel, gallery shows, and artist residencies in places I had to Google, he still made time to spoil the hell out of all of us when he was home. He adored both his wife and his daughter and openly admitted it was his joy in life to give Tía Sal and Dahlia anything they wanted.

Raised by a widowed immigrant father who worked his fingers to the bone for everything they had, Uncle Z made sure that Dahlia knew it was a privilege he enjoyed giving her, not an obligation she was entitled to. He was kind yet stern, slow to agitation, and I honestly couldn't remember a single time Dahlia had actually been in trouble. Not that she gave him much reason to be mad.

Even when he was gone, he was never like gone, gone. Uncle Z was like a satellite orbiting around us, always tethered to his family.

Tía Sal was his opposite. She'd get ruffled if the wind blew her hair out of place. Between her and Mom, Salvia got most of the Costa Rican spice, loving fiercely and with her whole soul. I was more like Tía Sal in that respect.

Dahlia moved through the kitchen with the same unflappable grace my mother had. The kind of person who could find a lost key in a hurricane without raising her voice. She didn't need to command the room. S-he simply anchored it with a gentle capability that resonated in the very air around her. The deep well of her empathy undoubtedly fueled the haunting beauty of her music.

I stepped in from the deck to sneak a few strawberries myself. Tía Sal turned when she saw me, a streak of flour on her cheek. "Don't even think about it, my gorgeous, glowing disaster of a niece."

I held my hands up in submission. Uncle Z handed me a glass of rosé without asking and kissed the top of my head. "My second-favorite girl," he said, winking.

"You can say I'm your favorite. Dahlia's not here."

"Rude," Dahlia called from outside.

We all laughed.

Dining alfresco was the Eze family's favorite way to eat. We ate on the deck, barefoot, the sunset bleeding gold and lavender into the ocean. Z had grilled fresh mahi as Sal plated everything as though she was going to create a painting of it for the gallery. They bickered playfully the whole time, about lemon zest, about grill time, about whether figs belonged on pizza. They did, Sal insisted. Z called it fruit heresy.

They moved around each other like the music Dahlia created. Z kissed Salvia's shoulder as he passed. She tucked her head against his side when she sat down. They laughed loud. Fought fair. Touched constantly.

And I watched.

Not with envy, exactly. But with a soft ache in my chest.

This was what it was supposed to look like when two people still wanted each other and saw each other, even after all the years of distractions.

It was different from my parents' love.

Or whatever was left of it.

At home, silence had replaced the space where affection used to be. My mom came home from work and disappeared into a bath or a glass of wine. My dad muttered about firewalls and contractors. They rarely touched. Rarely laughed. They were together, technically. So was the earth until one good jolt split it apart.

Here? This was joy.

Z brought out the strawberry tart Sal made earlier, swearing she'd infused it with "the essence of Van Gogh's ghost." He set a slice in front of me with a single edible flower on top.

"For the one who holds the universe together with sarcasm," he said.

"You're the best, Uncle Z."

He grinned. "Don't you forget it."

After the dinner dishes were washed and loaded into the dishwasher, Dahlia and I went to stretch out on the beach, as we usually did, no matter the season.

As the stars broke through the last burn of twilight, we sat in the sand with our feet buried, the house glowing behind us.

"You know," I said, "your parents are actually gross."

She smiled, gazing back at the windows where Z had Salvia in a close embrace, slow dancing in the kitchen. "I know. It's the kind of gross I want someday."

The tide had pulled far back, leaving a ribbon of wet sand in front of us. Dahlia was mid-story about an embarrassing Brevard mishap when her phone sounded from her pocket.

Her hand darted for it. Her face lit up, though her smile was ever so hesitant. I peeked over her shoulder.

"Jared?" Just saying his name out loud settled a weight on my chest.

She ignored me, thumbs flying. I leaned over to look again, but she angled the screen away. Still, I caught enough.

Jared: *Wish I could see you right now. Bet you look gorgeous with moonlight on your hair.*

Jared: *Do you ever think about me when you're out there? I think about you. A lot.*

Dahlia's cheeks flushed pink. She bit her bottom lip, something she did when she was deep in thought. "He's... sweet."

"Sweet?" I snorted. "He's not sweet. He's extra."

Another chime.

Jared: *No one else looks at you like I do, right? I'll always know if people are looking at you.*

Dahlia's grin faltered for just a second, then smoothed out. She typed back something, her fingers hovering before hitting send.

"How did he get your number?" I asked.

She shrugged, eyes still on the glowing screen. "He said he got it through a friend of a friend. I don't know, Jen, he just figured it out."

"That's not exactly reassuring."

She waved me off. "It's kind of romantic, right? Like he *wanted* to find me." The words came out softer, less certain.

I shoved my toes deeper into the sand, staring at the tide as if it could wash the entire conversation away. "Oh, I'm sure he wanted to find you. You know that's not exactly normal, right?"

Her eyes rolled defensively, her stubborn chin tilted, but her eyes flicked back to the phone like she wasn't sure she wanted to see the next message. A shadow passed across her face, gone before she smoothed it into another smile.

Her screen glowed again. This time, she didn't read it, only pressed her lips together and locked the phone.

I wanted to grab it, hurl it into the waves. Instead, I hugged my knees, biting back words I wanted to say.

Her eyes tracked something behind me, toward the dim line where the dunes met the walking path.

"What?" I turned. I saw nothing, just a shadow shifting at the edge of the streetlight's reach before it slipped away.

"Nothing," she said quickly, tucking her hair behind her ear. "Probably a tourist cutting through." Her tone had that too-bright edge I recognized.

I tried to joke it off. "Guess we're not the only ones admiring your parents' gross PDA from afar."

She didn't laugh.

"You okay? What did he say?"

"Nothing. I'm fine. Just wondering whether it's still considered PDA if the make-out session is in their own house."

"Good point."

I let the sound of the waves fill the space between us. The air had shifted, cooler now, heavier. When we finally went inside, Dahlia checked the lock on the sliding door.

Twice.

ELEVEN

Cataleya

A GAIN, I WAITED UNTIL I was sure Nick was asleep before slipping from the warmth of our bed. I made my way down the stairs, trying to avoid squeaky boards, then eased the front door shut behind me.

Cool night air wrapped around me, dimpling my skin as I stepped out onto the porch, making me second-guess what I was doing. The warmth of Nick's body was far more enticing than roaming around a dark, foreign, mostly deserted town in the middle of the night.

Kelly's shop wasn't far, though it had closed hours before. She'd mentioned living above it, and I needed answers. Needed to understand what was happening to me.

I could feel the change in my marrow vibrating through every cell, impossible as that was. Ever since those crimson waters.

I knocked as hard as I could without splitting my knuckles open on the hardwood of the shop's door, the CLOSED sign bumping against the door as I pounded. A moment later, a soft glow illuminated one of the upstairs windows. Kelly appeared, peering down at me through a parted curtain. She waved and vanished from sight.

Seconds later, there was a crash, followed by the grumbling of a few curses, then the door opened.

"Have questions, do you?"

"Questions?" I exhaled. "Yeah, you could say that. Did you know what would happen down in the pulpit?"

My breath came fast. I wasn't exactly scared, but the flash flood of all that was exciting and impossible threatened to drown me. Nothing *bad* had happened, especially the new sexual sensations I'd experienced. However, everything had changed. The hows and whys invaded all of my thoughts. How was this possible? Why me? Was this part of our Auchter bloodline?

"All I did was give you a slice of truth and a breath of knowledge," she said calmly. "I hoped you'd come tonight. It's easier to show than to tell. I'm meeting with my group. My coven, if you will."

"Coven?" I blinked. "Seriously? Are you telling me I'm some kind of witch now? I was mostly kidding the other day. You told a great story, I'll give you that. This is going a little far, don't you think? What's next? Vampires? Or, oh my god, werewolves?"

"Awoken, love. And don't be ridiculous." She chuckled. "There's no such thing as vampires or werewolves."

I stared at her. I wasn't so sure anymore.

"Come with me. Just feel. See. Trust. Then I'll explain everything." Kelly wrapped a cloak the color of deep red wine over her long ivory dress, then held out her hand.

I hesitated.

Kelly wasn't danger. She was sunshine after the rain. A half-remembered song, a face from a dream. Safe as my own heartbeat and familiar as my skin.

I took her hand.

"You'll be quite safe, I promise you."

I nodded and followed her into the woods.

It didn't take long to reach the clearing, though it might as well have been miles from civilization. It was a different world in those trees. The air was fresh, thicker, and singing with life.

I could hear them before I saw them. Feminine voices, soft and threaded with laughter.

I followed Kelly into a clearing where a bonfire was already blazing, sparks swirling upward like fireflies. Still holding my hand, she led me to a fallen log. With a smile and a nod, she let go, then stepped away to join the others.

The women, different ages, body types, and backgrounds, were all part of one entity. I could feel it, feel *them*. One group. One purpose. Most of them had long, natural hair waving in the breeze along with their flowing white or ivory dresses, their feet bare.

As soon as Kelly walked up to them, the conversations quieted. The soundtrack of the wildlife surrounding us and the snapping crackles of the fire became the only sounds of the night. They lined up in front of the fire. The ritual, the enchanting beauty of it, felt ancient and familiar.

Kelly stepped forward first. She lit a bundle of sage, which she then used to light her candle. Once the wick was lit, she blew out the flame, letting the smoke billow. She waved the curling smoke around her candle, then herself from her head down to her feet. Kelly lit the next woman's candle with hers, handed her the smoking sage, then stepped back into the silent line.

One by one, they repeated the movements, a quiet rhythm, a passing of light and intention. Once all the candles were lit, they stood silently with their heads bowed. At once, they all moved, forming a circle around the fire. Each woman placed her candle at her feet, then joined hands, all elegantly synced with each other, a single heartbeat. Even Kelly moved with a grace that usually eluded her.

A young woman with long, wavy blonde hair began to sing. A Celtic melody, haunting and raw. Others joined in, their harmonies clear, perfectly blended.

I wasn't sure what it all meant, but I could feel the emotion, the pain, the joy, the build of power, a connection to these women I'd never met before. My breath caught in my throat as hot tears ran down my cheeks, that recurring tingle of energy rippling along my skin.

I was part of it. They were me, and I was them, though I had no explanation for it.

A whisper tickled the breeze around me. Words so faint they blended into the crackling of the fire. The other women were still singing, no one looking over at me.

I heard it again. Definitely words from no visible source.

The hair on my neck and arms stood up. The voice was one I hadn't heard in decades, and now twice in the last couple of days. My mother's voice hummed along to the rhythm of the tribal song swirling around me. I closed my eyes, feeling her there. In the air, in the soil under my feet, in the warm caress of the flames.

Had she been here? Were these women somehow part of her as well? I'd come with questions that were no longer important, melting away in the firelight, so many new ones blooming. As the voices of the women sang on, my mother's whispered in my ear.

Welcome home, my love. Though always remember, not all power protects.

It was a warning. One full of love, comfort, and heartache. I was only two the last time I heard her sing to me, read me a story, or laugh. And then she left us. Even so, there wasn't anything I wouldn't do to feel her arms around me.

The tears spilled over, sliding down my cheeks.

Another voice reached me as Kelly approached. "Would you like to meet your sisters now?"

"I'd like that very much."

As I was introduced to each woman, I found *I already knew them.* My other sisters. Their names, their eyes, the feel of their hands in mine. My soul recognized theirs, puzzle pieces sliding into place.

I lost track of time as we chatted around the fire. Each woman, a constellation of experiences, shared what led her to this part of her journey.

It was when the oldest of them, Maeve, a tall woman with silver hair and haunting eyes of bright amber, took my hands that the conversation shifted.

"I knew your grandmother," she breathed, her gaze unfurling like a sail into the past. "Ivy, they called her."

Hearing someone else speak her name stilled my breath. "You did?"

"Yes," she murmured, a ghost of a smile gracing her wrinkled lips, not of fondness but of recognition. "And I knew the man she loved. A formidable pair, etched in time, until fate intervened."

"What happened?" The question tumbled out, desperate.

Maeve's eyes sharpened for a heartbeat, piercing into mine, then softened, veiling the past behind them once more. "This is not the night for that story to be told. Some truths shouldn't be unearthed before their time."

But she didn't let go of my hands. Instead, she leaned closer, her voice lowering to a tremor of memory.

"Ivy Auchter was unlike the rest of us. She carried the old blood, the kind that made even seasoned Awoken uneasy. There are those who still whisper her name in reverence, and others who spit it like a curse." Her gaze flicked toward the fire, flames reflecting the cataracts in her eyes. "When she walked into a room, the air shifted. Candles bent toward her flame. Water rose higher in glasses. Even the earth seemed to listen. An Awakening like that draws hunger. Always."

My throat tightened. "What happened to her?"

Her mouth curved, though sorrow hollowed it. "The Awakening is never lost, child. It only changes hands."

Before I could press her further, she released my hands with a final weighted squeeze and drew back into the circle of women, leaving me adrift in the wake of her words. The fire crackled, throwing sparks into the night.

Finally, as Kelly and I walked back to town, she turned toward me.

"Are you ready for all of this?" she asked as we reached the edge of the woods.

"I've always had this need for *more*. I was terrified that I'd never find it. That I'd die without ever being truly content." I looked up at the moon, the stars blinking overhead, a new awareness and appreciation of everything in the natural world around me. "It was always this. Waiting for me."

Kelly smiled. "This is only the beginning. We all follow our own paths, but we are one. We share the joys and sometimes the burdens that very few understand. Obviously, yours is that of the healer. The naturalist. Listen to the world around you. Open your heart. And remember, being Awoken is a celebration of all life. A dance with energy, healing, and balance. That is

your first lesson. The law of balance always has to be, well, balanced."
She laughed.

"Balance is a law?"

"It is *the* law," she said. "Without rules, there is no balance. Without balance, there is only chaos. Remember what I told you before. Awakening is the ability to manipulate natural energy. And that energy must come from somewhere. You can't create something from nothing. Since you're a healer, you understand this already. You wouldn't be able to run a hand over a wound and, poof, the wound is healed. The amount of energy it would take to do that would be astronomical. Instead, you can find a disease, feel what is wrong, and then use what nature gives us to help you heal it. Mother Earth has given us plants, the knowledge of what they do, their components, and how to use them to heal. Just be mindful of who or what you give your energy to. There is always a cost."

I nodded slowly, thinking back to the baby. The choking, then the exhaustion afterward. But nothing like that had happened during the crazy, hungry sex with Nick. That hadn't felt like taking, it was more of an exchange after which I was energized, exhilarated. "That kind of explains what happened earlier," I murmured. When Kelly only looked at me, I told her what had happened at the pub and behind the cottage.

Kelly's expression shifted. Curious, then cautious. "Those are potent abilities," she said. "To happen so soon..." She studied me, worry deepening on her brow. "I knew it the moment you walked into my shop. The power within you is stronger than I've ever sensed in someone untrained. I'd like to look into your ancestry, if that's okay?"

"Yes, please. The only thing is, we're leaving in the morning."

"Luckily, we live in an age of video calls and text messages. Never farther than a few taps."

"Very true." I smiled, suddenly reluctant to leave. "Thank you. For all of this. For giving me my life back."

"I did no such thing," she said, pulling me into a hug. "Everything you've experienced, everything that's Awakened, that's all you. I only shared some of the knowledge rolling around in my head." Kelly smiled, squeezing me hard, then pulled back with a mischievous glint in her eye.

"Now go disperse some of that beautiful energy on that hunky man of yours." She gave me a playful nudge.

Twelve

Jenna

THE FIRST NIGHT MY parents were home, everything clicked back into place. We were a unit again. We talked, laughed, and ordered pizza. Not fancy artisan stuff, just the greasy, paper-plate kind that left oil stains spreading like halos.

Dad flipped open the box with mock reverence. "Behold! The feast of champions! Or, you know, exhausted people who can't cook."

Mom chuckled. "You can cook when you put in the effort. You just choose mayhem instead."

He gasped. "Excuse me, I'll have you know I was actually praised by an aggressively charming Scottish cab driver for my culinary skills."

"Oh God, here we go," Mom groaned, already smiling.

But he was off and running, hands waving as if he were reenacting a war story. "There we were, lost in Edinburgh, hungry, jet-lagged, and desperate for a drink. The cabbie tells me, 'Aye, ye'll nae survive on crisps alone, lad!'"

His accent was terrible. Like a pirate auditioning for Shakespeare.

Mom nearly choked on her slice. "He did *not* sound like that."

"Sure he did," Dad said, puffing out his chest. "He even invited us to his flat for haggis. Haggis, people! That's trust."

I shook my head, laughing. "That's not trust, Dad. That's pity. He probably couldn't stand watching another American trying to survive on vending machines and gas station coffee."

Mom laughed so hard she snorted. A full laugh-snort combo that made me lose it too, filling the kitchen with laughter I'd been starving for, rich and unguarded.

We stayed up too late. Ate too much. Talked over one another until the house rang with voices. For one night, home was the version it used to be before the distances and heavy silences had crept in.

And Mom was different. I noticed it immediately. She was lighter, as if a layer of weight she'd been carrying had been peeled away. Her eyes sparkled, her voice was softer, threaded with a warmth that wasn't always there. She even pulled me into a spontaneous dance in the kitchen, her hands warm on mine, her laugh bright against the hum of the refrigerator. Dad cut in, twirling her as if they were on a ballroom floor instead of linoleum tile, and for once I didn't roll my eyes.

"We should travel more," she'd said when he spun her around.

"Agreed," I'd laughed. "But not if you're going to be this annoyingly zen afterward."

I watched them, smiling. The way they gravitated toward each other, as if whatever happened in Scotland had stitched them back together. Dad looked at Mom as if she were still his favorite thing. My chest ached with the hope that it would stay like this. Their relationship wasn't perfect, but it was real and it was strong.

As they laughed together, their eyes sparkling, optimism surged. Maybe love like that wasn't just a fairy tale. Maybe, just maybe, it was possible for me too.

Later that night, as I walked past her room, I saw her standing in front of the mirror, her silhouette against the glow of the bedside lamp, brushing her hair, each stroke deliberate, slow. It wasn't the ritual itself that stirred unease, but the look in her eyes, as if searching for something in her reflection.

I leaned against the doorway, my voice a hesitant whisper. "Hey."

She startled, the reverie broken. Then, a fragile smile bloomed. "Hey, baby."

"You okay?"

"Yeah," she murmured. "Just thinking."

The smile remained, a painted mask that failed to reach the depths of her eyes. I lingered, watching her in the reflection, the lamplight gilding the delicate features of her face. She was luminous, almost otherworldly.

"What about?" I asked, stepping into the room, drawn by the irresistible force that was my mother.

Her gaze met mine in the mirror. "Scotland mostly. It was..." She paused, searching for a word that could capture the elusive essence. "Different."

I perched on the edge of her bed. She laid the brush on the vanity, turning to face me. Her hair cascaded down around her shoulders in waves of midnight that caught the light like captured starlight. She resembled one of those beautiful figures from Sal's paintings. A woman steeped in mystery and untold stories.

She shook her head, a faint smile playing on her lips. "It's hard to explain. It was like coming home to a place I didn't know I'd left."

The tone of her voice sent a shiver tracing its way down my spine, an ominous hush before a storm. I fought to ignore the threat of impending change that hung in the air.

"That sounds kind of creepy."

Her laugh was soft, tinged with wistfulness. "I guess it does."

"You're... different," I blurted, the words escaping before I could cage them.

Her eyes sharpened as if I'd stumbled upon a hidden truth. "Different how?"

I picked at a loose thread on the blanket, heat rising in my cheeks. "In a good way. You seem, I guess, calmer? But also distracted. Like your mind's somewhere else."

Mom tilted her head, studying me with that familiar intensity, the way she did when she suspected a lie about brushing my teeth or finishing my homework. This time, the weight of her gaze was heavier, measuring me.

"I am a little different," she admitted, her voice a low, resonant hum. "Trips like that, they change you. You return not the same person who left."

Her words hung in the air, and for reasons I couldn't articulate, a sudden sting pricked behind my eyes. There was so much more she was holding back. I yearned to ask what she meant, what transformation she had undergone. But the gravity in her tone served as a silent barrier. Instead, I moved closer, resting my head against her shoulder, seeking solace in her familiar presence.

She wrapped an arm around me, her fingertips tracing patterns on my arm, tiny spirals, an absentminded caress.

"Don't grow up too fast, Jenna," she whispered into my hair, her voice thick with unspoken emotion.

"I'm already grown," I retorted, attempting lightheartedness that sounded thin even to my own ears. But she held me tighter, as if she possessed knowledge I lacked, a secret understanding of the journey ahead.

For a fleeting moment, there had been a subtle alteration in the atmosphere. Something Dad didn't seem to notice. If he did, he pretended not to.

By Friday, a whole two days after their return, Dad had already slipped back into his routine. Work, computers, the constant phone calls from clients, checking the status of this job or that one. He still talked about taking another trip.

"Maybe Costa Rica," he'd said over dinner. "Somewhere with fewer ghosts and cheaper coffee."

Mom smiled at that, but she didn't laugh. Instead, she watched him, disappointment settling back into a familiar expression.

Just like *before*.

Tía Sal started a group chat about Mom's birthday party, full of her chaotic energy and lots of cake emojis.

Tía: *Caterer is booked. Don't fight me. We're doing this.*

Mom: *So we're pretending 40 isn't terrifying?*

Tía: *Please. I made 40 my bitch. You will too.*

Dahl: *I'll be in charge of the bonfire and cake.*

Tía: *Jenna, bring your amazing guac and good vibes.*

Me: *I'll bring the guac with a side of deep emotional repression. Is that festive enough?*

Tía: *So dramatic.*

When I prodded about the party, Mom offered little more than a nod. Her lips tightened with a cryptic, "I trust Sal will do what she does best."

I didn't miss the shadow that flickered across her face.

THIRTEEN

Cataleya

J ET LAG HIT DIFFERENTLY in your forties.

The tiredness was only part of it, disorientation was even worse. The world seemed to have tilted a few degrees while I was away. Nothing quite aligned. The house looked the same, smelled the same, even the plants had survived in my absence.

Thank you, Jenna.

It was different nonetheless.

Maybe because *I* was.

I stood in the kitchen, barefoot, fingers wrapped around a mug of coffee I didn't remember making, staring at the Carolina humidity pressing against the window, thick drops of condensation trickling down the glass. I missed the Scottish chill already, the way the air was crisp and alive with history. How every corner whispered things when you stood still long enough to hear them.

Jenna padded in, her hair a wild knot on top of her head, rubbing sleep from her eyes.

"You're up early," she mumbled as she opened the cabinet to grab a coffee mug.

I offered a tired smile. "Still on Glasgow time."

She poured herself a mug of steaming coffee before leaning on the counter across from me. "You filled me in on the funny stories and some other stuff. But how about the rest of it? You and Dad seem... good."

I hesitated, trying to find a way to answer.

Nick and I. Those moments had been magic in themselves. And already they were fading. All our problems had been waiting to greet us the moment we returned, tearing away the beautiful passion I'd gotten a tiny taste of. Having just a nip was worse than never having it at all now that I knew what we could be and all that I was missing.

Then the Awakening. I'd probably said more than I should have last night. Or had I? If this Awakening was hereditary, it would affect Jenna as well.

"It was all beautiful," I said instead.

Jenna nodded, looking at me as if she understood. "Well, you look happy, Mom."

Her eyes bore into me. It almost all came out. The pulpit, the women. My mouth began to form the words. But her phone chimed, breaking the moment.

"Tía has been texting like crazy. She wants you to call her about your birthday thing," she said around another yawn.

Of course she did. Salvia, planner extraordinaire. Another opportunity to shine.

"I've already tried talking her into doing something low-key. Just family," I sighed, forcing my voice to be light. Socializing with the number of people I knew my sister would invite layered another level of fatigue on top of my current jet-lag zombification.

Jenna sipped her coffee, giving me a sideways glance. "You okay, Mom?"

I blinked. "Yeah, why?"

"You can talk to me about stuff, you know."

I smiled again, this one more forced. "Just tired."

It wasn't a lie. Not exactly. Though there was more. There was always more.

"Okay. Well, I gotta pick up stuff for the guac and then head into the animal shelter. Let me know if you want anything special from the grocery store." Jenna took another sip of her coffee, then gave me a quick kiss on the cheek before going back upstairs.

My phone dinged. A text from Sal.

Salvia: *I'm calling you right now. You better answer. We have party things to talk about for tomorrow night. Don't even try to say no. We're celebrating you properly. Besides, it would be really awkward to have a birthday party with no birthday girl.*

I stared at the message and sighed again. It should've been touching. Instead, my stomach knotted. On top of my to-do list multiplying by the hour, I was still trying to figure out why I could taste the air now. Why the sky was brighter than it had ever been before.

My phone started ringing with a video call.

"I haven't missed one of your birthdays in forty years. I'll be damned if I start now," Salvia insisted, her stunning face filling my phone screen, which was propped against the laundry basket.

I shoved yet another load into the machine. "Seriously? You've never missed a single birthday? That makes me all warm inside," I teased.

"It should, you spoiled little *mocosa*."

"I'm a spoiled brat? That's rich. Kettle, meet pot."

"When have I ever been spoiled? I've been taking care of you and Papi since I was six."

"Oh, boo-freaking-hoo," I joked, laughing. "Says the successful, gorgeous woman whose equally gorgeous husband built a damn pedestal for his queen's throne to sit upon."

"Okay, that's true. It's the universe compensating for my stolen childhood."

"My god, you're dramatic. No matter what you might think, Papi was always good to you. To us. He did everything he could. I don't understand why you can't forgive him for Mom. It wasn't his fault she left us, you know."

Salvia looked away from the phone, the old hurt and anger gathering on her brow. "Let's not spoil perfectly good party planning with all that. It's time to celebrate, remember?"

Only when it came to our father would she shut down immediately, refusing to engage.

"You should celebrate Dahlia's birthday. I'm old, and mine has already passed. Hers is on Sunday. Do the party for her." Salvia stared at me through the phone, which did nothing to soften the ice of her appalled expression. "Fine. What time do you want us there on Saturday to help set up?"

"Have I taught you nothing? *Your* party means you're waited on and worshiped. You never engage in meaningless tasks such as helping. Besides, I have a crew."

"Of course you do."

She ignored me. "Be here at three sharp. I was going to make it a formal thing. Forty is a big deal. Then Dahlia threw a full teenage fit. Apparently, she's sick of 'sophisticated gatherings' and wants to 'slum it in sweats.' Her words."

I laughed. "Can't blame her. You and Z drag her to every gallery opening and gala imaginable. A backyard barbecue sounds pretty perfect. Barefoot. No heels. Remind me to kiss Dahlia for at least trying to reintroduce you to the real world."

"You and your bare feet. I swear, you're a pedicurist's worst nightmare. Besides, you're full of it. Don't pretend you don't love a fancy event. I've seen your closet."

"I do. Once in a while. Who doesn't love a reason to get a new dress and to see their man in a tux? But not for turning forty. I'd rather sneak into middle age unnoticed. In fact, I'm reverse counting birthdays from now on."

"Reverse counting?"

"Yup. This year, I'm forty. Too late to get out of that one. Next year, I'll be thirty-nine, the year after that thirty-eight, and so on."

"No way. Be proud. If our parents gave us nothing else, they gave us great genes. Wear that number like a crown, 'cause you're still hot. Maybe even the hottest you've ever been."

"You got the good genes. You look twenty-nine, not forty-four."

"I know. That's what I'm saying."

I rolled my eyes and grinned. "I've got to finish this list if I'm going to make it to the party you're so sweetly throwing me to remind me that I'm old, but apparently still hot. Love you, *hermana*."

"Love you back, *hermanita*."

Fourteen

Jenna

A s I did three mornings a week, I went to the animal shelter where I'd been volunteering for two years. I thought it would look great on vet school applications, a shining star on my resume.

Then I fell in love with all the animals. Taking care of them, giving them the attention they were so often deprived of. Especially the hardest cases. The ones deemed unadoptable, who waited out their allotted time behind lonely bars, their fate usually inevitable. The least I could do was show them affection once in their lives before their time ran out.

The shelter proved that I had found my calling in life, even a talent for it. Never once had I been bitten, not even by those branded as vicious or dangerous, too broken, too scarred by cruelty to endure human touch. I tried to shower them with love, despite the shelter workers' warnings and worried glances. Those kinds of dogs mostly cowered away from me in corners, their fear palpable.

My heart broke every time. I would speak in a soothing voice, a gentle murmur as I refreshed their water and offered them food and treats. Occasionally, one would grant me a fleeting reward. A quick, tentative lick to my hand, or a quiet snuggle before retreating once more into the desolate corner of their cages. Small miracles I never took for granted.

The shelter was the one place where the noise in my head quieted. The minute I walked through the door, the smell of kibble and disinfectant wrapped around me like a comforting embrace, the chorus of barks rising in their messy, joyful greeting.

That's when I saw him.

Curled in the far corner of kennel seven was a reddish, sand-colored boy who bore the noble stamp of Boxer and the soft-eyed sweetness of a Lab. His eyes, the color of wet earth, held a depth that contradicted his shelter-battered coat. He watched me with unnerving intensity, as if he recognized me beyond mere curiosity.

I knelt, my fingers finding the cold barrier of the chain-link. "Hey, handsome," I whispered, the sound barely audible above the song of dogs around us.

He didn't bark, didn't flinch. He remained still for a long time, his gaze never leaving mine. Then, slowly, he unfolded his large body and moved toward me, pressing his nose tentatively against my fingers. A warm, steady exhale brushed my skin, a reciprocation of recognition, soft yet undeniable.

Marisol, one of the other volunteers, came up behind me. "We named this one Bramble. They found him wandering around Rainbow Row for weeks before they could finally catch him. Skittish with everyone, except apparently you."

Bramble. The name was perfect. An echo of his untamed spirit, wild and rooted all at once.

I unlatched the gate and stepped inside. The loud clank of the metal latch resonated behind me. He leaned into me, as if we had shared a lifetime of such gestures. My hands sank into the warmth of his dirt-patched coat, and the world around me dissolved.

By the time my shift ended, I'd already signed the adoption papers.

The dog trembled with equal fear and excitement during the entire drive to Dahlia's. The moment I pulled up to the curb of the beach house, excitement won out. Bramble's thick tail whipped with the strength of a turbine.

"Okay. Okay. Hold on, big guy."

The moment I opened the car door, he jumped out and took off, leaving me with the leash in my hand and my heart galloping as fast as the dog was running. He had been in my care for less than six hours, and I was going to lose him, proving I was the worst pet owner ever.

But then he stopped at the front porch, turning in excited circles, looking back at me, impatiently waiting for me to catch up.

I chuckled, jogging up to him. "All right, I'm coming."

Again, he dashed ahead when I opened the front door, straight to the back slider that led out to the deck. He whimpered, looking out, then back at me. If I didn't know any better, I'd have thought he'd been here before.

On the deck, Dahlia's fingers danced over her guitar strings, the ocean breeze tugging at her curls and carrying fragments of a song still finding its shape.

"This time, no running off, got it?" He looked up at me with those big brown eyes, his long tongue lolled out of his panting mouth. The dog was literally smiling at me.

"I'm serious."

I opened the slider, and off he went, darting straight for Dahlia. My first worry was no longer that he'd run off. It was that he'd clobber poor, unsuspecting Dahlia with his eighty-plus pound body.

"Bramble! Get back here!"

His nails slid to a stop on the wooden planks before his massive red-yellow body halted. He slunk back over to me, as dramatically as possible, with an ashamed look on his adorable face. I watched in awe. There was no way he already recognized his new name.

"Good boy, Bramble." I reached down and gave his head a good scratch.

"Bramble, huh?" Dahlia set her guitar aside, smiling at the overly excited dog at my side.

With a wag of his tail at his new name, he glanced at me, then at Dahlia.

I laughed. "Go ahead. Easy this time."

He left my side to trot over to her, gave her a quick sniff, then rolled over, exposing his belly for Dahlia to rub.

"Does your mom know?" Dahlia asked, raising an eyebrow as she gave Bramble what looked to be the rubdown of his life.

"Not yet."

Dahlia chuckled. "I'm actually surprised you don't have ten dogs already. Not to mention who knows how many cats. Birds, pigs, goats. Really, you should have a farm by now."

"Funny."

"Seriously," she smiled sweetly. "Let's take him to the water, see if he's going to be a true beach pup."

Beach pup he was. He dove in and out of the waves with restless fervor. I threw a chew rope until my arm felt like it was going to fall off.

When I fell to the sand in defeat, Bramble finally settled at my feet, his head resting on his paws, his gaze fixed on the endless expanse of water. His ears twitched every so often, listening to things beyond what the rest of us could hear, while Dahlia and I sat on the beach listening to music and the waves lapping, chatting about everything and nothing, like we always did.

"Your mom seems different," Dahlia said.

I looked at her. "You noticed?"

She nodded. "Yeah. In a quiet way. Like she brought something back with her."

That gave me chills.

Brought something back.

I shook it off. "She needed the break."

"Don't we all," Dahlia muttered, pulling her knees up to her chest.

We fell quiet, the air now charged between us.

Her foot was tapping, her nervous tell. And she kept glancing toward the trail that led from the beach to the side of the house, as if she were expecting someone.

"What's up?" I asked.

"Hm? Nothing," she said too quickly. "Just twitchy. Too much lemonade." Her smile didn't quite meet her eyes. She shot another glance toward the dunes before leaning in and whispering, "It's... Jared, actually."

"Yeah?"

"I keep seeing him. He's been showing up in random places. Once at the gas station. Then the bookstore. All of a sudden, he's popping up *everywhere.*" She shook her head. "Never mind. I'm just being dramatic."

I studied her face. "Dramatic how?"

She shrugged, picking at a thread on her shorts. "Like, I'll think I see him, and then when I look again, he's gone. Other times, when I see him somewhere, I feel him looking at me. But as soon as I look up, he's suddenly busy doing something else. I'm sure it's just in my head."

The way she said it didn't sound like it was *just* in her head.

Bramble lifted his square head from where he was sprawled between us, ears flicking toward the dune path, the same direction that Dahlia had looked earlier. A low rumble started in his chest, barely a growl, enough to put my guard on high alert. I followed his intense gaze down the path, but saw only shadows.

"You want me to say something to him?" I asked.

Her eyes flicked to mine, sharp for half a second before she softened it with a laugh. "God, no. That'd make it weird. It's nothing." She reached for her phone, pretending to scroll, her shoulders still tight.

Bramble didn't take his eyes off the path. His tail was still, his whole body locked in that alert way dogs get when they've decided something doesn't belong.

Dahlia flinched when a gull screeched overhead, its shadow passing over us.

❧

When I took Bramble home, he had much the same reaction, excited to see his new home. He darted ahead, waiting for me on the first step.

My dad was the first to see us walk in. He was leaning against the counter, scrolling on his phone with one hand and nursing a beer with the other. His eyes flicked to the dog, then up to me.

I froze in the doorway, holding my breath like I was trying to sneak contraband past airport security. My best attempt at an innocent, awkward smile probably didn't help. I should have asked, or at least called to warn them what I was bringing home. But I'd been so enamored by Bramble that everything else fell away.

Deep laughter broke from him, warm and unguarded. "It's about time, kid. I thought you'd have brought home half a dozen by now."

"Why does everyone keep saying that?"

He gave me a sarcastic, amused look over the rim of his glass that screamed, *you know why.*

Bramble wagged his big tail as he meandered to my dad.

"Hey, big guy. You're a handsome one, aren't you?"

That giant tongue fell out again, pure bliss trembling through him as Dad gave him a good scratch.

Before I could call him back, the sound of soft footsteps on the stairs pulled Bramble's attention. The second my mom stepped into the kitchen, barefoot, her dark waves falling in front of her shoulders, a mug of tea cradled in her hands, Bramble froze.

It looked like he might cower and hide. But he wasn't frozen or fearful. He was listening. His head tilted, ears cocked forward, eyes locked on her in a way that made the tiny hairs on my arms rise.

Mom stopped too, meeting his gaze. Neither of them moved. The space between them buzzed with an invisible current. Then her mouth curved into a smile. Not her distracted, polite smile, but slow, pure adoration.

She bent, holding her hand out. Bramble moved immediately to her, plopping down at her feet. He pressed his nose into her palm without so much as a sniff, melting against her hand, his eyes fluttering shut as if he'd just been touched by sunlight. His tail thudded so hard against the tile that I worried it might break off.

"He's perfect," she said, glancing at me with that same softened look.

"Yeah, he is," I murmured in awe.

When she finally straightened and padded back upstairs, Bramble let out a soft whine. He stayed at the bottom of the stairs, watching until she disappeared from view. Only then did he turn and press himself into my leg, his eyes searching mine with an intensity that made my throat tighten.

FIFTEEN

Cataleya

A s I slipped earrings into my lobes before Salvia's party, I caught my reflection in the mirror. My skin glowed as if I'd been lit from within, my eyes catching light in a way that wasn't usual. I wasn't sure whether it was beautiful or dangerous.

Nick came up behind me, his reflection appearing over my shoulder.

I let myself imagine it, his hand reaching around my waist, the other sliding down the curve of my neck, his lips brushing the place where my pulse beat wild. I could feel the wanting in him, see it in the way his gaze lingered at my throat, the faint shift of his weight like he might lean in.

My whole body tensed, aching for his touch. I waited, breath held, certain he would reach for me.

But then he hesitated, his hand falling back to his side. In the mirror, his smile was warm but guarded.

"You look beautiful," he said, voice careful.

I smiled back, wanting to believe him. Instead, stinging disappointment edged in. He adjusted his collar beside me, the moment vanishing.

I touched the base of my throat as if to hold on to the ghost of what almost was. Under my fingertips, that faint tremor pulsed, alive with possibility, insistent and new.

"Jenna, let's go! Dad's already waiting in the car." I called up from the bottom of the stairs as I gathered my things and stuffed them into my small purse.

Footsteps pounded above before Jenna appeared at the top of the stairs, a playful grin plastered on her face. Bramble trotted down beside her, nails clicking against the wood, tail swishing as if he was in on whatever joke she'd just cooked up.

"What are you wearing?" I asked, chuckling as I took in her frumpy sweatpants and one of Nick's old oversized T-shirts. "Are you trying to give Tía Sal an aneurysm?"

"Don't worry, it was Dahlia's idea," Jenna said, slinging a backpack over her shoulder as she descended the stairs. "Just a little joke. I have a change of clothes in here."

"Just make sure my sister knows I had nothing to do with this rebellion," I muttered, locking the door behind us.

Bramble jumped into the backseat before Jenna even got the door fully open, settling in with a huff, his head resting on her knee, exactly where he belonged.

The scenic drive more than made up for the twenty minutes it took to get from our house in the old village of Mount Pleasant to Sullivan's Island.

The drive over the bridge through the marsh, watching the long, green grass sway along the shoreline, shifted whatever was now inside me. Subtle at first. A tremor under my skin, humming with vividness.

Colors grew louder, the air alive and threaded with currents that tugged at me. My senses became hyperaware, catching on small things like the way the tide breathed against the shore in time with my pulse.

As we passed a cluster of live oaks, Spanish moss cascading from their branches, I thought I could hear birds singing from their perches. Bramble lifted his head at the same moment, ears swiveling toward the trees. His gaze tracked the passing greenery, and for a second, we were both tuned into the same frequency.

Which was ridiculous.

Of course, I couldn't *hear* the birds in the trees from inside a speeding car, over the hum of the tires and the blast of the air conditioning.

I didn't know what it all meant yet. Only that I was awake in a way I hadn't been before.

Bramble's tail thumped twice, as if in agreement, before he curled back against Jenna's side. She was happily scrolling on her phone, oblivious. His eyes stayed half-open, tracking the trees until they faded from view.

I pulled my eyes away and focused instead on distracting myself with my own phone.

SIXTEEN

Nick

THE MOMENT OUR BOOTS hit Carolina soil, the routine swallowed us whole. Since we'd been home, I got busy, and she'd gone quiet again. Worse, the fragile ember Cat and I lit didn't survive the flight home.

In Scotland, she'd kissed me, remembering me, wanting me. Her body opened to mine again, not just out of habit or duty, but hunger. Need. Her laugh had returned, her eyes softer. I saw pieces of the girl I'd fallen in love with wrapped inside the woman she'd become. I'd made love to her against a cottage wall like we were twenty again. And now...

Now, her thoughts were always elsewhere. Not in that exhausted, hard-shift-in-the-NICU kind of way. She was pulled tight. When I touched her, sometimes she melted into it, and other times she... flinched.

Jenna noticed, though she said nothing. It was the way she watched us over the rim of her coffee mug each morning.

I watched Cat get ready for her birthday party Salvia had insisted on throwing. Beach house, big food spread, all of their high-profile artsy friends, and the rest of the family invited. Cat had groaned about it when we were still in Edinburgh, but she'd never say no. Not to Sal. She'd never liked disappointing her family, especially her sister. It had been wired into her since childhood. Guilt and obligation were part of her bloodstream. I could see it in the tension in her shoulders.

Cat stood at the mirror, putting on earrings. She looked stunning, of course. Hair half up, neckline soft, those curves she didn't think I noticed still stole my breath after all these years.

"You look beautiful," I said, stepping behind her. I wanted to lean in, pull her hair to the side so I could brush my lips against her neck. Taste her skin.

In Scotland, I would have without a second thought. Home, however, was less-charted territory.

I started to lean in, but her expression in the reflection stopped me. She was studying me, as if I'd somehow done the wrong thing.

She offered a small smile. "Thanks. You're not bad yourself."

Fumbling with hands that no longer knew what to do, I adjusted my collar in the mirror beside her. "Hey, you doing okay?"

She hesitated a beat too long. "Yeah. Just a lot on my mind."

"Work?"

"Sort of."

I waited. Nothing more came.

The dread or grief, or both, hit the center of my chest. She was slipping away again.

She turned, grabbed her bag, and headed for the door. "Ready?"

Not really. I nodded anyway.

The thing was, I didn't *mind* going. I actually loved Salvia and Z. Not only were they family, Z had been my best friend since Sal brought him into our team. Z was the guy who never asked too many questions, yet always had my back. Hanging out with him was easy. No pressure, just a string of beers and dry humor.

Diego would be there too.

Cataleya's dad had never liked me. Not really. He tolerated me. Had from the start. Back when I was just the scruffy neighborhood kid who fell for his youngest daughter. Even after twenty-plus years, a mortgage, a child, and multiple thankless family holidays, I could still see it in his eyes.

Not good enough.

I didn't let it get to me anymore, at least not much. Tonight, with everything already off, I wasn't exactly looking forward to the cold once-over and passive-aggressive comments about how *real men worked with their hands.*

At least there'd be cake.

Cataleya was quiet as we drove. She stared out the window, her fingers tapping absently against her thigh. The sun slanted low across her cheekbones, catching in her lashes. It reminded me of her in Scotland again, how she glowed that morning after we... Just thinking about it made me shift in my seat, grateful no one was paying attention.

We passed a stretch of trees along the coastal road before we hit the bridge, and she turned to look. Really *watched*. Eyes narrowed. Head tilted, as if something invisible had caught her attention.

The damndest part about it was that the dog did the same thing at the exact same time. Bramble's head had shot up from Jenna's lap and mimicked Cat's gestures. As if he heard and saw what she did.

"What's up?" I asked.

She blinked and turned back toward the road, smoothing her hand over her lap. "Nothing. Just... do the trees seem greener than usual?"

I chuckled softly. "It's Charleston in summer. Everything's trying to show off."

She didn't laugh. Just smiled faintly and kept looking out the window. Bramble's tail thumped in agreement with Cat. I'd never seen a dog so in love with two women. Clever pup.

By the time we pulled in front of Sal and Z's beach house, she'd gone quiet again. Not in that sullen way. She was humming. Some low, absent tune I didn't recognize.

She stepped out of the car before I even killed the engine, eyes sweeping the street. Cars lined both sides as far as could be seen.

"Little get-together?" Cat muttered as we turned the corner. The full spread of Sal and Z's beachfront party came into view. A long white tent dominated the sand, and smoke billowed from the grill, a meat-lover's incantation.

"I'm sure Z's not the one manning the grill, either," I added with a laugh, slipping my hand lightly to the small of Cataleya's back. I enjoyed touching her again. Needed to. Even if she didn't always lean into it. "I'd hate the guy if he weren't so damn nice."

"Sure you would," she said with a smile, the corner of her mouth curling, knowing I was only half serious. "You two have been inseparable since Salvia introduced him, what is it? Nineteen years ago now?"

"Because he's such a damn nice guy," I said as Z walked up to us. "Not to mention the man is eye candy."

Z came striding up the walk, his white linen shirt rolled up at the sleeves. Confident. Calm. That effortless Z-cool that I still hadn't managed to imitate after nearly two decades.

"Hey man, you're not bad to look at either," he said, pulling me in for a hard-patting man-hug.

"And that accent? Unfair advantage," I grinned, giving him a few slaps back.

"Should I be jealous?" Cat teased, giving Z a hello hug. "Maybe let you two have a moment?"

Z wrapped her up in one of those signature hugs that somehow looked both protective and flirty. He leaned in, whispering, *"Il n'y a pas besoin d'être jalouse, chérie,"* in his smooth bass, heavy with Creole French.

She blinked. "Yeah, Nick's right. That's definitely hot. What did you say?"

"I said, 'There is no need to be jealous, darling,'" Z translated with that infuriating grin before kissing her cheek.

His eyes jumped behind us to Jenna striding up in her combat boots and sweats. He burst into laughter.

"You too?" Z shook his head in mock dismay. Jenna beamed at him. Bramble gave a happy bark of agreement.

"Are you sure you still want to walk in like that?" Cat asked her, grinning.

"Oh, all this big fanciness is going to make it even more hilarious," Jenna said with that mischievous sparkle in her eyes, the one she got from me, whether she wanted to admit it or not.

She took off ahead, no doubt in search of Dahlia, her other half.

"Those two," I chuckled, shaking my head.

"Careful," Cat warned, nudging me with her elbow. "You look proud."

"Hell, I *am*." I leaned in and pressed a kiss to her temple. She didn't pull away. She didn't lean in either.

"I swear you love poking the bear in my wife," Z said, smirking as we followed the girls into the crowd.

"I do what I can to stay entertained," I quipped.

"Better you than me, brother," Z said as he led us toward the crowd. "Make yourselves at home. It's your party, after all. Happy birthday, *chérie.*"

I glanced over at Cat.

Her gaze scanned the large crowd, a sheen of panic settling over her. She went still. I knew she didn't do crowds well, even though her natural charm always pulled them in.

"Bar?" I bumped her hip.

"You read my mind."

⁂

We made our way through the crowd. The way she smiled at them, the effortless sway in her movements, the light in her eyes. It was all Cat. Turned up. Amplified.

As I followed, I couldn't help but feel like I was always a step behind, made to watch instead of being her partner. A few steps later, I heard a voice beside me.

"Uncle Nick," Dahlia said, raising a brow. "You look like you're thinking about something dangerous."

I laughed under my breath. "I always look like that. It's just my face."

She sipped from her lemony drink as she scanned the crowd. "Tía Cat looks good. Like, glowy."

"She does," I agreed.

Dahlia tilted her head. "Different, though."

I looked at her sideways. "You're not wrong."

She just smiled, far too grown-up for her age. "It's a good different. I think."

She spotted Jenna and Bramble across the beach and gave me a soft nudge. "Don't overthink it, okay? Go tell her she looks amazing before someone else beats you to it."

And just like that, she fluttered away, a butterfly in the wind.

I turned back to find Cat laughing, really laughing, with Salvia in that warm, unguarded way she hadn't done with me in years. The sun painted her in gold that made her glow in a way that had nothing to do with me.

She used to tilt toward me like that, head tipped back against my shoulder when we were younger, the sound of her laugh soft against my neck.

As I watched my wife from across the patio, sharp jealousy twisted through me with nowhere to land. I knew I'd been the one to let her slip away.

Seventeen

Cataleya

THE ENORMITY OF THE crowd at my *little* birthday party was overwhelming, to say the least. Once Z left our side, I was exposed. Too many people I didn't know. Too much noise. Too much sun. Too much everything.

I stood caught in the blur of clinking glasses, perfumed embraces, and strangers offering smiles like we were lifelong friends.

A raw and unfiltered kaleidoscope of emotions that weren't mine slammed into me. I could feel the energy of the crowd. *Literal* energy, a current crackling beneath my skin.

The wind off the ocean carried more than salt. It carried *feeling*. Fragments of other people's joy, discomfort, sorrow, pride, sadness, greed, happiness. All of it soaked into me without permission, a floodgate swinging wide open. My skin vibrated, tingling with static. The air heated as clove and sandalwood churned with the aromas from the barbecue.

My lungs were desperate for the breath I'd been holding and my feet wanted to bolt back to the car where it was quiet and safe.

Instead of running, I remained anchored, my entire body trembling.

A woman approached, reaching out to shake my hand, saying happy birthday and something about not looking a day over thirty-five. Muttering a quick thank you, I tried my hardest to look normal by making eye contact, though I hesitated to take her outstretched hand. Her face contorted in confusion as she walked away.

Nick placed a hand at my waist, pulling my attention back to him. I focused everything on his touch. The light pressure of his fingers, the warmth of his palm. I moved my eyes from the crowd to my feet, staring at the one spot near my sandaled toes where a small white pebble rested. I blew a breath out slow and deep, inhaled the same way, giving all of my focus to that rock and the weight of my husband's hand.

Finally the noise faded, and the world righted itself to a normal decibel.

Nick reached for my hand. I squeezed it back, grateful, even though it made me ache. He still thought we were celebrating the same thing. For me, this wasn't just another birthday.

It was my first as an Awoken.

Salvia waved to me from down the sand, radiant as ever. But the light around her was too bright, the sun clinging to her longer than it should, gleaming along Salvia's long, dark hair that cascaded down her elegantly clad back. Of course, not a single one out of place. Her flawless white blouse and pants fluttered in the breeze, contrasting the blue-green of the ocean behind her.

I blinked against the brilliant glow. Her shape blurred, then sharpened, a shimmering aura pulsing faintly around her shoulders. I took a step back, blinking harder, refocusing my eyes. The aura slowly faded away.

Affluent-looking guests hovered around her, offering cheek kisses and empty praise as she greeted them. It was enough to tighten my stomach into a knot of anxiety.

"Bar?" Nick bumped my hip.

"You read my mind."

As the bartender handed me a glass of Chardonnay, a familiar voice chimed behind me.

"*Hola, mi querida hija. Feliz cumpleaños.*"

"Papi." I smiled, kissing my father's cheek. "Finally, a face I recognize."

"Nick." Though my father had been in the country since he was twenty years old, his accent stubbornly clung to his words. Slight. But still there.

"Diego." Nick nodded, shaking Diego's outstretched hand. Civil yet still cool, even after all these years.

My father had never quite let go of how young we were when we got together. Or that we married the moment I turned eighteen. Or that Jenna had appeared less than a year after that. A quarter of a century later and he was still giving Nick a hard time. Not as intensely, but sadly, they wouldn't be having a beer together anytime soon.

Just then, Dahlia's laughter rang out. Salvia had spotted the girls. She charged toward them, taking both by the arms, leading them back toward the house. I chuckled. Salvia's ability to hold her composure was phenomenal. She was ironclad. I knew her well enough to see the red rising beneath her olive skin.

The girls were right, it *was* pretty funny. I was definitely going to get an earful about our spirited little jokesters.

The laughter died on my lips when I noticed my father watching me. Rather, the *way* he was watching me. Observant. Suspicious.

"What's up?" I asked, raising an eyebrow.

"Nothing. What do you mean?" He quickly looked away, the strange look disappearing as he stared down into the suddenly fascinating beer in his hands.

"You were *looking* at me..."

"I wasn't looking at you."

I stared eye to eye with him, playing the blinking game. A game I always won.

My father was not a tall man, but he'd always held his ground. My mother had been even shorter. Where Salvia and I had gotten our height, albeit an average five-seven and five-six, I'll never know.

"I only wondered how your trip was. You haven't told me much."

"It was great. Definitely the break Nick and I needed."

"Good." He hesitated, still looking at me, as if waiting for something more. "Good," he repeated, softer this time.

"I wasn't trying to keep anything from you."

He only nodded.

"What made you pick Scotland?"

I shrugged. "I've always wanted to see where Mom's side came from. We've been to see Abuela Carmen in Costa Rica a few times. But never Scotland."

He nodded again, his lips pressed together. "Did you see or do anything unusual?"

"Unusual?" My brow furrowed.

"Scotland's an old place. Old places hold things. Sometimes people feel... different there."

"Different how?" I asked, pretending to laugh, though something about his phrasing tugged at me.

He didn't answer right away. His gaze drifted past me, where the evening light was thinning. "Some people sense things others don't. History, memory, energy. Whatever word makes you comfortable."

"Energy," I echoed carefully. My father was entirely too close to hitting the nail on the head. Suspiciously so. The way he said it made goosebumps rise, as if he wasn't guessing. I forced a small smile, though my pulse had quickened. "Like ghosts?"

That earned the faintest twitch of a smile. "Maybe."

I shifted my weight, pretending to study the condensation on my glass instead of him. "Nothing was really *unusual*, except that it all seemed... familiar?"

His eyes lifted to mine. "Familiar," he repeated.

"What are you really asking, Papi?"

He studied me for a long moment, the lines around his mouth deepening. "You look different," he said at last.

My heart stumbled, though I kept my expression even. "Jet lag, maybe."

Diego kept watching me, that same old instinct in him working quietly, his need to read people, to uncover what was unsaid. "Some places remember us, even when we forget them." A solemn expression passed over his face before he glanced away.

Nick, standing quietly nearby, glanced over, honing in on the strangeness of my father's behavior.

"Was that what it was like when you went there with Mom?"

"Yes. Well, for your mother."

"And for you?"

He was silent for so long that I thought he wouldn't answer. Until a low whisper finally came. "It took something from me."

"What?" I asked.

"Everything."

I was taken aback. Never in forty years had I seen any darkness in my father. Not only did I see it, it rippled from him.

He placed his hand over mine. It was supposed to be a gesture of comfort, but the moment our skin touched, a flash of heat radiated through my palm, up my arm. The edges of my vision blurred, my mind transported, focusing on my father's eyes, diving into them. Through his cornea, past his now dilated pupils.

The movie played, traveling down the optic nerve, into the vessels, speeding into the prefrontal cortex of his brain. A cluster of tissue, darker than the rest around it, lay still while neurons fired all around it. The movie lingered there, then it dove into the dark tissue. Another movie played. A series of quick flashes. My mother's face, her sweet smile so bright. So much love in her eyes. Then, a piece of paper. A letter. Blurred words I couldn't make out. Then, my father falling to his knees in the mud, anguish crippling him.

My vision pulled away, speeding backward out of him until I was just staring at his face. The wine glass in my hand shattered, white wine spilling onto the white tablecloth, a few bright red splotches of my blood dripping with it.

"Jesus." Diego grabbed my hand, assessing the cut, then pressed a napkin into my palm. I pulled away, afraid I'd see more.

"Are you all right?" Nick asked as he took my hand, dabbing the blood away with more napkins.

"It's fine. Just a little cut."

"You sure?"

"Yes. Yes, it's fine." I hissed, fully aware people were now looking over at us.

"Okay. I'll get you another glass." Nick kissed my palm, then turned back toward the bar. When he was out of earshot, I looked back at my father.

"Papi—"

Another voice broke in.

"Diego, looking debonair as ever." An older woman I recognized from Salvia's circle approached us at the cocktail table we were standing at.

"Mrs. Mitchell. Good to see you," Diego awkwardly hugged the woman when she pulled him into her arms.

The strangeness of the moment faded quickly as I watched the expression change on my father's face when the woman pulled him in suggestively. I had to bite my cheek and look away to hide a smile, while Nick didn't bother hiding his amusement as he walked back with two fresh drinks in hand.

"I'm not *Mrs.* anymore, silly. Not for a year now. I insist you call me Cora. I was meandering through one of Zion's galleries the other day and, of course, ran into Salvia. She has such exquisite taste. Her eye is impeccable. Anyway, it made me think of you and how we still have never gone to that lunch we promised each other. How about next week? I'm free Tuesday afternoon." The woman flipped her hair, then rested her elbows on the table, giving Diego an excellent view of her cleavage.

"*Cora*, I don't usually have time during the week. My job tends to get in the way of that," he said flatly.

"You're such a funny man. Oh, Stacey, dear. I've been dying to talk to you..." With that, Cora disappeared.

"Short attention span," Diego muttered, taking a long pull from his beer.

"She's nice looking, recently divorced, and obviously willing. You should go for it."

"Why on earth would I *go for it*?" Diego snorted, taking another long drag of his beer.

"Because you should have a woman in your life. I don't think I've ever even seen you date. I mean, I'm sure you have. I hope you have. Which is great. Live a little."

"*Mija*, I would never do that to a woman."

"Do what?"

"Your mother, *ella era el amor de mi vida*. My heart will never belong to another woman."

"She left us, Papi. A long time ago. You deserve happiness."

He pulled me to his side and kissed my forehead. "I *am* happy. You, Salvia, Jenna, and Dahlia, you girls *are* my happiness."

"We are?" Salvia joined us, kissed our father's cheek, gave Nick a quick hug hello, then me.

"You girls are the very fiber of my heart," he said softly, pain flickering behind his smile. A deep, old pain that often appeared in Salvia's presence. "You know this."

"Okay." Salvia turned her attention to me. "Happy birthday, baby sister."

"This is a lot, Sal. You didn't have to."

Salvia clicked her tongue. "This? I scaled way back. Besides, it's what I do."

"I'm not one of your galleries. I'm just a simple girl."

"Don't I know it? You'd rather be barefoot and braless."

"Who wouldn't?" I kissed my sister's cheek. "Thank you, though. This is all gorgeous. As usual."

"Even though I never balk at an opportunity for an elaborate celebration, you're worth celebrating. You're my best friend."

"Still?"

"Always. From cradle to the grave."

"So, what happened?"

"What always does. Life."

EIGHTEEN

Jenna

BY THE TIME WE'D redressed, the DJ had gone quiet and the deck lights glowed soft and golden against the twilight. A piano had been wheeled close to where the speakers were set up, its white lacquer gleaming under the deck lights.

Dahlia slipped onto the bench, her hair catching the sun, fingers hovering above the keys.

"Happy birthday to my favorite Tía." She found Mom in the crowd and gave her a bright smile before she began to play.

The first run was classical. Demanding, fierce, a storm of notes that belonged in a Vienna concert hall. But then, as natural as breath, the melody bent and softened, weaving into my mom's favorite song. The shift was seamless, the notes pouring out as if they were meant to be part of each other, waiting for Dahlia's hands to free them.

The breeze lifted strands of her hair as she swayed, every chord alive. She wasn't just playing the piano, she was part of it, part of the air itself. Her music braided with the salty wind and the gentle lapping of waves along the shore.

Guests leaned against the rails, hushed. Even Tía Sal stilled, her face softening with bright pride glinting in her eyes. And Mom. She pressed her hand to her chest, eyes wide and glazing over, as though the music had struck something tender and hidden deep inside her.

A shift of a shadow beyond the dunes tore my attention away from Dahlia. Bramble lifted his head, ears twitching. But when I blinked, the space was still again, and Dahlia's music carried everything else away.

The last note lingered, trembling in the air before it slipped into the sound of the tide. Silence, then applause, warm and real, rose from the deck and bonfire below.

I leaned into Dahlia as she stood, her face flushed and luminous.

"If you had only added the words, that would've been over-the-top amazing."

She swatted at me, laughter spilling out. "Don't be crazy. My parents are here."

"Exactly. Best time to blow their minds." I grinned.

"Or die of humiliation," she muttered, rolling her eyes, but her smile gave her away.

As the party dwindled down, the last die-hard guests remained around the bonfire. Dahlia and I had slipped away to the deck with Tía Sal's homemade lavender-lemonade, watching the gulls spiral above the waves, silver against the bruised sky. The breeze carried laughter from below while Bramble snored at our feet.

It should have been relaxing, but there was an undercurrent running between us in the way Dahlia's foot tapped. After the second time she looked back toward the dunes, I looked too. Standing just in the shadows was a still figure. Too still. Most likely a pole, or a guest who had too much to drink.

Even Bramble was picking up on Dahlia's tension. He lifted his head, ears perked, a low rumble in his throat sounding as his eyes followed my line of sight. I tried to focus on the figure, but nothing moved.

"Brams, hush now. You'll freak out Tía." Or Dahlia, for that matter.

"I need to get you back out on a board," I said, laying back on the cushioned lounge chair.

Dahlia's shoulders lifted in a half-shrug. "I don't think so. That was an epic failure last time."

I nudged her elbow. "You live on the beach, Dahl. You should probably know how to surf. Let me try to teach you again." I mimed a wobble, my arms flailing.

Dahlia giggled. "I fell off so spectacularly you nearly drowned laughing." She pushed me playfully. "I want to be fearless, like you. You don't care about looking silly."

I bumped her back. "If you loosen up a bit, you too can be fearless and silly."

Her phone buzzed on the table between us. She frowned, swiped it up, and the color drained from her cheeks. I leaned closer. It was a photo. A far shot, but unmistakable. Dahlia at the piano earlier, playing Mom's song. The angle was zoomed in haphazardly, as if taken from far away.

My stomach iced over. "Who sent that?"

She swallowed. "Jared. He says he heard about the party from the gallery crowd."

Before I could spit out what I thought about that, footsteps sounded on the deck. Jared emerged from the shadows as though he'd been waiting, his hands tucked casually in his pockets, a grin that was all charm and teeth plastered on his face.

"Hope I'm not crashing." His voice slid out smoothly. "Word travels fast in the art world. Big night for the Ortega-Eze family. Thought I'd stop by, see for myself."

Dahlia blinked, caught between flustered and pleased. "Oh... uh. Sure. I mean, hi." She tucked her phone away, pushing a curl behind her ear.

A low, steady growl rumbled from Bramble, his whole body tightening. I placed my hand on his back, trying to calm him.

When Jared crouched, feigning interest as if he meant to scratch his ears, Bramble's lips peeled back, his teeth flashing in the lights. A guttural snarl ripped from his chest as he hunched low, ready to lunge.

"Bram!" I grabbed his collar with both hands, muscles straining as he surged forward. For a fraction of a second, I wanted to let him go, see Jared knocked flat, teeth sinking into that pretty face. Let the outside show what I already saw. But morals won. I dragged Bramble back against my legs, his body vibrating with rage.

Jared straightened slowly, eyes narrowing on Bramble, then on me, before his smile slid back into place. He smoothed the cuff of his shirt, all composure again.

"It's okay, boy. I'm family now," he quipped, voice light but edged. "Nice setup," he said, glancing toward the bonfire. "Family, friends, the sea. Beats any gallery opening." His eyes landed on Dahlia and lingered just a beat too long.

"Yeah. It's nice." Dahlia laughed, either nerves or, *gross*, flirtation twisting it into something like agreement.

Nice? That was how she described being stalked and showing up uninvited?

She didn't see the edge beneath his smile.

But I did. And Bramble did.

Tía Sal looked up at the sound of Dahlia's laughter. She paused, her gaze sliding past us toward Jared. Her expression sharpened. Measuring, deciding whether he belonged or not. Then her eyes shifted back to Dahlia, softening for just a breath.

She crossed the sand toward us, a tray of rolled bruschetta balanced in her hands, but I didn't miss the way her eyes fixated on Jared.

"Uh oh. Do you think she's still mad at us?" I whispered to Dahlia, nudging her with my elbow.

"Can you two get down there and at least say goodbye to what's left of our guests?" she asked, her voice brisk, but the note underneath was different.

Protective, edged.

I caught Dahlia's elbow, steering her gently toward the steps. "Come on. Tía wants us down there." My tone was light, but my grip wasn't.

"We have to go. See you later?" Dahlia said absently to Jared, her worried gaze focused on Sal, who returned to Uncle Z's side. She motioned for Dahlia to join with a stern nod.

Jared straightened, his gaze shifted to me. He smiled again, wider this time. "I'll be around," he said. Not goodbye. A promise.

From the bonfire, Uncle Z's laugh rang out, deep and warm. But when his attention tracked upward and landed on Jared, his smile faltered. He shifted closer to Sal, brushing her arm in that quiet way he had of letting her know he was paying attention.

And Dad, next to him at the bonfire, noticed too. His dimple faded, replaced by that furrow that came out when he didn't like one of my dates. He wouldn't say anything, at least not in front of the other guests. But I knew that look. A silent warning meant for later.

"Tonight," Sal called out, her impatience flushing her olive skin.

"On it." Dahlia skipped down the stairs to the beach.

I saw the familiar lift-and-drop in Dahlia's chest, already knowing what ran through her mind. We'd talked about it so many times.

Music was the art that spilled out of her. When Dahlia played, she was fluid and daring. Until she overthought pleasing her mom.

No matter how many times I tried to reassure Dahlia, it did little to settle her anxiety that she wasn't good enough. But that was Dahlia, always striving to be the perfect student, perfect hostess, perfect daughter.

Not that Tía Sal had ever been cold or cruel. She was the complete opposite. In fact, Salvia was wrapped around her daughter's finger, though Dahlia never saw it that way. She only saw her mother's successful, fancy art gallery curator side, where Mrs. Salvia Ortega-Eze had to wear her name like a crown, keeping it and the gallery's reputation gleaming with perfection.

NINETEEN

Jenna

"I'M GOING TO STAY for a while. Dahlia can bring me home."

"Dahlia?" Mom laughed and kissed my cheek as I walked them out to their car.

Across the street, a shadow leaned against the fence near the edge of the neighbor's yard. I couldn't see a face. My heart did a double beat. Jared again, squatting in the dark? I scoffed at my absurdity.

Probably just a stray guest.

Beside me, Bramble gave a low, quiet growl, barely more than a vibration under my hand where it rested on his collar. His gaze was locked on the figure, body stiff, tail straight and still.

Or was it?

"You okay?" Dad asked.

"Yeah. Just thought I saw someone." I stroked Bramble's neck to calm him, even as my pulse kicked. "This guy still needs to get used to people."

Dad's eyes stayed on the fence line. "Who was the guy earlier?"

A shiver ran through me. Dad and his radar. In for the win again.

"Someone crushing on Dahlia," I said. "Unfortunately."

"We don't like him?" my mom asked, not even trying to hide her smirk.

"Not particularly. But it's her life."

Dad's jaw twitched. "If he keeps hanging around, I'll have a word with Z."

"No way, Dad. She'd murder me." I wrapped Dad in a quick hug, done with giving Jared more oxygen. "I'm going to convince Dahlia to let me teach her how to drive. Again."

"I don't get it. You chomped at the bit to get your driver's license." My dad's dimple deepened as he smiled at me, remembering how much I hounded him to teach me.

Randomly, he'd throw me his keys and let me take him around the neighborhoods of Mount Pleasant. We'd always end up getting ice cream on our impromptu Driver's Ed sessions.

"That's what I'm saying. She's missing out on freedom."

"Be careful. Not too fast. Only go on side roads. The—"

"Mom. I know. Love you guys." I waved as I walked away. Always so protective. She forgets I'd been driving for five whole years already. Bramble trotted close to my leg, glancing back toward the fence line twice before following me up the path.

⁂

I pulled my Honda into the driveway. Bramble jumped out the second I opened the door, circling once before standing sentinel near the front bumper, ears tuned toward the curve in the road. Dahlia hovered at the driver's door, arms wrapped around herself.

"Come on," I coaxed, spinning the keys around my finger. "You've got to learn sometime, right? And better with me than with some boring instructor."

Sal and Z watched us from the front porch. Worry plastered on Tía Sal's face, while Z looked amused.

Dahlia cast a glance at her parents, then down the deserted lane, where streetlights winked on one by one.

"What if I stall and everyone's watching?"

I gave her a sideways smile. "Then we'll stall spectacularly, just like surfing. Only this time, I promise not to laugh. Too hard. Besides, it's automatic."

Salvia's lips twitched, and a sparkle of laughter rang out.

"Z, go with them," she suggested as she also wrapped her arms around herself. Like mother, like daughter.

"Jenna is perfect for Dahl. She actually listens to her." He laughed and winked at Dahlia. "Give her hell, Jenna. Just don't kill her."

Dahlia bit her lip. "You're always so brave. Me? I panic if I can't find the turn signal."

"Then I'll teach you the turn signals first." I handed the keys to Dahlia. "Get in. Start it."

Bramble hopped into the backseat, curling up behind us with his chin propped on the console as if he intended to supervise the whole lesson.

Finally, Dahlia crawled into the car, clutching the steering wheel with a white-knuckle grip, her posture iron-straight.

"Relax. Pretend you're at your piano in a room full of people waiting to hear you sing." I grinned. "Except the room moves."

A nervous laugh escaped Dahlia. "Great analogy."

I took her through the controls. Gas. Break. And of course, the turn signals.

Dahlia eased her foot. The car rolled an inch, then two, then five. She stiffened.

"Breathe," I teased, my hand patting Dahlia's shoulder. "You're doing amazing."

Dahlia pressed the accelerator. The Honda crept forward, slow, confident. She grinned, the first spark of triumph lighting her eyes.

"I'm driving. I'm really driving."

I glanced at the speedometer. Fifteen miles per hour. "Hey, slow down. We're not drag racing," I joked, my voice playful.

Dahlia's laugh bubbled out. "Shush, you."

"Today, you claim freedom. Tomorrow night, you claim adulthood. You can drive us on the open road to *Shadow & Silk*."

Dahlia glanced toward the curve leading back to the main road. "The open road sounds downright terrifying."

I softened my expression. "You've got me. Always. No matter how scary."

After a while, Dahlia relaxed. We even got up to twenty-five miles an hour. As we rolled down another quiet road, Dahlia stiffened.

"How do you know if you're being followed?"

I peeked in the side mirror. A black SUV was behind us.

"Probably just someone heading home. Other people do occasionally use these roads."

She nodded, her knuckles turning white on the wheel again. Bramble stared out the back window.

"Maybe it's Jared, your not-so-secret admirer."

Dahlia gave a quick glare in my direction before focusing on the road again. "Not funny."

"Hey, having a stalker is hot these days. I bet if you ask, he'd go shirtless while wearing a mask for you."

"Still not funny."

"I mean, I did try to warn you about him."

"Oh my god, Jenna. He's not *that* bad."

"At least this SUV isn't right on our ass. Let's make our way back. I don't want you killing us in the dark." I reached over and turned up the music.

Twenty

Cataleya

Nick and I weren't able to slip away from the party until later than I'd wanted. By the time we did, I was hoping, perhaps foolishly, to rekindle that fire. To feel his lips burning on mine again.

At the party, I saw a glimpse of that heat. The way he watched me, his touch finding me, a hand on my back, an arm around my waist when we'd first gotten there. It didn't take long before we went our separate ways, as usual. He found his group of people to mingle with. I'd found mine. The touching and sideways glances evaporated into mist.

When we pulled into our driveway, the air between us had cooled completely, washing away with the summer rain that fell steadily.

"I hope Jenna and Dahlia aren't still driving around."

Nick didn't look at me. He didn't respond at all. He just kept walking, leaving me to talk to myself.

By the time I got into bed next to him, he was already snoring peacefully. The slow cadence of his breath, the gentle rise and fall of his chest, were as familiar as the tides. Part of me wanted to reach for him, snuggle into him. More of me wanted him to reach out.

Instead, I turned away, shut off the lamp, and closed my eyes, trying to ignore the riptide of want.

The darkness brought a flash of memory from Scotland. How his hands gripped the curve of my hips as he ground himself into me, giving me that taste of the passion we'd been missing. Yet, every time we returned to our normal life, he forgot I existed all over again.

My eyes welled up as I listened to the light rainfall outside the window. Couldn't he feel it, too? How could I be the only one living in the racing current of hurt and stinging pain, while he was happily adrift on a calm surface?

The tears got harder to hold back as I cried quietly. I was giving up on myself. On him. On us.

There was no use trying to shock the asystole of my heart back to life.

The devastation pressed down on my chest as I tried to quiet my sobs. They overtook me, wracking through my body.

I slipped out of bed, going to the kitchen, my path blurred by tears no longer swallowed. I grabbed a glass and a bottle of whiskey, taking them to the table where I poured a generous amount, shot it back, then poured another, hoping the heat would burn away the numbness.

The house was silent except for the steady patter of rain against the windows, a tempo to the grief I could no longer contain. My hand trembled as I brought the glass to my lips. The rush of emotion heaved my body with fierce sobs as I cried into the silence.

When I heard footsteps sounding down the hallway, I didn't even try to hide my tears. Nick appeared in the doorway, bleary-eyed, hair mussed by sleep, scratching the back of his head.

"What are you still doing up?"

"I'm..." I ran a trembling palm over my face, wiping away tear tracks, unable to look at him. I picked up my glass, watching the amber liquid swirl, and took another sip before answering. "Couldn't sleep."

He stepped into the kitchen, leaned on the doorframe. The space between us miles instead of mere feet. The half-smile on his lips died when he looked at me.

"You okay?"

A soft, broken laugh escaped me.

"That's the thing, Nick. I'm not. I haven't been in a long time. And I don't think you are either." I took another sip. "I think we've gotten really good at pretending, though. Haven't we?"

Nick walked over slowly until he stood across the table from me. He didn't sit.

"Cat, talk to me."

I lifted my tired, red, swollen eyes to meet his.

"I don't know what to say. I just..." My voice broke in a guttural sob. My eyes drifted to the picture of us on our wedding day. I'd wanted forever with him. We got halfway there. "We used to be this fire, and now we're just smoke. Every morning I wake up, when I reach for you, it's like you're already gone."

He swallowed, throat bobbing. "I'm here."

"Are you? Because I swear I've been married to a ghost for years. A ghost who remembers anniversary dates but doesn't know my favorite song. A ghost who knows how to laugh, but not how to reach me when I'm bleeding inside."

His face crumpled. He sat across from me, hesitating before he reached out, his fingers trembling as he took the bottle and my glass, filling it. He took a long sip before speaking.

"You've been pulling away," he whispered. "I thought Scotland would be our reset."

I shook my head. "It was a spark. Sparks die if there's nothing left to burn," my words muffled in the tears that came back. "Nick, I'm not angry. I'm just... empty."

"I've been trying." He swallowed hard, as a tear slipped down his face, unbidden. "Just tell me how to save it."

"I don't know how, and I'm all out of fight," I confessed, staring down at the tiled floor, the one I painstakingly picked out. "I don't even know when we started fading. One day I woke up and realized I couldn't remember the last time you really looked at me."

Nick reached across the table, taking my hand. For once, I didn't pull away. We sat there, fingers entwined, soaking in their warmth.

"I literally have no regrets. We were too young, but we weren't. I like the way my life has turned out. Why don't you?"

I couldn't answer. Not because I didn't want to. I would give anything to be able to answer that question. Maybe then, I'd find what it was that would finally ease my heart into contented happiness. Nick deserved an honest response, but all I could manage was a weak shrug of my shoulders.

"I love you. I'll always love you, Cat. Even if it doesn't look the way it used to," he said, his voice rough as he pressed my hand to his cheek. His breath was warm, his tears hot on my fingers. "I'm sorry I haven't been enough."

I shook my head, unable to find the right words. In that moment, I was just a woman too broken to hold on. I wanted to believe him and feel hope flicker again. But how many times had I already done that? All I could do was let my fingers tighten around his, a fragile bridge between us. No words, just the heat of his palm against mine.

"I'm sorry," I whispered, the words a death knell.

"What do we do?" Nick asked, his voice wobbling.

"We let each other go."

"You can't be serious." He let out a sharp breath of frustration.

"What else can we do?"

"A hell of a lot more than just giving up," he snapped, his hand slapping down on the table. His voice thundered, but the tremor in it betrayed him. He glared at me, but the thin mask didn't hide the devastation underneath. His shoulders sagged, fury dissolving into the quiet desolation of a man who knew the truth behind the hurt.

"Like what, Nick? This didn't just happen all of a sudden. It's not going to fix itself overnight either. We need time away from each other."

"And if I don't want that?"

I had no answer. There was nothing more to say. We sat in silence, the bottle of whiskey, the empty glass, and the weight of more than twenty years between us in the quiet grief of a marriage ending. Not in fire, but in the slow, gentle hush of rain.

His hand tensed around mine, an echo of the boy who once held me like I was everything. Releasing my hand, he stood, his shoulders hunched, carrying every memory we'd built, and every crack we'd ignored.

Then he walked away.

My heart plummeted as I watched him leave. My throat ached with words that might have saved us. But I kept them locked in.

It was his turn to fight, not mine.

He never looked back.

And I said nothing to stop him.

TWENTY-ONE

Nick

The kitchen was still. Only the slow tick of the wall clock proved that time was still moving. I used to know how to read her, how to reach her, until each excuse paved another brick in the wall between us.

Now I'd lost her, with no idea how to find my way back. I wasn't even sure she wanted me to.

I stood from the table on heavy legs with an ache in my tight chest, and my stomach flipped inside-out. If I looked at her, I'd beg, blubber. And I'd get angry. All of which would get me nowhere.

Without making a sound, I made my way upstairs. I opened the closet, pulled a bag from the back corner, the one we'd used in Scotland, and tossed in the essentials. Nothing folded. Nothing thought out. Just movement. A toothbrush. A couple of shirts. Socks. Chargers. My work badge.

I shoved the bag closed, the zipper snagging, tempting me to tear the whole damn thing in half.

I looked around the room, at our bed, still made. Her pillow. Mine. The photo on the dresser of the three of us in the mountains. Jenna on my back, Cat laughing.

I ran my finger along the smiling faces.

Hopefully, all she needed was time. I could give her that, no matter how much I might resent her for it, and pray it wouldn't mean losing her for good.

The kitchen was dark by the time I went back down. Cataleya had disappeared somewhere in the house where I wasn't. The half-full bottle of whiskey glaring at me from the table. Our fingerprints pressed together on the glass beside it.

We made it twenty years. And we unraveled in twenty minutes.

The thought tightened my chest with an anger that was both hot and ugly at how easy it had been to lose everything. I poured myself one more drink. The waste of all the years scorching hotter than any whiskey could.

This wasn't what I wanted.

But *wanting* hadn't been enough.

I ripped the keys from the bowl, metal biting into my palm. I opened the front door, glancing over my shoulder into the house we'd built over decades. It stared back at me, hollow, stripped of everything but silence.

I walked out into the night. The rain had thinned to a mist, clinging to my skin. There was nowhere in particular to go, just somewhere that wasn't here. It would have been Z's. But her sister was there, Dahlia, too. There was no way I could handle another female disappointed in me at the moment.

A small chain hotel near the office came to mind. One of those places that offered a sad continental breakfast and weak coffee, the kind you don't really notice. It wasn't much, but it would do. I'd driven past it a thousand times on my way to work.

Work had always made sense. Clean logic. Systems you could fix. Problems with solutions. I'd poured so much of myself into it over the years, thinking if I was good at *that*, the rest of life would follow. It hadn't. And now all I had left were pieces.

In the driver's seat, I sat for a minute before starting the truck. My fingers hovered over the ignition as I glanced up at Jenna's dark window.

Jenna.

She was going to be gutted. We hadn't even prepared her. Not that there was a way to. She'd believed in us more than I had, and now I'd given her every reason not to.

I slammed my fist against the steering wheel. How the hell was I supposed to tell her that the laughter had stopped? That her mother didn't want to fight anymore? That I might not either?

For a second, I wanted to storm back in and demand Cataleya fight for us. Instead, I pressed my forehead against the wheel I'd just assaulted, trying to swallow down the knot building in my throat, forcing back the tears that pressed behind my eyes.

I would have expected a fight. Some kind of loud, messy blow-up. Anything. Not frostbite. She didn't yell. She didn't even flinch. And that was so much worse.

Part of me expected her to call me back.

She didn't.

Instead, she'd said the words that gutted me. *We let each other go.*

I started the truck, pulled out of the driveway, the headlights cutting through the mist, the house shrinking in the rearview until it was nothing but shadow.

Did she watch me go?

I didn't look back. It would kill me.

TWENTY-TWO

Cataleya

THE CHAIR CREAKED SOFTLY as I pushed away from the table after Nick walked away. Each footstep he took was a hammer blow to my heart.

I couldn't sit there another second, not with the walls pressing too close.

I slipped out the back door onto the patio. The damp night air pressed against my skin, mist clinging to my hair. I stood beneath the eaves, arms wrapped around myself, watching droplets bead along the railing.

The night held its breath when the truck rumbled to life out front.

Headlights sliced through the wet trees and then were gone.

My heart stuttered. One word, just one, and he would have stayed.

But I didn't move.

The silence afterward was unbearable. I pressed a hand to my mouth to hold it in. The scream, the plea, the sob. The shattering.

I didn't watch him go.

Because if I had, I would have crumbled. Fallen to my knees in the wet grass, swallowed every last piece of myself, and begged.

TWENTY-THREE

Jenna

T HE SUMMER SUN BLAZED through the window. I rolled over, pulling the blanket over my head. I definitely needed to invest in blackout curtains.

Because it was a rare morning when I didn't have to jump up and rush out, I let myself lounge in bed, getting my base coat on, apparently. Org Chem was done, thank god, and I didn't have a shift at the shelter until Tuesday. Two whole days off.

Bramble, my faithful shadow, was sprawled at the foot of the bed, paws twitching in some dream-run. I reached down to rub the top of his head. He gave a low, satisfied sigh, stretching out his long body.

It could have been a leisurely day spent curled up with an adorable dog and a good book, actually reading for pleasure. Except it was Dahlia's birthday and eighteen-and-over night at *Shadow & Silk*. The club I wasn't exactly looking forward to. Celebrating my bestie, however, was always a good time. Which also meant I'd have to find something to wear.

With an overly dramatic sigh, I hauled myself out of the cocoon of sheets. Bramble stirred in my wake, his eyes following me to the closet, his tail thumping against the mattress. As I approached the door, a strange sound sliced through the morning's tranquility.

Bramble's ears perked as well, swiveling toward the hallway a fraction of a second before my mind registered the sound.

Crying.

Crying was a foreign sound in this house.

I eased the bedroom door open, my head cocked, straining to pinpoint the sound's origin. It was coming from my parents' bedroom. Bramble padded ahead, pausing at the corner, his gaze flickering back to me as if awaiting orders.

Before I reached the door, my heart was already breaking. Bramble whined softly, his tail tucked low, as he nudged the door open with his nose. My mother was sitting on the edge of the bed. Broken.

Trying to clear the lingering fog of sleep, I pressed my eyes shut. I'd never seen my mom like this. I approached her, keeping my hands at my sides. Bramble settled himself at her feet, nudging her hand with his wet nose, emitting a series of mournful whines.

"You're crying," I whispered, the shock ringing in my voice.

She looked up at me, her eyes swollen and red, her face blotchy. By the look of it, she'd been crying for a long time. The pillow on her bed was wet, and my dad's side of the bed was still made and unwrinkled. She just looked at me, not saying anything. I wanted to hug her, comfort her. Instead, my body stood frozen.

"I have something I need to tell you. It's not great news."

A new panic set in. Dad's side of the bed hadn't been touched. Where was he? She wouldn't be crying like this. Unless...

"Is Dad okay?" Terror sharpened my words as I rushed to her side, my heart hammering against the bones in my chest, the burn of tears stinging the corners of my eyes. My dad's face flashed in my mind.

He couldn't be gone.

My mom's fingers intertwined with mine, her grip surprisingly strong.

"Dad is fine..." She took a breath. "...our marriage is not."

My eyes flew open. Wait. He's not... He just... what? Left? I scanned the room quickly. The untouched bed, the closet door open, a bunch of empty hangers on Dad's side of the closet.

"You kicked Dad out?" My breath rushed out.

She shook her head. "No. Not exactly. It just fell apart. It's complicated." She pressed her palm to my knee.

"But... why?" I asked as tears blurred my vision.

"The last thing I want is to hurt you in all this. I'm still your mom, and he's your dad," she said, her words catching. She cleared her throat, struggling to regain her composure. "I'm also a woman, Jenna. I need to know that, even after all these years, the man I love still wants me. That he *sees* me. That I matter."

I shook my head. "It doesn't sound ridiculous. I understand."

Finally, I gathered my mom into a fierce, protective embrace, her sorrow a tangible weight against my chest. Bramble edged closer, resting his chin on her knee, his eyes locked on her face as though he knew exactly how broken she was.

"I didn't expect you to be the one comforting me," she murmured into my hair.

I pulled back, wiping the corner of her eye with a gentle finger. "For what it's worth, I've seen the way he looks at you when you're not watching."

She blinked, surprised.

"There've been a few times, but my favorite one was when you were dancing horribly in the kitchen to some weird song. He walked in and just stared at you, smiling. Like you were the most beautiful thing he'd ever seen. His whole face changed, like he was falling in love all over again. Those kinds of moments, that's what I want one day. I'll never settle for less."

A sob slipped free from her. My arms tightened, and Bramble pressed himself against both of us, offering his silent support.

"When did you grow up on me?" she whispered, pressing a kiss to the top of my head.

"Maybe when you needed me to."

❦

"Just remember this moment tomorrow morning when you wake up feeling like death. Happy birthday, Cuzz." I clinked my champagne glass to Dahlia's, the last of the bottle we'd opened while getting ready.

The night out suddenly didn't seem so bad. It wouldn't hurt to get my mind off all the things happening at home, either.

Already the air had been sucked out of the house, and it had only been hours. The glaring changes were immediate. Dad's shoes were gone from the hallway. The spot on the entryway hooks where his Atlanta Braves cap used to hang, tilted sideways like always, was empty.

You're an adult now, I told myself. *You'll be okay.*

I didn't feel okay. I was five again, sitting on the back porch swing, waiting for my dad to show up with hot chocolate and awful jokes that always made me laugh.

Only now I was grown, and he was gone.

I wasn't about to tell Dahlia tonight, of all nights. Tonight was hers to celebrate. She should be happy and excited. I wasn't about to bring it all down.

"I won't regret a thing. I'm already having more fun than I've had in my entire life." Dahlia hiccupped as she clinked her glass against mine.

"That's because you're already buzzed. Drink." I handed her a bottle of water, then finished putting her hair up on one side with a few pins. "There. All done. Gorgeous as ever."

"Not bad. You should be a groomer instead of a vet," Dahlia slicked on a layer of lip gloss, smacked her lips together, then turned.

"Cute." I rolled my eyes at her, snatching the lip gloss to apply some myself.

The notes of "Bad Moon Rising" drifted from the speaker, making me stop mid-swipe. A quick pulse of unexpected dread threaded through me. I shook it off, laughing. "Why is *this* song on your party playlist?"

"It wasn't. She must be moody. She does that sometimes, picks her own songs."

"She?"

"Yeah, Alexis."

"You mean Alexa."

"No, I mean Alexis. She has her own identity."

I laughed, shaking my head.

A notification dinged on my phone. "Uber is here. Ready?"

"I was born ready."

"Word of advice. Never say that again." I chuckled, pushing the bottle of water at a giggling Dahlia as we walked down the stairs.

Yeah, I'll definitely be holding her hair by the end of the night.

Bramble paced in front of the door as Dahlia and I approached, nails anxiously tapping against the hardwood.

"You have to stay here."

His tail was still, his head low, eyes flicking between us and the front door.

"It's okay, buddy," I told him, bending to scratch behind his ears. His muscles were tense under my hand.

Dahlia grabbed her purse, putting the lip gloss inside, checking her reflection in the foyer mirror one last time. "He doesn't want us to go."

I laughed. "What, like a doggy sixth sense?"

Bramble let out a sharp huff, then turned to face the front window. He stayed there, unmoving, watching the dark street beyond the glass.

I tried to shrug off the unease as I grabbed my purse and checked my phone. When we stepped outside, he padded to the door, pressing his nose against the crack, pulling long, loud sniffs as if he could follow our scent all the way to wherever we were going.

As the Uber pulled away from the curb, I glanced back at the house. Bramble watched us, unmoving, a dark silhouette in the window.

Twenty-Four

Jenna

WE BARELY MADE IT through the first hurdle. The bouncer eyed Dahlia with suspicion as he held her ID up to the light.

"How much have you had to drink tonight?"

"Why, not a sip, sir. I'm only eighteen." Dahlia giggled right before I pinched her side. She clamped her mouth shut, fighting a grin.

He looked at me, then back at her for way too long, then finally smirked. "I've seen you at Joe's. You're pretty amazing."

He stamped my hand with a gaudy black ghost, then held his hand out to Dahlia. "Your wrist."

She held her arm out to him but pulled back when he went to put a neon green wristband on her.

"Everyone under twenty-one has to wear these pretty bracelets," the man said as he placed it on.

"You couldn't find a more clashing color?" Her face twisted in disgust as she twisted the wristband around her wrist.

The giant man chuckled as he unlinked the red velvet rope that had been the barrier between a dazzling night at *Shadow & Silk* and a walk of shame back to the Uber.

"Happy birthday and be smart, girls."

"Yes, sir!"

Lights strobed through the haze, deep bass thumped through my body. Dahlia turned, speaking to me, but her words were lost in the noise.

"What?" I shouted.

"Let's get a drink," Dahlia yelled, pointing to the bar on the other side of the room.

I followed her through the crowd of bouncing people packed so tight it was suffocating. I swallowed the annoyance. This was Dahlia's night. Not mine.

Her glow was undeniable, her face full of wonder as she looked around, dancing along with the music. Her joy was contagious, and I made myself lean into it, trying to match her enthusiasm. I'd promised her a night of fun, so I'd give it to her.

Once we had our drinks in hand, we made our way to a spot close to the dance floor, though there was really no designated area for dancing, as everyone was swaying and bouncing where they stood. A spot miraculously opened up at a high-top table. Yanking on Dahlia's shirt, I led her over, quickly placing my drink to claim it.

"You're gonna have to go out there with me," Dahlia shouted, lifting her chin toward the dance floor.

I forced a smile. "No way."

"You seem a little distracted," she said, her brow furrowing. "Everything okay?"

I hesitated, then nodded. "I'll go out there with you after a shot of something strong."

"So get a shot then. Bring me one, too."

"Funny. I'm going to go to the bathroom, and then I'll grab us a couple more drinks. You want another Coke Zero?"

"Let's go wild, make it cherry." Dahlia flashed her megawatt smile, batting her lashes.

I made my way to a ridiculously long line for the women's restroom. I hated leaving Dahlia for too long. But she'd been right when she said our entire family was overprotective of her. Including me.

After making it through the bathroom line and another at the bar, I was finally pushing my way back through the crowd, balancing our drinks. Dahlia was no longer alone at the high-top.

Some guy, broad-shouldered, sweaty, and too old for her, was leaning over her, gesturing with his drink, way too close. Dahlia's smile was polite, but not welcoming, her shoulders drawn in. I started weaving faster through the crush of bodies.

A familiar person materialized.

Jared.

"Hey. Back off. She's not interested." Jared slid between Dahlia and the guy. His arm came around the back of her chair, casual on the surface but pulling her firmly into his orbit, while the rest of his friends appeared at the table.

The other guy muttered something like "not worth it" before disappearing into the crowd.

By the time I reached the table, Jared was already perched on the stool beside her, his jaw set, his gaze scanning over Dahlia.

"You really are a stalker," I snapped, slamming down our drinks too hard, splashing their liquid contents onto the table.

"Whoa there, Spitfire. We were making our usual rounds when we saw this lovely birthday girl had a vulture circling. I figured it was the gentlemanly thing to do to keep this fine young lady company."

"Well, she's not alone now. You can go."

"Jenna, geez. Rude much? That weirdo really was bothering me before Jared and his friends chased him off."

Jared leaned back, smiling at me with that arrogant eyebrow cocked.

I sighed in defeat. Maybe I *was* just hell-bent on being rude to a guy I couldn't stand for no good reason. He'd never *actually* done anything bad to me personally. And I promised her I would loosen up tonight. I took a deep breath after rolling my eyes, of course, looked at Jared, and tried my best to sound sincere.

"Thanks for sending off some random. And sorry for being rude." It came off way more sarcastic than I meant. At least I tried.

"No worries. We're happy to protect and serve." Jared gestured at the others. "You know Sebastian, Bryce, and Tyler?"

As if on cue, a bartender arrived with a tray of neon shots.

"Perfect timing. Let's make amends," Jared said as he started handing out the shots.

"You get table service from the bartenders?" I watched the bartender share a silent nod with Jared before going back to the bar.

"Perks of being regulars here."

Translation: Money talks.

I looked at Dahlia, who was shining with adoration, then grabbed one of the neon drinks and downed it. I hissed out a breath as the too-sweet and oddly salty burn slid down the back of my throat.

"That's the spirit." Jared handed Dahlia a shot.

She glanced at me first, seeking approval. I shrugged, letting her decide for herself.

With a subtle glance around, though I suspected this group got away with whatever they wanted here, she took a miniature pink glass, put it to her lips, and swallowed down the contents.

Once I let go of my hate, at least for this *one* night, we had a good time. Dahlia dragged me onto the dance floor. We danced, laughed, joked. Had another fluorescent shot.

My brain swam, light, a reprieve from the animosity. The thoughts in my head quieted, a strange nothingness filling the space. Which rarely, if ever, happened.

My tongue got thick and heavy, my words tangling into each other, as my feet stumbled awkwardly. The edges of the room feathered and spun.

"I'm not feeling so great. I think it's time to get an Uber." It took an immense amount of force to keep my eyes open and look across the table at Dahlia.

Her forehead was pressed against the sticky tabletop. *Gross.*

"Dahl, you all—all right?"

Why wasn't my mouth working? It was like trying to talk through cotton.

She gave the smallest nod.

I fumbled with my phone, trying to see the blurred screen. The app was in there somewhere. My phone was snatched from my hand.

"Hey!"

"An Uber will take forever. I'll drive you." Jared was already leading Dahlia out. Sebastian had his arm around my waist, steering me along.

My arms didn't want to move. I shook my head, or I thought I did. It didn't want to listen either.

How did I get so drunk so fast? Two shots shouldn't erase my hands.

Then we were at a car. A black SUV.

What was with all the black SUVs in this town?

I woke up in the back seat.

Leather. Cold air blasting. Dahlia's head resting on my shoulder.

My eyes slid shut.

Just for a minute.

A whimper.

Not me. Dahlia?

I tried to open my eyes. They wouldn't budge. Tried to lift my arms. Couldn't.

Hard floor. Stale cigarettes, pot, mildew. Voices through a tunnel a thousand miles away.

"No one else gets this. She's all mine."

"You're being an idiot. They're not supposed to be ones we know."

"This isn't business. This is all pleasure. My pleasure."

"You're gonna get us caught. No DNA. No names. No mess. We got way too much on the line for this shit."

"Fuck my father. We work our asses off for them."

The floor beneath me began to shake.

"Dude. Is that one awake?"

"Handle it."

Blackness took me under again.

TWENTY-FIVE

Cataleya

THE MORNING OF MY first day back at work had been rough. I walked into our—no, *my*—bathroom half asleep and, for a moment, I'd forgotten. I could still smell him. The scent of his cologne clung to the air. The realization pained me, stealing my breath.

He was gone.

After struggling through a shower and then my first cup of coffee of the day, I was finally able to push it all down deep enough to function.

Everything was coming apart, and yet, I'd never been more myself.

The routine fifteen-minute drive from my house to the hospital buzzed with that strange hyper sensation that came over me when we drove out to Salvia and Z's beach house. The vibrant blue of the sky, the sway of the Spanish moss caught in an invisible breeze, the taste of saltiness in the air coming off the ocean.

My marriage was drowning while everything else pulsed with life it hadn't had before.

I parked my car where I usually did, beeped the locks, and made my way inside. Same as always. Until the automatic doors slid open.

And it all hit me at once.

The world was suddenly too sharp. Alarms shrilled. Antiseptic stung. The fluorescent lights burned overhead. Things I'd long grown accustomed to over my years as a nurse pushed down on me. Every sensation coming at once. So much illness. So many things wrong. Cries of infants pulled at me, demanding that I move. Act. Heal. Now.

My hands trembled. My heart pounded. I was hyperventilating as I scrubbed in. It took everything not to run back outside.

What the hell was happening to me?

Instead of taking off screaming, I closed my eyes, trying to focus on one thing at a time, consciously quieting all of my other senses, centering myself with deliberate intention, on the sensation of the scrub brush over my skin, the bristles over my fingers, up my arms. Breathe in. Breathe out. I repeated this rhythm until the one-minute timer buzzed, and the room quieted again.

Today was going to be interesting.

Morning report passed without further incident. I went through my normal routine, checking orders and lines, cleaning my station, and reviewing charts. Nothing unusual until my first assessment when I placed my hands on the baby.

Like in Scotland, in the pub, my palms heated, the warmth intensifying as that hint of sandalwood and clove wrapped around me.

I could see inside him. Clear, impossible, absolute. A movie of his internal composition played in my mind. Past his trachea, along the tiny cilia, down through the bronchi, and into his lungs. Fluid pooled where it shouldn't. Stagnant. Dangerous. Bacterial growth beginning to fester.

I yanked my hands away with a gasp.

On the monitor, his vitals were okay. Though a little fast on his respirations, and his oxygen saturation was on the lower side of normal. Everything else looked fine.

I looked over the baby again. His color was also nothing to be concerned about, his muscle tone appropriate. Temperature normal.

Still, I *knew* what I saw was true.

The neonatologist walked into the unit for his morning rounds. As soon as I saw him, I jumped at the chance to snag his attention first.

"Good morning, Doctor. Before you round, I have a quick question about one of my babies, bed twelve." I recited the baby's history, voiced my concerns, all while downplaying my inner anxiety. He listened, checked the baby.

"He looks okay. His morning labs are also unremarkable. Keep an eye out. If anything changes, let me know."

The rest of my shift followed the same strange rhythm. My hands telling me their stories, windows into my tiny patients.

When I touched my second baby, admitted for feeding issues, the same sensations came over me. The heat tingled in my palms when I touched her. Another movie ran through my mind, the internal anatomy of the baby's brain, letting me watch new neural pathways growing in hyper-speed in front of my eyes.

Nothing happened when I laid my hands on my third patient, a former twenty-six-weeker about to be discharged now at thirty-seven weeks. Which made sense, since he was healthy and ready to go home. There was nothing more to be done.

By the end of the shift, I was barely upright. The abnormal amount of caffeine I'd consumed did nothing to help. My limbs were heavy, my eyes gritty. I was trying to stifle yet another yawn when an alarm on one of my monitors started blaring.

Bed twelve.

His oxygen saturation was plummeting, along with his heart rate.

I rushed to his bedside, reaching into the isolette to stimulate him. As soon as his vitals recovered, I assessed him again. He was working harder to breathe, his little chest retracting with the additional effort. His temperature was low. Too low. His color changed before my eyes to a sickly green-gray. His movements bordered on lethargic.

I called the doctor and started a full workup. New labs. New X-rays.

The results came back quickly. Sepsis. The cause, pneumonia.

Aggressive treatment was started immediately. We'd caught it just in time.

It *was* real.

My Awakening.

The rush that came with truly knowing and being right was unlike any rush I'd ever had. It was intoxicating.

I could save lives.

In that moment, I wasn't the woman whose marriage had collapsed. I wasn't the daughter still carrying her mother's absence. I wasn't just the nurse.

I was the healer.

The walk to my car was a blur, as if I'd been awake for days instead of hours. I crawled into the driver's seat and blasted the air as cold as it would go to wake me up enough to drive.

I nodded off, just for a fraction of a second. Long enough to veer off into the oncoming traffic lane. Thankfully, the road was empty. I rolled all the windows down, letting the hot, damp wind slap me back into awareness.

This kind of fatigue was new to me, short of when Jenna was a newborn and I only slept in two-to-three-hour stretches for months on end.

What I'd been doing all day, healing, seeing, knowing, one baby after the other, drained me, rendering me useless.

Maybe a call to Kelly would be helpful. Tomorrow though, after some sleep.

Inching out of the car, I made my way into the house. I kicked off my shoes at the door, dumped everything out of my pockets, stripped off my scrubs, and face-planted into bed, where I instantly fell asleep.

Until my alarm went off the next morning. Ten hours of sleep, yet I was still beat. I could've slept ten more. Easily.

I called Kelly on the drive back to the hospital. She picked up on the first ring.

"It's a bit early for you over there across the pond," Kelly's voice resonated through the speakers in my car. "What happened?"

I told her everything. About my patient, the vision, the exhaustion.

"That's not surprising, love. Energy work takes *energy*. It has to come from somewhere. And right now, that source is you."

"I figured," I sighed. "I don't want to stop. I *can't* stop."

"We'll have to figure out another source you'll be needing for your abilities. Taking energy from yourself is unsustainable, for sure. If you have nothing left to take, then you'll have nothing left to give to those precious babies."

"There's no way to turn it down, is there? A way to use it only when I need it? I have two more shifts this week, and now that I know I can do this crazy, amazing thing, there is no way I could ever *not* use it. If I can save a baby's life, I'll give all the energy I've got. I'll Uber home if I have to."

"I don't know the answers to those questions. What I do, what I've experienced, is nothing like what you do. I make teas, poultices, and I help people protect their peace. You have abilities I have never seen in my lifetime of practice. If my grandmother were still lucid, not ailing like she is, I could ask her. This is a lot, and very new to me. And I've been doing this since I was a young girl, which was a long time... Wait, it's about timing!" Kelly's voice jumped with excitement.

"Timing?" I asked, wary.

"Of course! That has to be how your Awakening is so strong so quickly. Okay, here is the short version of the long story. You already know that when we Awaken many things need to align. Lineage, of course, and also place. But the most powerful force of all? A woman at her turning point."

I rubbed the back of my neck, the dull throb of a headache already forming. "Turning point?"

"Yes. The Maiden, the Mother, and the Crone," she said, her voice a whisper, reverent. "Each carries her own kind of magic. The Maiden who is in discovery of herself. The Mother is the creator and protector. But the Crone, she carries the wisdom and experience of both. Her body has quieted, and the energy she'd once spent nurturing everyone else returns to herself. And you, Cat, Awoke on your fortieth birthday."

I exhaled a shaky laugh. "You make it sound like perimenopause is a superpower."

"In a way, it is. For you, at least," she chuckled. "Still, you really need to be careful. It's a gift, yes. But without balance, it'll burn through you. Who knows what this kind of chaos will do to you. There have to be other ways to draw energy without depleting yourself. I'll work with the coven. Maeve, the older lady you met at the fire? I bet she'd be a fountain of information. For now, I'll email you some protections to use."

"Thank you. Really. In the meantime, I've got to run. Another shift."

"Just promise me something," Kelly said gently. "Promise you'll protect yourself, too."

I didn't answer. I wasn't sure how to keep that promise.

Never again would I have to lose a precious, innocent life. I'd never have to tell parents they've lost their child or hear a mother's wail of grief.

I could save them all, one baby at a time. If it cost me, it cost me.

This was all I had left.

Twenty-Six

Jenna

B LINDING LIGHT EXPLODED THROUGH the room, ripping me from a strange, shapeless nightmare. Sandpaper lined my eyelids as an elephant stampede pounded through my head. I raised a hand to shield my eyes, blinking against the intrusion of light.

I was in a bed, but not my own.

Dahlia's.

Dahlia!

I shot upright. The room spun as the burn of vomit rushed up my throat. I stumbled to the bathroom quickly. When I opened the door, Bramble darted out.

How did—

The vomit rushed into my mouth. I barely made it to the toilet in time before the contents of my stomach expelled from my body. I pressed my forehead against the cool ceramic for several minutes until I was sure the worst was over.

After rinsing my mouth, I made my way back to where I'd woken up next to Dahlia. Bramble already lay at her feet, head up, eyes on me. His ears twitched once before he rested his chin on his paws. A slow, long whimper escaped him, his gaze never leaving my face.

"How'd you get stuck in there, big guy?" I rubbed his head as I checked on Dahlia.

Dahlia was curled on her side, her chest rising and falling steadily. Just the three of us. In her room. The balcony door was cracked open, letting in a sultry breeze of ocean saltiness.

I tried to remember getting home. Nothing was there.

I hadn't drunk *that* much.

The more I tried to reach into the fog, the farther away the memories slipped.

I looked down at Dahlia. Her shirt was *wrong*. It was one of those tops that looked similar both front and back, and hers was now on backward. As I reached down to wake Dahlia, I noticed a bruise on my bicep.

Bramble's head lifted again, watching me with that same fixed, un-blinking look. I pushed my sleeves up. A faint, thumb-shaped bruise on my inner arm stared back at me. I rotated my arm. Three more ovals on the back side. The other arm too, lighter, but there.

What the hell?

I tried harder to think about getting back. Closing my eyes, all I could remember were the strobing lights, the bumping of the bass. And then Jared and his friends. They said they'd give us a ride. I'd stumbled. Sebastian caught me. That must've been how I got the bruises.

Right?

"Dahl, wake up." I nudged her softly. A throaty moan muffled from the pillow where her face was smashed.

"Dahlia." I nudged her harder.

She groaned, her face still buried in the pillow. "Why? Just, why?"

"Do you remember getting home?" I forced calm into my words, my throat closing as I whispered them.

Dahlia's body went rigid next to me. Slowly, she turned to face me. Mascara streaked beneath her eyes and trailed down her cheeks.

"No." Her lip trembled as her eyes welled.

"Don't cry. It's okay. We... we just drank too much," I said, tears filling my own eyes.

"I'm sorry," Dahlia whispered.

"For what?"

"I pushed you to take me there. I wanted to go so badly."

"Everyone wants to go there. You have nothing to apologize for."

Dahlia started crying again, pulling up her knees, burying her head against them. I stroked her back, her curls bouncing with each stroke.

"Dahlia, what do you remember?" My heart beat hard in my throat.

"That's just it. I don't remember *anything*. We were dancing, having fun, and then it's like the light switch got turned off. There's nothing. I feel wrong, like my skin doesn't fit. Sounds so stupid."

"No," I said softly. "It doesn't."

I hesitated, gathering enough courage to ask what I was terrified to know. "What about... down there? Are you sore or hurt?"

Dahlia looked up at me, her tears spilling down her cheeks. "I don't know."

I wrapped my arms around her. "We should talk to our parents."

Dahlia recoiled as if I'd struck her. "No! We can't tell *my mom*. Not *ever*."

"Dahlia, I think something happened—"

"Forget it. If we tell her, she'll never forgive me."

"What are you talking about? We didn't do anything wrong."

"I'm eighteen, not twenty-one."

"It's not like our parents didn't dabble in an underage drink or two in their day."

"You don't get it," she snapped. "She'll never look at me the same. She'll just see me as this damaged nothing." Dahlia was sobbing now, uncontrollably.

Bramble shifted closer while she cried, resting his head against my hip. The weight of him grounding me, even as my chest caved in. His tail stayed still, his body tense.

"Hey. She won't. She loves you more than anything." I rocked with her for a minute. "Can we at least tell *my* mom? She's a nurse. She'll know what to do."

"No, Jenna, please. Swear to me you won't tell anyone."

"I don't understand why—"

"Swear it. Or I'll never forgive you!"

She shoved me away so fast that the room spun again.

I swallowed the word that wanted to come out.

No.

"Okay," I said instead. "I won't say anything."

"We don't know that anything happened." She paced the room, her hands working one over the other, again and again. "I'd know. I would. No, we just got blackout drunk, and they dropped us off, like they said they would," Dahlia said, more to herself than to me, looking off into the sea beyond her balcony.

"I'd *know*," she whispered.

I heard a voice, Jared's voice, in my mind.

She's all mine.

"*If* something happened, and we say nothing, they'll do it again. To someone else, Dahl."

"Do what? Nothing happened. I'm taking a shower." Dahlia didn't look at me as she shoved past, slamming the door to her bathroom behind her. Bramble followed her, sitting at the closed door, letting out a low whine. Seconds later, the shower turned on.

I collapsed back onto the bed, praying the nausea would stop churning my stomach, closed my eyes, and ran my hands over my own body, searching.

Did anything hurt, feel sore, or different? Other than the bruises on my arms, nothing felt... violated.

Dude. Is that one awake?

Was 'that one' me? Did they hold me down while they did the unthinkable to Dahlia?

Why couldn't I remember?

A scream tore from me as I pressed my face into the pillow. I yelled until my throat was raw and I was spent. But then I heard Dahlia crying through the running water.

Wiping my tears away, I walked into the steam-filled room and saw her curled in the shower, knees to her chest, water raining over her. Without hesitating, I stepped in, clothes and all, and sank down beside her.

"I don't know why I'm crying. Nothing happened."

I didn't respond. Just held on and let her weep.

TWENTY-SEVEN

Cataleya

I T STARTED AS A thrill humming under my skin every time I stepped into the NICU, the energy vibrating through my veins even before I touched the babies. My hands glowed with possibility as I'd rest them on my patients. Clove and sandalwood would surround me as the heat radiated through my palms and up my arms, allowing me to see what no one else could.

Fluid in lungs. Causes of heart murmurs. Infections before they festered. I could see it all. And I could help. Every life I could save was a spark in my chest, a reminder that I wasn't useless.

Until I paid for it.

My Awakening, I was learning, came with limitations. And consequences.

At first, it was fatigue. More than what I brushed off as long shifts, not enough sleep, coffee not doing its job. Then it started to show in the shadows under my hollowed-out eyes, the soreness in my joints, the migraines that never really eased. The weight loss was a side effect of skipping meals, not intentional. Food became an afterthought to staying upright. I was just too damn tired to eat.

Each triumph carved a deeper canyon, the energy that should have nourished my own cells flowing outward instead. I kept pushing, picking up extra shifts. The hospital became a sanctuary where I could forget everything else failing in my life.

An empty house was all that waited for me. The sink piled with dirty dishes, mail unopened, the bed still neatly made. Work left little time for anything else. Which was the point.

Nick had walked away. I hadn't heard from him for weeks. Not that I should be surprised. Nor should it have stung that he'd vanished so completely.

Working helped me stop thinking about Nick, at least for a few hours. Where he was. What he was doing. *Who* he might be doing it with. The thought of which killed me more than any Awakening.

Then Jenna. When she was home, a rarity these days, she stayed in her room. It broke my heart that our separation was hurting her more than she let on.

Guilt squeezed tighter, knowing I'd been too busy to be there for my daughter. Yet I still went back for more. Another shift. Another rush saving those little lives.

Late one night, after guiding a preemie back from the brink of NEC, I staggered to my car. My fingers trembled as I reached for the steering wheel. A few wet drops hit my arm.

Blood.

I wiped my nose with the back of my hand. More blood. It took several minutes before the bleeding eased.

My phone buzzed beside me, the screen lighting up with a video-call icon. Kelly.

I'd been avoiding her. Every time we spoke, she reminded me of the cost I wasn't ready to hear about.

"Cataleya," she said the moment I'd forced my sleepy eyes open. She sat wrapped in a wool blanket, a shelf of books behind her, the wind howling outside her window. "You look terrible, love."

"Appreciate that."

"I keep telling you that you have to find balance. Have you been reading the books I sent you? Or tried working with herbs, or done some grounding work, or please tell me you've learned how to do protective work at the very least."

"With what time? I've been working..."

"You can't bleed yourself dry for everyone else. Until you learn how to ground and redirect, that's all your Awakening knows how to do. Take from *you*."

"Redirect how?" I asked her.

She sighed. "That's what I'm trying to figure out. Until we do, slow down."

I pressed a hand to my forehead. "I can't just stop. I save babies."

The world tilted.

"Not if you collapse."

She stared at me. She was worried. The thousands of miles between us couldn't hide it.

"Can you at least promise you'll call me on your next day off and I'll guide you through a grounding? It might be a Band-Aid on an artery, but it should help a bit."

"Sure. I promise." I sighed, too tired to argue further.

She hesitated. Then, with that spark of mischief that usually preceded trouble, said, "Actually, the reason I called was to get you some of that help now."

"What do you mean?"

Kelly balanced her phone against a stack of books, the camera angled toward a cup of tea. "I've brought in reinforcements," she said, grin widening. "Maeve. I think you'll recognize her. She's been practicing since before I was born. Said she once danced beside your grandmother, Ivy. Can you imagine?"

My smile froze. A cold, weightless second stretched out before the screen split in two.

The face that appeared was the same woman who had circled the flames in silence months ago, bare feet pressed into the dirt, her gaze old but still intense. I remembered her hands taking mine, her words.

There are those who still whisper her name in reverence, and others who spit it like a curse.

The old woman smiled, her amber, cataract-filled glinting. "Cataleya. We meet again."

I could taste the smoke from that night, even here, oceans away. "You were there," I breathed. "At the ritual. You told me you knew my grandmother, Ivy."

Maeve inclined her head. "I did. And Bloom, too. Though Ivy fled the Second Circle when Bloom was still quite young."

"The Second Circle?" Kelly asked, frowning.

Maeve's expression tightened. "Your little coven plays with candlelight and salt. Ours dealt in blood and binding. Your friend's grandmother carried what those who knew the Old Ways sought to reclaim."

My body tensed. "Reclaim?"

"The gift that was taken," she said simply. "Ivy's bloodline should have ended after the Reaping."

Kelly blinked, uneasy. "Maeve, you're frightening her. And me. What is this about?"

Maeve ignored her. "Tell me, child. When you swam beneath the falls of the pulpit, did they answer you?"

I could barely speak. "How did you know?"

That dark smile again, slow as the tide. "Because I was there when your grandmother opened it. We did it together. Then she stole it all from me."

The connection froze. Buffering in short spurts. Kelly's voice rose. Maeve's image distorted, her eyes gleaming gold just before the screen went black.

I could only sit there, listening to my panting breath. The scent of the Scottish peat fire still clung to memory, mingling with the faint salt in the coastal air outside.

Kelly texted immediately afterward.

Kelly: *I swear I didn't know she was that woman. I thought she was harmless. Please don't vanish on me.*

I let the phone drop to my lap and blinked tears into the empty car.

TWENTY-EIGHT

Cataleya

I DROVE TO SALVIA's house without thinking.

I needed someone who knew me before the Awakening, before the whispers of Scotland. Before being threatened by an old, terrifying woman. Someone to talk to, to cry to.

I needed my sister.

I hadn't told anyone about Nick leaving, about our marriage disintegrating. Then there was this whole, *I have these amazing powers now. I'm saving babies and killing myself slowly in the process* thing. Good times, right?

Salvia's car was the only one in the driveway. I let myself in. She was curled on the couch with a sketchpad, a glass of wine beside her.

"Look who finally emerges from the grave," she said with a smirk. "You look like shit."

"Thanks," I croaked, dropping onto the armchair. "It's a vibe." My joints ached so badly I could barely shift. "Where's Z? I didn't see his car."

"He left yesterday to go gallivanting around Europe for the next month."

"Gallivanting?" I cocked an eyebrow.

"Fine, he's working. First there's the BIAF, then the Frieze Masters, all wrapped up with Art Shopping at the Louvre. And before you ask, yes, I'm a little bitter that I didn't get to go with him. I have to stay for a big Indigo gala in New York. I need to be there to represent." She took a sip of her wine and looked at me again.

"Pity," I huffed. "Sounds awful."

"Shut up." She threw a throw pillow at me.

I glanced over at what Sal was working on. I couldn't see much. She held the pad too close to her body. Growing up, I used to love watching her sketch out an idea that she'd later bring to life with pencils or paint.

"What are you working on?"

"It's nothing," she bit out, arching her eyebrow when I leaned closer to look. "Worthless," she muttered, snapping the pad of paper closed.

I reached out and touched her wrist. "It's never worthless."

I caught a flash of gratitude in her eyes before she turned away. "Cat, you really look bad. Almost as bad as Dahlia lately."

"Her too? Did Dahlia and Jenna have a fight or something? Jenna's been moping around. When she *is* home." Or when *I* was home was more accurate.

"Honestly, I have no idea what's going on with those girls." Sal hesitated, took a long drink of her wine before she looked me in the eye. "Dahlia gave up Juilliard."

"What? *Why?*"

As I looked at my sister, I could see it all in the deepened lines on her face. Worry. Doubt. Insecurity. Salvia brought me up to speed on what had been occurring in her home, crushing another anvil of guilt down on me.

I'd been so caught up in my drama with Nick, and playing God trying to save all the babies I could with these new abilities, that I failed to see that my own family was breaking all around me.

"I'm so sorry. I should have seen it." My words came out barely above a whisper.

"What are you saying? How could you possibly *see* this going on? Unless you're suddenly some kind of psychic," Sal scoffed with an incredulous laugh.

When I didn't laugh with her, she noticed.

She studied me, eyes narrowing. "You've been different since you got back. What happened in Scotland?"

Of course she would see it. Of course she would know.

I hesitated, my throat closing around the words. Then, finally, I told her everything.

What happened at the pulpit and the crimson waters. The Awakening that had slid into me like light through a crack in a dam. The energy. The babies. About Kelly and the eerie conversation I'd just had with Maeve.

Then I told her about Nick. About what had really been happening over the years, and that he'd been gone for weeks. The final blow in our love story. And how I missed him terribly.

She didn't interrupt once.

"I don't know exactly what to call it. Kelly calls it an Awakening."

She stared at me for a long time, then said, "So you mean to tell me you've been living in a real-life fantasy novel while I've been here with wine, artist egos, and a broody teenager?"

A pause filled the silence between us. Then we both laughed. It was like breathing again. She reached out, taking my hand in hers, and squeezed.

"Why didn't you tell me any of this sooner?" she asked, her voice thick with worry.

"I didn't know how to explain it. And I wasn't ready to admit that I'd failed in my marriage."

"Are you okay? About Nick, I mean." Sal's question hung in the air, her expression laced with love and concern. She understood my heart, she always had.

I shrugged, then shook my head. "How can I be?" I breathed.

Salvia moved closer to me, wrapping her arms around me as I cried. When my tears quieted, she stood silently, then disappeared into the kitchen.

When she reappeared, it was with a bottle of wine and another glass in her hand. She opened the sliding door that led out to the deck.

"Come on," she said, gesturing for me to follow her out.

She sat on one of the overstuffed deck chairs, filled the glass, handed it to me, then refilled hers. "Drink up. It's going to be a long night."

It had been too long since we talked like that. About her art, the galleries. Funny stories about artists, and Z. We talked about my work, the babies, the Awakening.

And we talked about our parents. For the first time, maybe ever.

"Why *do* you hate Papi so much?"

"I don't hate him. I know he tried his best for us, and I love him. I do. I can't really explain it."

"Try."

Salvia took a long sip from her glass, then quietly refilled it, giving herself the time to find the words she didn't want to say out loud.

"Because of Mom," she finally said. "I can't shake it, Cat. Papi... he had something to do with Mom." She paused, the silence stretching, thick with unspoken fears. Then, her gaze locked onto mine, the raw emotion in her eyes. "I don't think she *left*, Cat. Not really."

"Of course she did."

"I *remember* things that don't add up. You were two. You can't possibly remember much of anything."

That was true. Sometimes I'd have a flash of memory. A warm smile, a toy I'd loved. Nothing tangible. Salvia, on the other hand, had been six.

"What are you saying? That Papi—"

"No." Sal's voice dropped low. "I don't know. After Mom left, there were cops at our house. Papi was acting strangely. And the neighbors said and did awful things. They accused Papi of doing something to Mom." Her eyes glazed over, lost in memory, staring out at the ocean. "Then he packed us up, and we left in the middle of the night."

"You never told me any of this."

"Why would I? You were a baby. *I* was a baby. After the years started passing, I didn't want to crush you. You idolize Papi so much. And because I didn't want it to be true. I *don't* want it to be true."

Silence lingered for a few minutes while I tried to wrap my mind around everything Sal had revealed. "I always thought they were so in love."

"That's just it. They *were*. Then, all of a sudden, she's gone. It's never made any sense."

"At my birthday bash, Papi said some strange things about Scotland." I told her about the odd interaction that had happened. "It probably has nothing to do with anything. Still, it feels like it might?"

"Maybe someday we'll find out. The important thing is that history not repeat itself in our relationships with our families." She shrugged, signifying she was done with the whole childhood topic.

The conversation drifted to the girls, what was happening with them lately. Dahlia's announcing her deferral from Juilliard, the disconnect between them. And how much it broke her heart. Jenna had been acting similarly, beginning around the same time Dahlia had. We tried to figure out what had been happening between them. A fight? A boy? Neither of us was sure.

As we talked about our daughters, a coldness settled in. Heavy. Looming.

"It's something else," I interrupted her.

She looked over at me, pondering as she sipped her wine. "Is this part of that new witchy thing?"

I shrugged, the dark presence of what was happening pressing down. "I can't explain it yet."

She watched me with a mixture of concern and doubt. "Got anything a little more concrete?"

It was gone. Flitting away as quickly as it came. "Unfortunately, no. It's blocked? Maybe if I touched one of them. I mean, with intention, maybe I could *see* what's wrong?"

She considered it. "Two reasons why that's not a good idea. One, you look like you're about to keel over as it is. One more time might push you over the edge. Second, that feels like a major invasion of privacy. Babies, one thing, or for some kind of medical emergency. But for any sort of mind reading, totally different story. I don't need to give Dahlia any more reasons to shut me out." She quieted in thought again.

"Dahlia hasn't sung in weeks." Sal's voice was barely above a whisper when she spoke again. "She barely even eats. And Jenna. There's been a storm in that girl..." Sal's words drifted off. "So what?" she said, suddenly changing the subject. "If I go to Scotland, find a stone circle and chant to the ancestors, then I'll be able to do whatever you do?"

"Honestly?" I shrugged. "That's how it worked for me. Though it was more of an almost drowning in a deep creek type of thing."

She arched an eyebrow. "It wouldn't be fair if *you* got powers and *I* didn't." There was a thread of truth woven underneath her voice.

"What are we going to tell the girls? Our grandmother's blood runs through them as well."

My brain must have been more wrung out than I thought. It had taken way too long for Sal's comment to register. "Wait, you knew Dahlia sings?" Of course she did. As I did. Not that the girls had told either of us.

"First, we don't tell them until we figure out everything about this Awakening. Second, you think those girls can sneak off to Joe's without me knowing about it? She has so much talent, Cat." Tears wet Sal's eyes. "It kills me that she won't share that part of herself with me."

"I can see why."

"What is that supposed to mean?" Her eyes narrowed at me. A person could be killed with that glare alone.

"Think about it from her perspective for a minute. Her mother has this phenomenal talent, yet she calls it *worthless*. This, coming from a woman whose taste is renowned, whose judgment holds immense power. I'd be paralyzed by the fear of her opinion, of never measuring up." I watched my sister, waiting for the words to sink in.

Salvia cast her gaze over the water, the truth both cutting and opening her.

"It's never been my intention to make her doubt herself. To make her feel like she isn't enough. I don't want her to hurt like that. Even if she couldn't play a note, or sounded like Big Bird, she is more than enough. She's our whole world. My whole heart."

"Maybe tell her that."

She quieted as she wiped a tear away. I looked over at her again.

"Big Bird?"

"Yeah, you know..." Sal gave a squawking impression, flapping her arms wildly.

Laughter burst from me, spraying a mouthful of wine. "That's Scuttle!"

"Whatever. My point still stands."

We sipped our wine in silence for a while, staring out at the waves as they came in and pulled back again.

"She'll come back to herself, and she'll bring you in when she's ready," I said softly.

"They both will," Sal replied.

"Then why do I feel that the worst isn't over?"

For once, Salvia didn't argue.

It didn't take an Awakening to feel it coming.

Or that it would ask everything of us.

TWENTY-NINE

Jenna

I SAT IN THE car outside the campus lot, engine running, air conditioning blasting, yet sweat still slicked my neck. Not from the heat, but because I'd pulled onto this street.

My throat ached from swallowing down acidic bile.

This is fine, I told myself. *You've done harder things. You've survived worse.*

Lie.

I hadn't been surviving. Just breathing.

Though Dahlia and I had made it out with our hearts still beating, everything had changed.

Apparently, I couldn't drive on the street that housed the college without the phantom press of a drink in my hand, the taste of poison I hadn't seen coming.

And now I had to walk back into a world that was no longer mine. It was his. *Jared's.*

Just the thought of him made me shudder. He was here, walking around this campus like it was just another semester. For them, another clean slate. While mine was stained in places I couldn't scrub clean.

I stared at the entrance of the student center where dozens of people filtered in laughing, sipping iced coffees, sunglasses propped on top of their heads as if nothing bad could ever happen.

I used to be one of them.

Every group of guys walking in packs made my pulse stop. Just as every backward baseball cap made my skin crawl.

My phone buzzed in the center console.

Dahl: *You've got this. Just today. Just get through today.*

I didn't respond. There was no way to put into words how much I *didn't* have this. I still wasn't sure how I was supposed to sit in lecture halls pretending to care about syllabus week.

What would I do if I saw him? Or if he saw me?

Then I did see him.

Casual. Laughing. The group of them walked right past the entrance like they owned the place. Jared, followed by his crew. Sebastian, Bryce, and Tyler.

I lost the ability to breathe.

Loud, high-pitched ringing screamed in my ears as my vision blurred at the edges.

His voice filtered into the black space where memory should have been.

I ducked down, my heart hammering against the steering wheel. I pressed my forehead against the wheel, eyes squeezed tight, my teeth knocking together along with the rest of my shuddering body.

I can't do this. I can't.

Dahlia's face flashed in my mind. How she'd cried in my lap. How in the past weeks she'd vanished, whispering things like, *I don't know how to be here anymore.*

I couldn't let him erase her. I wouldn't let him win.

I straightened slowly, ignoring the burning behind my eyes and the fact that my hands were still shaking. Watching Jared laugh with his friends, the way he high-fived someone like he was just another carefree college guy, like nothing had happened, like *we* hadn't happened, ignited a fiery rage that surged up from somewhere deeper than fear. Deeper than pain. Deeper than the part of me that had been taught to be polite. To be quiet. To survive.

He doesn't get to live untouched while we rot.

Wiping my sweaty palms on my jeans, I grabbed my bag and opened the car door. My heart hammered in my chest, a frantic drum solo against my ribs. I didn't have any specific plan. What I did know was that I had legs that could still stand.

I slammed the car door shut.

I wasn't going to be the one hiding. I would not disappear.

Not for him.

Not for any of them.

The lecture hall was cool and dim, the overhead lights humming softly. Students filtered in, their voices muffled by the vaulted acoustics. Some scrolled through their phones. Others laughed, tossed back energy drinks, and shared notes across the aisle.

I kept my eyes down. One breath at a time. One second at a time. I just needed to make it to the end of the hour. I didn't have to be brave, just present.

I chose a seat near the exit, my escape route mapped and memorized. My fingers gripped the pen in my hand so tightly the plastic could've cracked beneath the pressure.

Then I heard it.

That laugh.

How deeply it had burrowed into me. Arrogant, familiar. My skin went cold.

Handle it.

I looked up slowly, already knowing.

Jared slid into the row two ahead of me, throwing his arm over the back of his chair, as confident as ever. His profile was lit by the glow of his phone. Same sharp jaw. Same smirk.

As though he felt the stab of my glare boring into the back of his skull, he looked back. His eyes met mine. An acknowledgment of recognition. Then a smug flick of his brow.

My whole body froze, my heart exploding into motion against the heat flooding into my chest. Too fast, too loud, every beat a fist against my ribs as my lungs refused to fully expand.

Tiny static pops skated across my skin as my fingertips burned on the desk. The air shifted, charged, curling around me.

The overhead light above Jared swayed, a low rumble following. His seat vibrated, then the rest of the room shook. Students held onto the desktops, casting worried glances around them. Someone yelped.

Jared flinched, cursing under his breath.

My eyes stayed glued to the back of his head.

The professor clapped for attention. "Just a little earthquake, people. Let's settle down."

The rumbling quieted along with the shaking.

"Easy for a California native to say," one student scoffed.

An uneasy chuckle sounded from around the room. People settled down. The incident brushed off as a fluke, no big deal.

Jared looked over his shoulder one last time. And this time, he didn't smirk. He looked unsettled.

The moment the lecture ended, I was on my feet. I didn't look up, just gathered my things with hurried precision and moved toward the door like it was the only lifeline in a burning room.

I made it to the stairwell.

"Hey, Spitfire."

My spine straightened as I turned slowly, heart thundering so loud I was sure he could hear it.

Nothing had changed about him. That's what shook me most. Baseball cap. Expensive hoodie. Same lazy, confident slouch, knowing nothing could ever touch him. Like he hadn't caused my world to split open.

"How's Dahlia?" He ran a hand over the back of his neck.

I took a step toward him, my voice spitting through my teeth. "You don't get to say her name."

"Whoa. What's the hostility about?" His tone had a practiced edge. Not kindness. Damage control. "Look, I just wanted to talk a little."

"Talk about what? The fact that neither of us remembers half the night?"

"Yeah, you gals had a good time."

"*A good time*? Is that what you call it?" The rage sputtered earthquakes through my body.

"Really, you should thank me for getting you home safe and sound. Even though your dog almost took Sebastian's hand off. We had to give him a sleepy treat so we could get you two in without her parents finding out how drunk y'all got."

"You *drugged* my dog?"

He shrugged.

His indifference reignited the rage.

"I may not remember the rest of that night, but I *know* what happened."

Jared looked at me then, really looked. And for the first time, he wasn't smug. He was angry.

The earth would swallow us both if I stood close to him any longer. I turned to leave. He circled around to block my escape. He shouldered me as I moved to shove past him, moving his face inches from mine, the warmth of his breath against my ear.

"Careful, Spitfire," he hissed. "People throw around accusations, things get messy."

No remorse. Just blatant threats.

I leaned in, ignoring the bile rising up.

"Good," I whispered. "Let it get messy."

He looked like he wanted to say something else, to minimize my words, but he didn't. Instead, he turned to leave.

Before he took two steps, I added, "I don't need to prove anything to crush you all into the ground."

He paused, jaw tight, then walked away.

THIRTY

Nick

H ABITS WERE A BITCH to break. Weeks in this motel, and my hands still wanted to steer toward the house that wasn't mine anymore.

I'd let myself drive by a couple of times. Check on things from afar, daring not to get caught by Cat. I wouldn't want her to think I wasn't respecting her wishes. Though every time I drove by, I had to fight the urge to say the hell with it and stop, just so I could see my wife, hear her voice. Take her into my arms.

Which would only make things worse.

The hotel wasn't that far away. Ten minutes from the house, tops. Close enough to keep pretending this was temporary. Far enough that I wouldn't run back every time I missed her.

Which was just about every night.

Mostly, I sat in the stiff corner chair, the vinyl biting into my forearms, room-temperature whiskey in hand, the TV flickering some meaningless generic late-night show, keeping the silence from swallowing me.

My bag sagged, still half-packed on the floor, the zipper broken. The shirts were wrinkled from too many wears without a wash, jeans slung over the chair back. My work badge hung on the doorknob. Proof that I was still functional, still showing up. Still trying to be the guy I used to be.

And I never stopped thinking about how I'd let it get this far.

Cataleya. Her name echoed with the ache of longing, and grief so profound it bordered on mourning.

Instead of sleep, flashes of that night at the dining table replayed endlessly. The tremor in her voice, the defeated slump of her shoulders. God, that look on her face. And I'd just sat there, letting her unravel in front of me without lifting a single thread to weave us back together.

I should've fought that night. For her. For us. For the life we've built.

I might not know how to fix what we'd broken, but I couldn't let her drift away. I *wouldn't*.

She needed space, so I'd given it. But enough was enough. For her, I would do whatever it took. Because she still mattered. She *always* would.

And then there was Jenna.

It had been four weeks since I'd seen her. The longest span of time since the day she was born, twenty-one years before. At first, I figured she needed space too. Her classes had started back up, which kept her busy. She was with Dahlia a lot, probably spending more time at Sal and Z's. I told myself it made sense, even when it didn't sit right in my gut.

My daughter was drifting away as well. She'd gone quiet. The kind of quiet that shatters. My daughter was hurting, and I didn't know how to reach her.

I unlocked my phone and tapped her name. Still no reply to my last attempt to reach out. So I called. It went to voicemail.

"Hey, kiddo..."

I winced at how tired I sounded.

"I keep missing you. Maybe you're not ready to talk yet. And that's okay."

I paused, picturing the swing on the back porch.

"When you were little and something was bothering you, I'd sit next to you on that back porch swing and not say a word. I'd just... wait until you were ready."

Another beat of silence.

"I'm still here, Jenna. I'll keep waiting."

I ended the call before I could overthink it, setting the phone face down on the table, then dragging both hands down my face.

I missed her more than I could say. And not just because she was my daughter, but because she was my favorite person. The one who challenged me, laughed at my bad jokes, roasted me for everything from my coffee habits to my playlists. Losing her was like losing air.

I was failing her too, losing both of my girls at once. My heart and my air. I might not know what came next, but I knew I wasn't giving up.

Not on Jenna. Not on Cataleya. Not on my family.

I picked up the phone again, my fingers finding Z's contact. I hit connect on a video call. I had no idea what time it was wherever he was in Europe. Really, I didn't care.

A few rings sounded before his face filled the screen. There was some kind of sculpture clump he must have been working on behind him, a beer sweating beside it.

"Hey."

"Reynolds," he said, squinting at me. "You look like hell."

"Yeah," I muttered. "Been a while since I've had an entire night's sleep."

He took a sip from the beer bottle that looked absurdly tiny in his hands. "Is this a social call, or are you working up to something?"

"What's going on with my girls?" The words came out harsher than I meant, though I didn't take them back. "Cataleya. Jenna. You know more about them than I do right now."

He didn't answer right away. Just took another slow sip of his beer, eyeing me over the rim. "You mean besides the fact that you walked out?"

I took the hit. "Yeah. Besides that."

"I don't know what's going on exactly. I just know Sal says they've been off. Guarded. Jenna hardly says a word. And Cat's been working a lot. Too much."

I swallowed hard. "I don't know how to fix it."

"Can't fix anything standing outside waiting to be invited in," he said, his voice dropping to that low, deliberate tone that meant he wasn't playing. "You've got to go to them."

"It's not that simple—"

"It's exactly that simple," Z cut in. "You don't get to wait until it's convenient to show up. You don't get to use 'giving them space' as an excuse for doing nothing. Do you want your family back? Kick the damn door down and don't leave until they know you mean it."

The words landed like a punch. I sat there, jaw tight, heart pounding.

"I'm not giving up," I said. I thought of Cataleya's tired eyes, of Jenna's name on my phone screen with no reply.

"Good," Z replied, leaning back. "Because if you do, Reynolds, you're not the man I thought you were. If you give up, I'll be the first one to call you a coward. And the last one to let you forget it." There was no trace of his usual smirk.

I ran my hand over my face, my gaze dropping to the floor as my gut tightened. "I'll fix it."

"I hope you do," Z said, nodding. Then he ended the call.

I stood in the middle of the wreckage that was my shattered life, consumed by regret that threatened to swallow me whole.

I dropped the phone on the bed, picked up the book that sat on the table and heaved it onto the ground.

"Fuck!"

How could I have been so stupid? I should never have left.

Ever.

The weight of that devastating truth broke me wide open.

They were the reason my heart beat. The reason I breathed. I'd spend every hour of every day fixing what I'd broken, proving that I would go to whatever lengths were needed to make sure both of the women I cherished more than my own life never doubted me again.

Whatever it took.

THIRTY-ONE

Jenna

DAHLIA STOPPED RETURNING MY texts, and my calls went to voice-mail. When I'd barge into her room, she would be sitting in the dark, curtains drawn. A book sat open, never changing pages.

She hadn't performed at Joe's for weeks. Not since *Shadow & Silk*. The piano and her guitar sat collecting dust.

Then she announced she was deferring her acceptance to Juilliard. Everything Dahlia had ever dreamed of.

While Tía Sal had lost it, Uncle Z sat silent. Which was one of the scariest things I've ever seen. All that big elegance looked downright murderous when he was mad. It was the first time I'd ever seen that side of my uncle.

The last few weeks hadn't exactly been kind to me either. I filled every moment I could with volunteering at the shelter, studying, and training Bramble. No matter what I did, my mind drifted back, replaying that night minute by minute, trying to fill the space where memory should be. Which inevitably led to dark bitterness that Jared was still walking around untouched, unpunished.

I'd known Jared for what he was, and still I let him near us. Now Dahlia was paying the price.

Part of me wanted to go to my mom anyway. To walk into her room, crawl into her bed like I used to when I was small and the world was too heavy. Let her pull me in, rub slow circles on my back, whisper, *I've got you, baby girl,* and let myself finally fall apart in her arms.

I missed her. Especially lately.

She was going through hell too. I could see it in the way she never really sat down anymore. The way she filled every second with extra shifts and endless to-do lists. How she worked late, came home exhausted. She didn't even pour herself a glass of wine anymore. She'd just stand at the kitchen sink for way too long, staring out the window.

Since classes had started back up, and fall was busy season at the shelter, I'd stop by to check on Dahlia, even if only for a few minutes, whenever I could.

Bramble stuck his head out the window, ears flapping in the salty breeze, as I parked my trusty Honda on the sand. He ran ahead of me as my phone vibrated in my back pocket. I let myself in, looking at my dad's face that popped up on the screen. I let it go to voicemail. Hearing his voice would drill a hole in the dam I'd built. If I talked to him, it would all crumble. My walls were fragile enough, barely holding everything together.

I listened to his message before walking upstairs. Even though it was only a message, an ache pierced my chest at the sound of his voice.

"Hey kiddo. I keep missing you. Maybe you're not ready to talk yet. And that's okay."

There was a pause.

"When you were little and something was bothering you, I'd sit next to you on that back porch swing and not say a word. I'd just... wait until you were ready."

A beat of silence. Then another.

"I'm still here, Jenna. I'll keep waiting."

Tears burned in my throat and flooded my eyes. I missed him. I needed my dad.

Bramble reappeared at my side in an instant, leaning against my leg, sensing the despair pressing on me. I buried my fingers in his fur, grounding myself. I wiped my face, took a few deep breaths, and then made my way upstairs.

"Dahl, are you here?" I called out when I found her bedroom empty.

"In the bathroom," she answered faintly.

I glanced around, picked up the book that sat open, face down, on her nightstand. Same page as the last time I looked. With a sigh, I shook my head, replacing it. I opened the curtains to her enviable view of the ocean and cracked the slider, letting out the thick, musty air and the cool ocean breeze in. The humidity had thankfully subsided in the early October days.

"I'm going to raid your fridge," I said to the closed door.

"K."

At the end of the hall, just past the staircase landing, Tía Sal's studio door was cracked open, turpentine wafting down the hall. Though she'd always been private with her work, it had been so long since I'd seen any of it I had to peek in.

I paused at the door, my gaze drawn to the single painting hanging in her studio. A woman with flowing brown hair, as if a breeze still stirred it, stood in a field of wildflowers, her profile serene and sure. It looked as though the wind would stir and the woman would look up at any moment.

I stepped closer, my socked feet silent on the plush, paint-splattered throw rug.

"Tía..." My voice cracked with awe. "She's so beautiful. Why don't you have this downstairs on display?"

Her paintings were breathtaking. Yet, she'd never hung any of them in any of their galleries, or even at home. I'd been to enough of those galas to know her work was better than most of what I'd seen go for a price that blew my mind.

"This is one of the first paintings I've ever done." She came up beside me, her shoulders a little too straight, her critical gaze looking over the painting.

"It's so real, like she could start walking at any moment. I feel her." I traced one of the loose brushstrokes with my eyes. "Who is it?"

Sal's lips curved into a distant smile. "My mother. Your grandmother. It's my last memory of her. I did it not long after she left."

"I thought you were only, like, six?" I tried not to let my jaw drop open.

Sal shrugged. She brushed a fingertip against the frame, reverence in that small touch.

Behind us, we heard a door close. My heart tightened as I glanced toward the doorway.

"Dahlia's been so quiet lately. I've tried asking, but she doesn't tell me anything." Sal glanced past me into the darkness of the hallway beyond my shoulder.

Everything in me wanted to tell her. About what happened. About why the light had faded away from Dahlia's eyes. Why she'd hidden herself in a darkness where I couldn't reach her. And how much Dahlia needed her now.

But that promise kept me silent.

"She's probably just tired. And with the whole Juilliard thing." I bit my lip, knowing I couldn't tell her anything more without breaking my word.

"If she needs anything..." Her words trailed off.

"I'll keep an eye on her," I promised softly, my words only empty place-holders as I stepped out of the studio.

For the first time in my life, I'd lied to my aunt. When she found out, I wasn't sure she'd ever forgive me.

Dahlia didn't look up when I walked back into her room. She was stoic, standing beside her bed, her face staring down at the floor.

"I guess we got our answer," Dahlia whispered.

"What answer?" I asked, closing the door behind me.

Dahlia held up an object. My heart seized.

"What do you mean, *our answer*?" I repeated.

"That *something* happened after all."

She was holding a pregnancy test. I crossed the room, knowing before I looked. The word was a sucker punch.

Pregnant.

My mind reeled. Dahlia had withdrawn from everyone, everything. Even me. She hadn't been seeing anyone, not since her first boyfriend moved away with his family months ago.

"Has there been anyone since Daniel?" I asked gently.

She shook her head. "No one. Ever."

"Wait, *never*? I thought you and Daniel..."

"Nope. If he hadn't had to move to California, then I would have liked him to have been my first. A few semi-heavy make-out sessions. That's it. We never even got close."

"Oh, Dahlia." My voice broke with tears, falling hot and fast as I wrapped her in a hug.

"We have proof now." My words spat out, rage surging.

Her laugh was bitter. "This proves nothing. He'll just say it was consensual."

She was right. The burden of proof would fall on her, not her perpetrator.

I breathed deeply, trying to steady myself.

"First, we need to make sure that bastard didn't leave anything else behind. Then we can figure out what to do next. Together."

She looked up at me with a brokenness that shattered me. With the slightest nod, she buried her face in my chest and cried. And I could do nothing except be there.

THIRTY-TWO

Jenna

THE CLINIC WAS SMALL, private, yet the humiliation was inescapable. Full blood panels would take a few days to come back, but fortunately, both of our rapid STD results were clean. Even though I'd somehow known that I hadn't been violated the way Dahlia had, I couldn't ignore the possibility. Just in case.

All was clear. Except for one small growth that the ultrasound confirmed remained in Dahlia's womb. Dahlia had no desire to look at the screen or the picture they'd printed. I held onto it for her, just in case.

"I know what you said before," I whispered. "And I hear you, I promise. But I have to ask one more time. Are you sure you don't want to tell anyone? Our parents?" We were sitting on a bench under a tree behind the clinic. The nurse had told us to take as long as we needed.

This time, there was no spurt of anger or insistence. Dahlia's eyes, once filled with tornadoes of anger, looked down at the floor.

Slowly, she shook her head. "No. It's too late. I want them to know only the girl I was before. Not this broken version."

"You're not broken," I whispered. "They love you. I love you. None of this was your fault. Do you hear me? None of it. I knew what kind of piece of shit he was. I let him get close to you..." My words drifted away in the tears that spilled over no matter how much I tried fighting them off.

Her hand closed over mine. "No more blaming ourselves. *He* did this. I just need to fix it. Forget it ever happened and get on with my life."

It took me a few seconds to answer. I wiped my face, cleared my throat, and took a few breaths. "Are you sure? We can't take it back once we do this."

"Yes, I'm sure." Dahlia wiped away her own tears. "Thank you for the 'we.'" She nudged me with her shoulder.

"You're not in this alone. I'll always be your emotionally unstable superhero."

A tiny smile tilted one side of her mouth. An hour later, we were back inside. Decision made. For better or worse.

We told the moms that Dahlia was staying over for the weekend. My mom would be at work, like she'd been most of the time since the separation, and my dad was wherever he ended up, we could hide from the outside world at my house. I'd tend to her, share the burden, and make sure she wasn't alone.

We read the instructions before she took the first pill. We set a timer for the next round. Then we watched a movie, pretending, just for a while, that we were normal girls on a normal night.

When the cramps hit, I held her hand as she cried from the pain and the weight of it all.

By Sunday, it was over, and the spark that used to live in her eyes was gone.

If I ever got Jared alone in a room again, there wouldn't be just talking. I wouldn't hesitate to murder him. Even with only my bare hands.

And I would not be sorry.

Tuesday blurred by in a haze of obligations. Classes bled into a full shift at the shelter, every hour grinding by. When I finally started for home, twilight was already swallowing the sky. Summer's golden stretch was fading into the crisp breath of fall, where every gust seemed to whisper that change was coming.

The next day would be brutal as well. My earliest class required rising before the sun. A cruel trade-off for dropping Jared's. Even the thought of sitting in the same room with him again was unthinkable. One more run-in and I'd probably end up in handcuffs. Fitting, really. The cherry on top.

I almost went straight home, just enough time for a shower, maybe a few minutes of studying before collapsing. But I hadn't seen Dahlia since I dropped her off Sunday night. I'd texted her. Her responses were never more than a few words, and today she hadn't responded at all.

She was at home alone. Tía Sal had left for New York on Monday for some gala, Uncle Z was somewhere in Europe, and Dahlia had refused to stay with me. She'd said she needed her own bed, the comfort of salt air, and the whispered hush of sea breezes.

I pulled into the driveway. The house was dark, no porch light, no glow from any window. Dahlia rarely went to bed before ten.

The hair on my arms stood up as a chill swept through me.

I let myself in with my key and checked the deck first, expecting to find her wrapped in a blanket, *letting the ocean winds calm her soul* as she had proclaimed on too many occasions to count.

She wasn't out there.

Upstairs, no light leaked from beneath the door. I opened it slowly.

"Dahlia?" my voice rasped, barely a whisper.

A lump lay motionless beneath the covers. Icy dread sank into me.

I reached out and nudged her lightly. Her heat radiated against my hand, fever-hot.

I snapped the lamp on. Her skin gleamed with sweat, her forehead slick and burning. A pain-strangled sound broke from her lips.

"Oh god. You're burning up." My voice cracked. "I have to get you to the hospital."

She didn't answer. When I tried to lift her arm, she let out a sharp cry and clutched at her abdomen.

"I'm so sorry." Stinging tears blurred everything. Her face, the room, my shaking hands. Somehow I managed to half-drag, half-carry my best friend down the stairs, out the door, into the night.

"Please don't die on me," I begged, my words breaking apart. "*Please.*"

I barely stopped for red lights, headlights slicing past like ghosts. Dahlia's head lolled against the window, her breath shallow and uneven, sweat glistening on her skin, each painful moan tearing into me.

"Stay with me," I whispered, again and again, my voice trembling. "Please, Dahl. Just breathe. You're okay." But *okay* was a lie. A thin, useless word dissolving under the sound of tires on asphalt.

The hospital finally rose out of the darkness. I swerved into the ER bay, slammed the gear into park, and stumbled out, screaming for help.

The doors burst open, a flood of blue scrubs and urgency.

"What happened?" A nurse's voice cut through the ringing in my ears.

"I... I don't know," I stammered. "She's burning up. She... she couldn't even stand."

Another voice said, "Get her on the gurney."

The world fractured into motion. Hands lifted Dahlia from the car. Her fingers slipped from mine, warm and then gone. Then I was running after them as they wheeled her inside.

Fluorescent light poured down in sterile sheets. The smell of illness and antiseptic hit like bleach to my lungs. The slap of shoes on tile, the shriek of wheels, the mechanical gasp of automatic doors assaulted my ears.

They vanished behind double doors marked *Authorized Personnel Only*. I stood there, helpless, the world narrowing to a single, deafening pulse.

A nurse appeared at my side with a clipboard. "Are you family?"

My throat was raw, burning with tears. "She's my cousin."

"What is your name?"

"Jenna. Jenna Reynolds."

She glanced up. Something like recognition flickered across her face. "Wait here," she said gently, but her voice barely reached me.

I sank into a plastic chair, its edges biting into my legs. It was too cold and too hot all at once. My hands wouldn't stop shaking. Her heat still clung to my skin, ghosting up my arms.

For one long, desperate moment, I wanted my mother. She'd know what to do and hold me in her steady hands. I couldn't breathe around the thoughts forming in my mind.

Maybe I'd waited too long.

Maybe she wouldn't wake up.

Beneath the fear, molten rose. Slow, certain.

If Dahlia didn't make it through this, I wouldn't shatter. I'd split open. The ground would crack, the air would burn, and Jared would be the first to be swallowed by the quake.

THIRTY-THREE

Cataleya

THE NICU WAS QUIET. Too quiet.

Most of my babies were stable for once. No alarms screaming, no heart rates dipping. On any other day, that silence might have been a blessing. Today, it prickled along my skin.

I was elbow-deep in charting when the phone rang, an unfamiliar hospital extension lighting the screen.

"NICU, this is Cataleya," I answered, half-distracted.

"Hey, Cat. It's Lydia from the ICU. I know this might break every HIPPA rule in the book. We already called her mom, but I thought you'd want to know as well. Your niece, Dahlia, is here. It's serious."

My pen slipped from my fingers, clattering against the tile.

"What?" I whispered. "Did you say ICU?"

"She was brought up from the OR about thirty minutes ago. Jenna's with her. She's asking for you."

"I'll be right there."

I don't remember leaving the NICU. One moment I was at the desk, the next I was pushing through the ICU doors, scanning every whiteboard, every face, searching for Lydia, or Dahlia, anyone.

I found Jenna first.

She was curled in on herself in a waiting chair, arms wrapped around her middle, holding herself together. Her eyes were red-rimmed, cheeks blotchy. When she saw me, a broken sound tore out of her. My knees nearly buckled.

"Mom," her voice broke as she flew into my arms.

I held her, instinctually, protectively, even as dread tightened in my gut. "What happened?"

She didn't answer, just shook her head.

Lydia appeared from Dahlia's room. "Oh good, Cat, you're here. I just gave Dahlia some pain meds. She'll probably be out for a bit. I'll give you all some privacy." She slipped out, closing the curtain halfway.

My eyes swept the room, taking in a sight I had seen too many times from the other side of care. A sight no family should ever have to see. The sterile scent of antiseptic hung heavy in the air as machines kept a steady rhythm beside the bed where Dahlia lay pale and unconscious, IV lines trailing from her arms.

"They said that she was septic," Jenna said, her voice cracking on the word.

My stomach dropped.

"I went to check on her. She was so hot and in so much pain. She kept bleeding. They said there was a complication. After the termination. Some tissue didn't come out, and it got infected. They had to rush her into surgery." Jenna's chin quivered.

"Termination?" Words left my mind. All I could muster were breathless, one-word responses.

Her shoulders hunched. She opened her mouth, closed it again, then whispered, "She didn't want anyone to know." Her voice was barely audible. "Something happened that night at the club."

My heart skipped. "Dahlia's birthday?"

Jenna nodded, then broke, collapsing into the chair as her legs gave out, hands covering her face.

"I think they drugged us," she said. "No. I *know* they did. Jared and his friends. We woke up and couldn't remember anything. Then Dahlia took a pregnancy test. It was positive. We went to the clinic so she could end it."

I caught the chair for balance before going to Dahlia's bedside. I hesitated to put my hands on her, afraid of what I might see, of what I might feel. The torrent of clove and sandalwood swirled, my palms already warming as I reached down. When I touched her balmy skin, the vision flared to life.

Her blood. The infection. Sickness running through her veins. It was everywhere. Then Dahlia's laugh, clear and bright, the way she sang, her soul braided with music. I pulled my trembling hands away from her.

"Mom. Your nose is bleeding."

I wiped my nose with the back of my sleeve, blinking against the dizziness. I checked the IV fluids hanging from her pumps, noting which antibiotics were dripping into her lines. My heart beat harder still as I turned to Jenna.

"Did they..." My voice shook. "Did they hurt you?"

Jenna's eyes brimmed. "I don't think so."

I exhaled, the breath of relief stumbling out of me as rage spun in my chest.

"Does Sal know?" I asked, although I already feared the answer.

"No. Nobody does. I promised Dahlia I wouldn't..." Jenna took a breath, trying to find the words. "She thought you'd all look at her like she was broken. Tainted. I promised I wouldn't tell anyone."

Her words cut. I opened my mouth and nothing came out. Before Jenna could go on, the curtain snapped open.

Salvia.

She stood in a formal gown, a sparkling clutch dangling from her hand. She must have come straight from the gala. Her gaze flicked from me to Jenna's tear-streaked face, then to the hospital bed. Her voice dropped, sharp as a blade.

"You promised Dahlia you wouldn't *tell me*?"

"Sal," I started, but she pushed past me, her face paling as she took in her daughter's motionless form. Her clutch slipped against her wrist as her hand curled into a fist.

"What the fuck happened?" she whispered, low and lethal.

"Sal—" I reached for her arm.

"No." She tore away. "You don't get to talk right now." Her gaze cut to Jenna, who flinched but didn't look away.

"I... I didn't know what to do. We were scared," Jenna blurted through her tears.

"You *lied* to me," Salvia interrupted, her breath ragged.

"I didn't mean to."

"She was in pain, and you kept your mouth shut!"

"Salvia, that's enough," I snapped, stepping between them.

Salvia blinked at me like I was a stranger, fists clenched so tight her knuckles glowed white against the crimson flush of her skin.

Jenna shook her head, eyes pleading. "She was raped, Tía. We were drugged. We don't remember much. He got her pregnant, and now she's really sick."

Sal went utterly still.

"She's pregnant?" she sputtered.

Jenna started crying again. "She *was* pregnant."

Salvia staggered a step back, then swayed forward again. I caught her elbow to steady her. But she jerked away, turning on me, her body violently shaking.

"You *knew*," she snapped. "And you didn't tell me?"

"I found out minutes ago." I stepped closer. "They were afraid to tell anyone, Sal."

"She could have died! You should have told me!" Salvia's voice shattered.

"I know!" Jenna cried harder. "I'm sorry. So sorry. She couldn't take it. She thought you'd be ashamed of her."

Then, like a dam bursting, Salvia let out a sound that didn't sound human. A deep, wounded growl, torn straight from the center of her.

"She's my baby," she gasped, crumpling into a chair.

"I know." I crouched beside her, my own tears falling freely as I pulled her into my arms.

"I was supposed to protect her. She's mine. I should have known."

"You couldn't have."

No one moved. The monitors kept time for all of us until Salvia looked up, her voice changed, vibrating with something that no longer belonged to grief.

"I need to know what happened. *All* of it."

As Jenna recounted their nightmare in halting fragments, my pulse answered with its own thrumming. The Awakening stirred inside, dark and unrelenting. The lights above us flickered. Deep within me recognized the fluctuation.

The same force that had answered in the pulpit now pulsed through me, raw and untamed.

THIRTY-FOUR

Cataleya

I T HAD BEEN THREE days.

Three days of catnaps curled in chairs too hard for sleep, blinking against worry and the mounting weight of rage. Rage at the world. Rage at the boys who hurt our girls. Rage at myself for not seeing it sooner.

The stark lights above hummed, casting a glare that needled into my skull, intensifying the headache that never truly left.

This was the new routine. A shift in the NICU, then down to the ICU, a few minutes of fractured sleep, then start all over again. Lather, rinse, disintegrate.

The pressures of each day left my body with an unrelenting hollowing, my insides scooped out and replaced with sand. Every hour blurring into the next. Even now, I was back in the ICU, sitting with Dahlia, my badge still clipped to my collar. I pulled it free, the sharp corners snagging on the threads of my scrubs. My fingers fumbled with it, too tired to unclip it properly.

I wasn't the only one spending every waking moment at the hospital. Sal was a constant presence, never leaving Dahlia's side. While Jenna was nearly as devoted, only stepping away for essential obligations like attending class or caring for Bramble.

She'd quit the shelter quietly, never mentioning it. My bright golden girl was dimming. Her frame had thinned, her shoulders hunched. Her smile hidden away, a constant sadness had settled in her eyes.

Jenna stood to hug me briefly. "I was going to get some coffee. You want some?" she asked, her voice raspy.

"That would be amazing," I said, trying my best to smile.

"Tía?" she asked Salvia gently.

Sal didn't look away from Dahlia. Didn't say a word. Just shook her head, the faintest of movements.

After Jenna left, I brushed Sal's dark hair from her shoulder and let my hand rest there. "How is she today?"

Another small shake of her head.

I sat beside her, every inch of me aching in protest. The machines whispered steady rhythms of my niece's fragile recovery. The soft sounds were so constant they'd become a lullaby. My eyelids drooped, trembling with the weight of staying open, the rest of my limbs following, gravity tripling its pull.

"Mom?"

Jenna handed me something, her voice sounded far away, an underwater garble. I blinked hard. Black spots bloomed like ink dropped in water, devouring the edges of the world.

The room tilted. My eyes rolled.

Then there was only black.

Before I even opened my eyes, I knew where I was. The scent and sounds were unmistakable. Then I noticed the IV in my arm, the site a little puffy from the tape, a liter of fluids dripping into me. The assessment was automatic before it hit me. I wasn't the nurse this time. I was the patient.

"No." It came out a croak, my throat raw. "No, I can't be here."

My vision swam as I tried to sit up, my head protesting in painful throbs.

"You collapsed." A doctor I didn't recognize stood at the foot of the bed. Her white coat open, her face unreadable. "You're severely dehydrated, likely suffering from extended exhaustion, and your daughter mentioned you've been experiencing tremors and nosebleeds. Is that true?" she asked evenly.

I said nothing. Just closed my eyes.

"She answered your phone when your unit called," the doctor continued. "They've been trying to reach you. She let them know what happened. Several of your colleagues came by while you were resting. They're all worried about you. Your unit supervisor recommended medical leave. I'm inclined to agree."

Mustering every ounce of willpower and strength to remain calm, I asked, "For how long?"

"First, I'd like to keep you overnight for some fluid maintenance and to run some labs. After that, I'd like you to rest for at least a couple of weeks. Minimum."

A strangled, bitter laugh escaped as panic wanted to curl tight around my lungs. "That long? I can't. What will happen to the babies? I can't disappear now."

"It's not disappearing. It's recovering. You have to save yourself before you can save anyone else."

She could have just slapped me. It would have hurt less.

I sat on the edge of the hospital bed, IV still in place, phone in hand. His name glowed on the screen, still marked with a little heart I'd added years ago, my thumb hovering over his name.

Nick.

The cursor blinked in the text box.

I miss you.

Three small words that meant everything. I couldn't press send. I didn't even finish typing them. Just stared at the screen until the letters blurred.

I closed my eyes and let myself drift back to a quiet Sunday morning. One of so many before everything slid sideways.

Jenna had still been asleep, and the house had that rare early hush. I remember how warm the sunlight was, slanting through the window in golden strips. I'd walked into the kitchen barefoot, wearing Nick's old T-shirt, and found him already there, mug in hand, reading something on his phone.

He looked up at me, smiled slow, that dimple peeking out.

"Coffee's hot," he said, leaning back, looking me over, his smile widening. "I like when you wear my shirts." His deep voice still raspy with sleep.

We didn't say much else. Didn't need to. He pulled me between his legs, wrapped his arms around my waist, rested his forehead against my chest and held me.

I hadn't thought about those mornings for so long. Hadn't let myself. I pressed a hand to my chest and couldn't seem to pull in a full breath.

I opened my eyes. The cursor still blinked. I started to type again.

I just wanted to say…

I deleted that, too. I didn't know how to finish that sentence. What I really wanted to say was: *I miss you. I'm not okay. I'm not strong right now, and I need you to love me anyway.*

I couldn't ask that of him, not anymore. I'd thrown it away like the fool I was.

I locked the screen and set the phone down face down on the bedside table.

It started as a flicker.

A ripple under my skin, static caught in the bloodstream. Not painful. More like a vibration that didn't belong. My pulse strengthened. The air warmed as the lights in the room dimmed, darkening the room.

A nurse walked past in the hallway. Her footsteps should have been faint, yet they boomed. I sat up, pressing my palms to my ears, willing the dizziness to pass, my limbs buzzing as if they were overloaded, shorting, fracturing from the inside out. Then the scent hit. Sandalwood and clov e… burning.

The Awakening.

Fraying.

It had been whispering for weeks. The exhaustion, the hand tremors, the nosebleeds.

The curtain swayed, though the air was still. A cool wetness pooled around my bare feet, rippling in concentric circles that widened without water to cause them.

I heard her voice then. Soft. Layered. Everywhere at once.

You can't heal what you won't let break, my daughter.

Bloom. My mother's whisper, warm and steady, echoed in a pulse of light wrapping around me.

The glow faded slowly, sinking back into my veins. The water receded until my feet were dry again, and the machines resumed their lullaby once more.

A warning.

If I didn't listen, I was going to break. And if I broke, those pieces would turn to ash.

THIRTY-FIVE

Cataleya

HAVING NOTHING BETTER TO do than stare up at white ceiling tiles for hours on end gave me too much time to think. Being reduced to patient, told to rest when every fiber of my being screamed to do anything but, was humbling beyond measure.

My phone vibrated on the tray beside me.

Jenna: *I'm coming from Dahlia's room. Do you want me to bring you anything?*

I stared at the message, then closed my eyes as tears slipped down the sides of my face.

The worst on my long list of recent failures.

Jenna.

Taking care of *me*.

She was the one who needed to be taken care of, not the one doing the caretaking. She should be studying, laughing, living. Not carrying the weight I dropped. Not holding everything together with trembling hands. The role reversal was cruel.

And Dahlia. Broken and bandaged and still fighting infection. How could *I* be the one in this bed when she was the one who had been so close to death?

I thought I could keep going, keep fixing, keep saving.

I'd poured everything into those tiny NICU fighters, believing that giving more of myself meant I was answering my highest calling. Somewhere in all that saving, I'd stopped seeing the ones who needed me most. My family became collateral damage, wounded by my absence.

If I'd been present, sensed Jenna's suffering, I could have seen Dahlia's infection before it got as bad as it did. Instead, while I was working all those extra shifts using the amazing Awakening that enabled me to do truly magical things, my girls were hurt. Violated. Drugged and dragged through hell.

And I wasn't there.

The door creaked open with a soft hush of caution.

Jenna peeked in, a styrofoam cup in one hand, a paper bag in the other. Her hair was pulled back in a haphazard bun, wisps of dark hair she got from me falling into her face, her sweatshirt hung off one shoulder as if she'd dressed without thinking. She looked older than yesterday.

"Hey," she whispered, stepping in.

I swiped quickly at my cheeks.

"You didn't answer, so..." She crossed the room and set the bag down carefully on the tray. "I brought you some terrible coffee and a muffin you probably won't eat."

I gave her a weak smile. "Thanks, baby."

Jenna pulled the visitor chair close, sat down, folding one leg under her, her eyes searching mine.

"Do you want me to call Dad?"

Yes.

"No. I don't want to worry him. I'm okay."

"You scared me," she whispered. "One second you were there, and the next you just..." Her voice caught. She looked down at the cup in her hands. "I thought you died. Just like that. No warning."

I reached for her hand.

"I'm so sorry I scared you," I whispered. "I didn't realize I was that tired."

"Yes, you did. You knew. You just didn't care," she said. Not unkindly. Just a necessary truth.

Still, I flinched.

"You don't stop, Mom. Not unless you're forced to." She brushed her thumb over mine. "And even then, I think you'd try to crawl out of your own hospital bed just to go take care of someone else."

I let out a brittle laugh. "It's hard to let go."

"I know," Jenna said, leaning in so our foreheads touched. "You have to. Just for a minute. You have to let someone else carry it for you."

I had to look down to keep from falling apart in front of her.

And through the ache, the faint hum beneath my skin still whispered, refusing to let go, no matter how depleted I was.

The hospital forced me to stay overnight. Long enough to flood my veins with fluids, stick a pulse ox on my finger, and confirm I wasn't dying, at least not in any measurable way. Then they handed me a prescription for rest, like that was something you could pick up in a bottle.

The leave of absence wasn't a choice so much as a surrender. I was forced to shift my focus to my family, who should've always come first.

My heart wanted to crawl into bed beside Jenna and Dahlia and make them soup and promise I'd never leave their side again. Though part of my brain wanted to reach for my phone and check in on the NICU.

When the hospital finally discharged me, I rejoined my family back in Dahlia's room, now downgraded out of the ICU, where we all stayed most of the day.

The light in her room was dim, the soft glow from the monitor casting faint shadows over her face. She was sleeping again, and finally stable. She still had potent antibiotics running through her IV, but the infection was lessening its grip on her.

However, the damage had been done. Not just to her body. To all of us. A boundary had been breached, obliterating any semblance of normalcy that once defined us.

Our family would never be the same.

A chilling truth settled in. This was only the start of our journey.

Salvia stood in the corner, arms crossed, in her new standing guard position. She hadn't cried again since the storm hit. Hadn't spoken much at all. She hovered. Stared. Held Dahlia's hand.

I, on the other hand, couldn't stop moving since I'd been released. The fluids and sleep reignited an energy I hadn't had in a while. Every time I sat down, the weight of helplessness threatened to suffocate me. So I paced, I cleaned. I rearranged Dahlia's things, refilled water canisters that were already full.

Anything that would keep my hands busy while my mind raced on the brink of obsession. Those boys, who they were, where I could find them, what I'd do to make sure they paid for hurting our girls.

The guilt was growing teeth. It now had focus, purpose. The tide of my anger now had direction. I wasn't about to let this rot in the dark like some shameful family secret. That was the favorite hiding place of boys like that. Let it fester in the dark and they'd be back at it the next weekend, the next semester, the next girl.

They thought they'd gotten away with it, that these girls would keep quiet. Too scared, too ashamed, too broken to fight back.

They didn't know us at all.

The system could only do so much with what they were given. But there were other ways to build pressure and expose the truth. Nick had skills. Salvia burned with a fury that could flatten buildings if you pointed her in the right direction. And I had the Awakening, a weapon I would learn to wield. We had tools. We had more than a motive.

"Papi," Salvia said sharply, ripping my thoughts away. My head snapped up.

Diego stepped inside the room, his shoulders pulled up, hands shoved deep into his jacket pockets. Shadows lingered under his eyes that hadn't been there before. He looked over Dahlia, slow and deliberate. That quiet sadness he carried spread through the room.

"How is she?" Diego asked, looking at the machines that were hooked up to Dahlia, taking a step closer to the bed.

Salvia didn't answer. Instead, she moved toward him, her eyes hard.

"What are you doing here?" she demanded, then scoffed, moving away from him before he could respond. "You know what, never mind. Let's get coffee. Jenna, text me when she wakes."

Jenna's eyes darted between the three of us, confusion and worry all tangled together, caught in the silent tension threading the air. She nodded. "Of course."

Salvia's fingers hooked around my wrist before I could think of a reason to stay, pulling me toward the door. Diego followed. She spun on him before we'd cleared the nurses' station.

"I thought you said you didn't want to come to the hospital," she snapped.

Diego didn't meet her eyes. His thumb dragged over the ridge of his wedding band, a restless loop he'd worn into the gold after all these years.

"I didn't want to bring this kind of energy into a place that's already hurting," he said finally.

Her brows furrowed. "What are you talking about?"

His gaze lifted to hers. I swear I could see the aura of our mother standing between them.

"Blame," he said. "The kind that is always between you and me, Salvia."

Her jaw flexed, her silence louder than any shout.

"You think I don't know you blame me? Even after all these years?" His voice didn't rise. "You're right. I shouldn't have come. Dahlia doesn't need this stress." Hurt was heavy in his words. He turned before either of us could answer.

I reached out instinctively. "Papi—"

He didn't slow down. I watched him retreat from us, vanishing down the hall.

"*Salvia.* What the hell is wrong with you?"

"They're going to get away with it." Her voice had changed, deep, dangerous.

I watched her, my mind trying to catch up.

"There's no evidence," she continued, her gaze still fixed ahead at where our father had disappeared. "The guys who did this? They'll go on as if nothing had ever happened. Like Dahlia was just another girl they broke and tossed aside." She looked up at me then. "We can't let that happen."

I nodded, my throat tight. "I know. I've been thinking the same thing."

"Do you remember any of the names Jenna said? Jared something and—"

"Jared Allon," I said, the name bitter on my tongue. "He goes to Jenna's school. Sebastian is a football jock and Jared's right-hand man. There are a couple of others. Bryce and Tyler." Salvia stared at me. "I told you, I've been thinking the same thing."

She paused as she pulled out her phone. "We can't go to the police with nothing more than accusations. We need proof. Recordings. Names. Timelines. I don't think our girls were the first. They've done this before. I *know* it. And they'll do it again. I don't care how long it takes. If the law can't do anything, I will."

"You're talking about gathering evidence ourselves?" I asked.

"We expose them, and we end them." Her voice didn't tremble anymore. It sharpened, a blade ready to cut deep.

I exhaled slowly, embracing the shift. The need for blood.

"We know who is involved. We know the club. And we should be able to find the motel they took them to on the *Find My* app." I looked at my sister. "They'll never see us coming."

Salvia's eyes sparked. "Damn right, they won't."

THIRTY-SIX

Cataleya

AFTER TEN DAYS IN the hospital and a full course of strong IV meds, we were finally able to bring Dahlia home.

At least my not-so-voluntary leave of absence from work would allow me to help take care of her and get Jenna out of the caretaker role she'd crammed herself into.

Being behind in her classes would ultimately cause her more stress, which was the last thing she needed. With me there, I hoped Jenna would feel better about leaving Dahlia. Mostly because of the conversation I'd overheard between them.

"Please, Jenna. Don't let me screw up your life any more than I already have."

"What are you talking about? You haven't screwed up anything. I'm just worried about you. I need to make sure you're okay. I don't want to leave you alone again. I was really scared, Dahl."

"I know." A pause. "I never thanked you. For saving my life."

"I didn't do anything. I drove you to the hospital."

"I was letting myself get worse. I wanted it to..."

"*Dahlia.*"

"If you hadn't come..." Another pause. "So, yeah, you saved my life. Now please go live yours. Get those goals. Don't waste any more time. I'll be right here, getting waited on by the moms. I'm okay. I promise."

I had to brace a hand against the counter to stay upright. Hearing my niece, my second daughter, in that kind of emotional turmoil, and knowing this Awakening was useless to her, nearly took my knees out.

Salvia and I went to work, spending hours at her kitchen table, our laptops open, notebooks scattered. When the coffee went cold beside us, we switched the mugs for wine glasses and continued deep into the night.

I pulled up the class roster from Jenna's summer course. Nick had access to university portals through his department, and I knew all of Nick's passwords. Typing in his credentials was like violating patient privacy, a sacred rule I'd never broken.

I ignored the pang in my gut as I typed, using his passwords behind his back.

I hovered over his name more than once, but never pressed call. I would have to eventually. He was Jenna's father, he had the right to know about what happened. For now, the less he knew, the safer he stayed.

The memory of his face hit me. How it was lined with hurt and exhaustion. But he hadn't yelled, hadn't said a word. He'd just left without ever looking back.

With him *truly* gone—no toothbrush by the sink, no terribly off-key humming when he made coffee in the morning—I caught myself missing the life that wasn't there anymore.

I *yearned* for him.

In the still moments, I'd find myself reaching for my phone before I could stop myself. More than once, I stared at his name until the screen went dark.

I needed to hear his voice. I wanted to feel his hand in mine again. God, I wanted to crawl into his arms, bury my face in his chest, and let the tears fall there.

Because our daughter had been hurt in a way we couldn't undo.

Because our niece had almost died.

Because I missed him. I loved him.

Now, when I needed him the most, he wasn't here. And I'd been the one to tell him to leave.

I had to push it away and focus on what we were doing. Names. Social media profiles. Check-ins. Likes. Photos from *Shadow & Silk*. We collected everything.

Sal barely blinked as she worked, clicking through profiles so fast I had to lean over to keep up. Her eye for detail, honed with years of training, missed nothing.

"They've been at this for months," she muttered, clicking through one of their Instagram accounts. "Look at these comments. Same club. Same hashtags. Different girls. They're cataloging trophies."

Acid churned my stomach.

"I wonder if there's a way to get access to private groups?" I asked out loud. "A way to become part of their world. Get them to do it again, only this time the bait will be ready."

"You'd do that?" Sal asked, pausing.

"I'd do anything," I said. "This is mine, too."

Dahlia was mine too. I'd held her, cared for her since she was a baby, danced with her at family parties, watched her light up a room with her voice.

She was my daughter's best friend, and she was my best friend's daughter.

And they had hurt my baby, too. Not like they'd hurt Dahlia, and I thanked all the powers that be for that. She was hurting nevertheless.

This was *our* war.

"I lied to Z. I've never lied to my husband before." Salvia gazed out the window toward the endless sea. "He doesn't know Dahlia was in the hospital, that she was attacked, that she..." Sal's words drifted away. "All he knows is that she was sick. That's all I could manage."

I took her hand in mine. "I think this is too important to be told over the phone a continent away."

Salvia nodded, wiped away a lone tear that escaped, then looked at me.

"So, what's your plan?"

I met her gaze across the table.

"Remember how you said we looked great for our age? Let's see how far that gets us. We play their game."

"And if that doesn't work?"

There was more I wanted these boys to endure. I wasn't about to give it all to a system that had already failed before it started. My mouth twitched. "Then we go full witch-hunt."

She smiled. Slow, wicked.

I should've been afraid of the look in her eyes. One that matched my own. But I wasn't.

The darkness coiled tighter with every photo we uncovered, every smirking face tagged in a post, every girl in the background whose story I'd never know. My rage wasn't loud like Sal's. Hers burned like wildfire. Mine burned like oil, steady and deliberate.

We were the wrong women to leave breathing after wronging us.

Before we made our move, I needed control.

My gift had been feeding on me for weeks, and I wasn't about to walk into this hollowed-out.

I picked up my phone and dialed Kelly.

"You were right about all of it. I'm ready. Will you teach me?"

THIRTY-SEVEN

Jenna

B RAMBLE, WAGGING SO HARD his whole body swayed, was the first to greet us. We heard him before we even opened the door, his nails clicking on the hardwood, a tap dance of excitement. A drawn-out, sorrowful whine escaped him as the door swung inward, escalating into a frenzy of joyous barks as he pressed himself against us. He sniffed Dahlia from head to toe, confirming she was still here, still alive.

Dahlia sank to her knees in the foyer, letting him paint her face with affection while she laughed for the first time in weeks. I hadn't realized how badly I needed to hear that sound.

"I missed you too, Brams," she breathed, eliciting another plaintive whine of devotion as he pressed closer.

Throughout the day, he remained her shadow, curled at the foot of her bed, head resting on his paws, his eyes diligently tracking her every move.

Late that night, when I couldn't sleep, I found him lying at the slider, watching. His ears twitched at the smallest sounds, his gaze always drifting toward the walking path past the dunes. Then he stood, his big body taut, ears forward, nostrils flaring, a low growl rumbling through him.

I got up quickly, opening the slider to see what had his attention. The dim moonlight caught a figure, a dark blur just far enough to be questionable. But the stance. The tilt of his head. Watching.

Jared.

He didn't move closer. Because he saw me, or because Bramble stepped forward, hackles raised, his deep growl rolled down the beach, so vicious it gave me chills.

I gripped the edge of the railing, my pulse pounding. Jared just stood there, watching. I glared back at him. Though every inch of me screamed to flee, I refused to let him back me down.

Not this time.

Then he turned and disappeared into the shadows beyond the trees.

Bramble didn't relax right away. He stayed at the slider, head swiveling, ears twitching at every creak and gust of wind. Only when he was convinced the beach was empty again did he glance back at me, checking that I was still there, safe.

I knelt down and buried my face in his neck. "Good boy," I whispered, though my voice shook.

Behind me, Dahlia stirred in bed, murmuring in her sleep. I slid the door shut and locked it. Bramble stayed pressed against me, his heartbeat steady against mine.

Early rays of dawn were barely bleeding through the window, and already Dahlia was up, looking out at the ocean.

"Did you sleep at all?" I asked, my voice raspy with exhaustion.

I sat up on the oversized lounger I'd slept on in Dahlia's room. She'd struggled with nightmares off and on throughout the night, a restless cycle of tossing, mumbling, and the occasional choked cry.

She shrugged. Behind her, the bright floral quilt we'd picked out together last summer, a lifetime ago, hung in tangled folds on the foot of her bed.

I pulled a blanket around my shoulders. "You hungry? I can get breakfast started."

"I'll try," she murmured as she retreated to her bed, scooting herself back into it.

I rose and sat opposite her, close enough to press my toes against hers, a silent connection. Outside, the gulls screeched, impatient for their morning catch. The sound jarred Dahlia, making her flinch.

"They want their breakfast, too." I reached out, steadying her. "Dahl, we don't have to be afraid."

"My mind won't let me forget. Even when I sleep."

"We'll drown it out," I promised, my voice firm with determination. "We can play music or audiobooks. I can definitely talk all night. We'll stay awake together if we have to."

She shook her head. "I don't want to be awake."

Dahlia stared down at our feet pressed together, her toes cold against mine.

"She's not okay," she said out of nowhere, her voice rough. "Your mom."

"I know."

"She looked like a ghost, Jen. Even before she collapsed at the hospital." Dahlia leaned back against the pillow, staring up at the ceiling. "That's what happens to the women in our family, isn't it?"

I frowned. "What do you mean?"

"They don't stop until they bleed," she whispered. "And even then, they don't rest. They just wipe it up and keep going."

I'd seen it in my mom. In Salvia. In Dahlia, too. Our inherited compulsion to fix, to carry, to hold steady when everything else was falling apart, no matter the cost.

"I used to think they were superheroes," I murmured. "In sarcasm and heels."

Dahlia gave a soft, broken laugh. "Turns out they're just really good at hiding when they're dying inside."

The silence stretched between us, long enough for the gulls outside to take over, their cries loud against the hush of the room.

"Do you think it's passed down? That inability to stop?"

Dahlia turned her head toward me. "Are you asking if it's trauma or hereditary?"

"Yeah."

She exhaled. "Both?"

"I don't want to be like that," I said softly.

"I don't either. But I already feel it happening."

The thought of Dahlia disappearing into survival before she had a chance to come back to herself ripped a hole in me.

I lifted her chin, forcing her to meet my eyes.

"Remember when we built that blanket fort in the living room and we used your mom's ridiculously expensive sheets over the furniture? You insisted on bringing in the flashlight." A laugh slipped free. "Not because you were afraid of the dark, but because you wanted to scare me. You read ghost stories until two a.m., that damn flashlight under your chin like some demented demon. I hid under the pillows, terrified."

She scoffed, a flicker of amusement in her eyes. "It was the only time I was the brave one."

"You've always been the brave one." I pressed my knees to hers.

She leaned forward, resting her forehead on her knees. "I don't know *who* I am anymore," she whispered.

There were no right words. So I gave her all I had left, my arms.

I scooted closer, wrapping myself around her trembling frame. She stiffened for a heartbeat, then folded into me, her tears warm against my neck.

"You are Dahlia Elizabeth Eze. Your parents are not only gorgeous, they're kind, just like you are. You play the piano and the guitar as if they possess you. And your voice isn't bad, either. You're the bravest person I know, playing in front of a room full of strangers without shaking. You're stubborn and brilliant and the best person I've ever known. Those bastards can't *ever* take *any* of that away from you."

Her tears slowed. She looked up, eyes clear. "What if I can never play again?"

I tucked a loose strand of hair behind her ear. "Music is part of your soul. You'll never lose it. It'll come back to you when you're ready."

Outside, the first golden beam slipped across the quilt, illuminating the florals into a bright glow. She nodded, a small, fierce movement, the barest spark of hope flickering back to life.

We sat close, listening as the gulls wheeled outside, their cries no longer menacing.

The rest of the house remained quiet, wrapped in early morning stillness. No one else should be awake. Yet faint voices drifted up from outside.

My body tensed, Jared's predatory stance flashing through my mind. But Bramble jogged to the slider, tail high and wagging. Then I recognized my mom's voice.

I crossed the room and peered down through the glass.

Below, Mom stood barefoot on the damp sand. Sal held a phone out, lit candles flickering around them, casting dancing shadows on the beach.

My breath caught.

Were they filming?

THIRTY-EIGHT

Cataleya

A s dawn broke, Salvia and I stood on the beach behind her house, a few candles flickering in the ocean breeze, casting a dim light around us as instructed. The air was already growing colder with winter's approach, chilling my skin, a promise of darkness coming. I focused on the cool sand beneath my bare feet, trying to stay present in the moment.

Salvia held her phone out with the screen facing me so that I could see Kelly on the video call. I waited for instructions while Kelly set up on her end. She placed a leather-bound book, decades old, if not older, beside her teacup. She leaned forward to adjust her camera angle.

I watched, horrified, as her hand drifted too far to the right. The full mug of hot tea tipped, amber liquid spilling across the gilt edges of the book.

"Oh no. Bugger!" she gasped, diving off screen. Seconds later she reappeared, cheeks flaming, tea-stained pages clutched to her chest. "All right. I may have baptized the book. One sec, I'll..."

She sputtered out a ragged apology while frantically blotting the cover with a towel. Her usual composure was gone, replaced by a frazzled grin that made me smile despite myself, something I hadn't thought possible for a long time. Even Salvia, who'd found nothing amusing about any of this so far, bit her lip to hide a smirk.

Finally, Kelly's now calm face flickered back onto the screen.

"We are going to focus on grounding. How it feels not only to draw energy but to give it back. Plant your feet," Kelly said, voice soft and insistent. "Heel to earth, toes splayed. Clear your mind. Listen to the ocean. Which is lovely, by the way. Imagine roots growing from your soles, burrowing deep into the sand. See the energy rising. From the earth into your feet, up your legs, your core, through your arms and into your fingers. Feel the heat of it. Slow, steady."

I obeyed, pressing my heels down, imagining brittle roots snaking from the sand into my body. To my surprise, the energy buzzed within me, the way it did when I would *see* into my patients. Warmth tingled in my hands, spreading to my fingers.

"Good," Kelly murmured. "Now. Hold it. Feel it. Let it pull you in."

What began as a hum became a vibration, stronger than I wanted. It was getting away from me, pulling me apart instead of holding me together.

"Breathe, Cat," Kelly said gently. "In through your nose. Hold. Out through your mouth. Once you have a hold of it, picture it leaving you. Down your arms, out your core, your legs, your feet. *You* control it. Don't let it control you."

I didn't know how. It got too strong. My body shook as I tried to inhale. The salty air turned to acid on my tongue. The gentle lapping of water had amplified into tall waves crashing on the shoreline. Instead of warmth flowing downward, it yanked out of me, pulling my blood with it. My calves went numb as the world spun.

Salvia caught my arm as I stumbled. The instant she touched me, energy tore from her and into me. Gasping, I pulled away, and she stared at her hand, the one that had touched me, wonder in her eyes.

"I..." My voice cracked. "I don't feel anything but panic." Static zapped across my skin.

Kelly's brows knitted. "That's okay. Sometimes the drain is too strong. Let it go. Release your shoulders. Trust the earth to take it back."

My heart pounded so hard I could feel it in my throat. A shard of Awakening, raw and furious, flickered at the edge of my vision as I lost control. I tried to clamp it down, to pull it back in, but it leaped away. A fierce wind whirled around us, extinguishing the candles in one sweep and every ounce of energy along with them.

"Cataleya, stop and breathe," Kelly urged. "Forget the roots. Come back to your body. Wiggle your toes. Open your eyes."

"No." Panic bloomed in my chest as I crashed to the ground.

Kelly's voice blurred into the ringing in my ears, Salvia asking if I was okay tunneled in the distance. I collapsed back onto the sand, dizzy.

The Awakening, instead of stabilizing, surged again, tugging at me instead of holding me steady. My pulse thundered in my throat. Every nerve buzzed with too much power and too little control.

"It's worse," I choked, chest heaving as I fought for breath.

Salvia reached toward me, but I jerked away before she could touch me again. Just in case. I lifted my head enough to see Kelly's face on the screen. Pale, wide-eyed, her hand pressed over her heart as if she could steady both of us at once.

I pressed my palms into the sand, focusing on the grains beneath my fingers. *Inhale. Exhale.*

At first, there was only a dizzying pull, like the tide dragging me under. Then, somewhere in the static, I caught it. The faint rhythm of my breath, the sand clinging to my palms, the solid press of earth beneath me.

I wasn't sinking. I was anchoring.

The realization rippled through me. I'd done this before without even knowing. At the party, when the flood of emotions nearly tore me apart. I'd forced myself still, focusing on the weight of Nick's hand until the noise quieted. Then again in the NICU, scrubbing in, the bristles of the brush against my skin grounded me when the energy threatened to spiral.

I *had* stopped it before. I could do it again.

The panic didn't vanish, but it loosened its grip. My pulse slowed. The spinning eased. The ocean's roar softened to its natural rhythm, the breeze brushed over my skin like a cool caress.

For the first time, I wasn't just surviving the current.

I was steering it.

Then, I remembered Salvia's essence. I'd pulled it in for a fraction of a second. I'd stolen it. I hadn't just grounded, I'd consumed. The triumph that had bloomed twisted.

The worst of the tremors finally eased. My breathing slowed. The sand was cold beneath me, the surf whispering instead of roaring. Salvia crouched beside me, cautious but close, her eyes wide with worry.

Kelly's voice crackled through the phone, gentler now. "That's it, love. You did it. You found your footing."

I swallowed hard, still shaking. "I didn't *do* anything. I just quieted it. Like before."

Kelly nodded, relief softening her features. "That's the point of grounding. It's not about silencing the Awakening, it's about learning when to *listen* to it. You didn't lose control, you found it."

Her words settled deep, the meaning unfurling with each breath. The fear that had strangled me loosened.

Kelly's expression shifted, a flicker of something like pride. "Just remember, control cuts both ways."

Salvia looked between us, the wind tossing her hair. "Then we make sure you stay on the right side of it."

I nodded, staring out at the restless sea. For the first time since my Awakening, I wasn't afraid of the power moving through me. If I could quiet the Awakening, I could also call it when I needed it most.

Kelly exhaled. "Well, that was enough of a fright for me today. We'll try again tomorrow. For now, rest."

Sal ended the call, then reached for me. "Come on, I'll help you back to the deck."

"Don't touch me!" It came out harshly, more than I'd meant.

"It should be okay now. You have nothing left in you to do it again."

I hesitated. It wasn't just the fear of hurting her. It was the fear that she'd be afraid of me. Or worse, repulsed.

"Cat, I'm fine," she said gently. "It didn't hurt. It just felt like a wind tunnel. Kind of tingly, like a quick high." She chuckled.

"It made you feel *high*?" Against all odds, I laughed. Then again, Salvia always could bring me back.

"Kind of. Hard to explain. Now come on. I need coffee, pronto. If I wait for your slow ass, it'll take forever." She offered her hand again.

After a long breath, I took it, trusting her more than I trusted myself.

THIRTY-NINE

Jenna

THE BEACH WAS WAKING up. Mist curled off the waves, the morning cloud cover still thick and gray. Everything still except for the slow breath of waves.

And the moms.

Mine was barefoot, standing in the center of a circle of lit candles, her dark waves dancing in the salty breeze. Tía Sal sat cross-legged outside the circle, facing the phone toward my mom. It didn't look as though she was recording her as much as showing her.

Whatever they were doing, the air crackled with it.

A woman's voice emanated from the phone. I could hear only fragmented phrases. *Energy. Grounding. Technique.*

"Dahlia," I whispered as loudly as I could without making my presence known from below. "Come see this."

We huddled together behind the curtain, peering through the gap.

Mom's posture was rigid at first, as if she didn't trust the earth under her. Then she inhaled so deeply her ribs visibly expanded.

"What are they doing?" Dahlia ducked her head to keep her voice low, her breath warm against my ear.

"No clue."

As we watched, a strange, sudden pressure pressed behind my ears at the same time my mom collapsed on the beach. When Sal lunged to catch her, a bright spark of light ignited between their hands, a visible discharge of energy. My mother recoiled, yanking herself away from her grip as if burned.

"What the—"

"Hide," Dahlia warned, darting behind the curtain, pulling me with her when they turned and headed back toward the house. We stayed hidden for a few seconds until we heard the door open and close from the deck to the kitchen.

"Did that look like..."

"What was that?"

"*Witchcraft*? But they're not..."

"...They wouldn't..."

The words tumbled out of our mouths simultaneously, a shared thought, a mutual disbelief. Then we just stared at each other.

Finally, Dahlia broke the silence. "That's not the only thing they've been hiding from us," she said, her voice mournful. "I think they're planning something... big."

"Bigger than that?" I asked, my pulse barely slowing.

"I overheard them talking about Jared and the others. They were talking about how there are other girls, that they've done this before. About trapping them before they do it again." Her voice cracked. "They've got names, photos. They're gathering proof."

I stared at her. "To give to the police?"

"I don't know. I don't think so." Her eyes darted toward me, as though pleading I'd tell her she was wrong. "The way it sounded, they want to do more. I think they *want* to do it themselves."

Heat crawled up my neck, my pulse a drum in my ears. I swallowed hard at the thought of our mothers rising to fight them alone. "That sounds..." My voice caught. "Dangerous."

"It is." Dahlia's hand slid over mine. "I'm scared and proud at the same time."

"Should we confront them?" My voice scratched its way out of my throat.

"Tell them we know? Or tell them not to go after them?"

"I don't think I want them to stop. I want to help them. Knowing that I could have stopped him from doing this to you—"

"Jenna, you couldn't have—"

"*Knowing* that I could have," I repeated, cutting her off, my voice rising with intensity. "I don't think I'll be able to live with myself if they do it again to someone else, and I didn't even *try*."

I had to stop to catch my breath. For the first time since everything happened, the rage that I'd shoved down for weeks was burning brighter than the guilt.

Dahlia looked away, avoiding my eyes. "I know, I get it. I don't think I can, though. I'm not ready."

"Hey," I said, nudging her lightly with a shoulder. "You don't have to. All you need to do is recover. I'll fight for both of us. I promise you."

"That's not for you to do."

"It is. You are my family. And you're my best friend. If not for you, then who?"

The kitchen, the heart of the house, had become a war room. Papers were spread across the table, a chaotic landscape of information. Photos, club schedules, even maps of parking lots, each piece of evidence a testament to their dedication, their unwavering pursuit of truth.

That's where I found them.

Mom had her dark, wavy hair pulled back in a messy bun. Her eyes were ringed with exhaustion, yet alight with a fierce purpose. Tía Sal paced beside her, phone in hand, jamming her fingers quickly against the screen, coordinating their efforts with military precision.

I hovered in the doorway, picking at the hem of my sleeve, trying to force the words out of my tightened throat. Mom glanced up, her eyes widening with a flash of worry, her expression softening as she took in my presence.

"Jenna, honey—"

I held up a hand. "I overheard. You're going after them. I want to help."

Her shoulders straightened. "Jenna."

I nodded, blinking back tears. "I have to. No one understands wanting justice, needing to make them pay for what they've done, more than I do. I can't just sit here and pretend it didn't happen anymore."

Dahlia appeared in the doorway. She slid beside me and took my hand in hers. "We're in this together."

Tía Sal looked at the two of us, her expression softening, her eyes glassy. She strode over to Dahlia, cupping her cheeks in her hands, kissing her forehead, brushing her hair away from her face. She looked at me, squeezing my other hand. Then she gave my mom a look, a silent communi-cation only they knew.

My mom let out a long exhale. "We can't let you actively participate in what we have planned. Whatever we do, whatever we get on these dirtbags, could be compromised if you were part of it. Besides, as your mothers, your safety is first, foremost, and absolutely non-negotiable."

I squared my shoulders, lifting my chin. "Why can't we—"

"However," Mom put up a finger to stop me, silencing my protest. "We can tell you what it is we're planning on doing. In fact, it might be smart to have a helpline waiting in the background if things go sideways."

My pulse hammered. I wasn't sure whether from relief or fear. "Just tell us what you need."

She motioned for us to join her. When I sat next to her, I noticed that my mother didn't just look weary from lack of sleep. She looked depleted, as if a part of her had been stolen, leaving an empty void.

A hot tear slipped down my cheek. "I'm sorry I didn't notice sooner. How sad you've been, how hard you've been fighting."

She placed a hand on my cheek, her eyes meeting mine. In that mo-ment I didn't see the strong, unshakable version of the mom I'd grown up with. I saw everything she was holding in. Hurt, love, sadness, guilt, and something that looked a lot like pride. It hit me harder than words ever could.

"There's nothing for you to be sorry about. I'm the one who needs to apologize to you. I wasn't there when you needed me most. I may not have been able to prevent what happened to the two of you, but I sure as hell should have been there holding your hand every minute after. I'll regret it for the rest of my days. I swear to you, it will never happen again."

She pulled me into a fierce hug and held me in a way that only mothers could as I cried against her shoulder. Her hand stroked my hair, smoothing it down my back until I could breathe again.

"We do this together," Mom whispered in my ear, her voice thick with emotion. Her hand found mine, squeezing hard.

Late into the afternoon, the four of us sat at the kitchen table, weaving ideas and preparations. As we outlined our plan, dates, locations, backup contingencies, our family had shifted from safe rhythms to something wild. Maybe even dangerous.

Whatever came next, we'd face it together. Even if together didn't look the same anymore.

FORTY

Cataleya

T HE LIGHTS OF *Shadow & Silk* shimmered across the pavement as we sat parked, watching people file past the velvet ropes. Music pulsed from inside, the kind of bass you feel in your bones before you even step in. I hadn't been to a club in over a decade, and this one oozed sinister malevolence even from the outside.

Sal sat rigid beside me, hands clenched in her lap. Dark jeans. No make-up. The same as me. Because no one was supposed to see us tonight.

"You good?" I asked.

Her jaw ticked. "Not even close."

"Sal, we're only watching tonight."

"I won't do anything," she snapped the words out, then softer, "Not yet."

Silence stretched between us. The bass thumped through the doors, steady as a heartbeat.

"I had this crazy dream. About Mom. I've had the exact same dream twice now. So strange," Sal whispered, almost to herself.

My stomach knotted. "Mom?"

Sal nodded, eyes fixed on the neon sign. "She was in her greenhouse at the old house in the Appalachians. She said, 'Don't follow the shadows.'"

A chill moved up my spine. "Sal... I've had that dream too."

Her gaze finally met mine, startled. For a beat, neither of us breathed. The air in the car was charged.

"Do you think it's a warning? Because it feels like one," she said.

"It does. But of what? This?" I whispered back.

"Shit," she straightened, scanning the line. "We need to change."

"What? Why?"

She scowled at the crowd. "Look at them. Then look at us," she said, jabbing a thumb toward the girls in glittery dresses, hair and makeup done. "*Not* dressing up will make us stand out."

She dug in the backseat, produced a makeup bag and brush, and got to work.

Ten minutes later, we walked toward the entrance.

We pushed through the crowd and found a corner with a partial view of the bar and the booths guarding the VIP area. The lights strobed, bodies pressed together, the music throttled like a heartbeat on amphetamines.

Sal flinched beside me. "I can't believe we let them come here."

"Don't do that," I murmured. "You were young once."

That earned me an eye-roll.

I could see the girls here. Dahlia laughing, dancing to the beat. Jenna beside her. Two bright, ordinary girls lost in the music. The happiness, the innocence they radiated before it was shattered.

A tear slid down.

"What's wrong?" She gripped my wrist, frantic.

"Just thinking of them happy. *Before*. It'll never be that way for them again."

Sal studied me, her expression going still in that dangerous way of hers. "We're going to make sure those guys spend the rest of their lives wishing they'd never met our girls. By the time we're done, they'll know what it feels like to be afraid."

We watched. We waited.

"They're not coming," Sal said after twenty minutes, voice tight with impatience.

"If not tonight, we'll try again tomorrow."

And then he came in. Jared. His arm slung around a buddy. Sebastian.

Fury blazed from Salvia. I grabbed her hand before she could move. "Don't. You promised."

"They're right there, Cat."

"And do what? Confront them? With what?"

She pulled free, clenching her fists at her sides instead. I caught her wrist. "Breathe. Slow in and slow out. Feel your feet on the ground."

She eyed me, an angry eyebrow cocked. "Grounding work? Really? Because it worked so well for you?"

"Just do it." I talked her through it again. And again.

Her chest rose and fell, breath ragged. "I still want to rip their fucking throats out."

A chuckle escaped. I didn't doubt it. Sal might not have any abilities from the Awakening, but she had rage in spades.

"Soon. Tonight we're here to watch. Not to burn it all down. Yet."

A text pinged on my phone. Jenna.

"Apparently, Sebastian is streaming everything they're doing right now." I read out lout. "He wouldn't be that stupid?"

"We can only hope," Sal answered through her teeth.

It happened quickly. Jared and his group moved with practiced ease, scanning the room, then zeroing in on two girls near the bar. Barely legal, flushed with alcohol and attention. Jared worked the charm.

Sebastian went to the bar and motioned. He waved the female bartender who went over to him away, signaling a different one instead. A male one. They exchanged some words, then money. A tip before service.

"Did you see that?" I asked.

"Yup. Looks like we're going to get some drinks from a certain bartender."

We watched the bartender take a tray of colorful shots to the table. He shot a quick glance around the room, then nodded to Sebastian as Jared kept the attention of the girls.

Then I saw it. The sleight of hand.

A vial. A pour. A finger stir.

I elbowed Sal. "Did you see *that*?"

"I saw it."

"Oh, god."

We didn't have to wait long before the girls were swaying, visibly altered within minutes. Jared leaned in, whispering in one girl's ear. She nodded dizzily. They started toward the back, arms around waists, half-carrying the girls out the rear exit.

We followed at a distance.

Out the back, past the dumpsters, a black SUV idled with its lights off. I recognized the driver from one of the many pictures currently scattered across the kitchen island. Bryce. Tyler sat next to him. They loaded the girls into the back seat.

We ran to our car. I peeled out of the space, following at just enough distance to avoid suspicion.

"They've done this a lot," Sal said, low. "Too smooth. Too easy."

"We can't let anything happen to those girls."

Sal nodded. "I wasn't planning on it."

FORTY-ONE

Jenna

TONIGHT WAS NIGHT ONE. Observation.

Dahlia and I were holed up at her place, phones charged, papers spread over the kitchen island like a battlefield map, ready to save any documentation or call for help at the first sign of trouble. Our little makeshift command center. Adrenaline coursed through me, making my hands shake.

At least we had an ocean view and the steady roll of the waves to calm our nerves.

"Dahl, I need a distraction."

She glanced up from her novel. "Me too. The words are just blurring." She closed the book and tossed it onto the couch. "Okay, run through the dossier again?" She pointed to the island.

We spent the next hour combing through everything the moms had compiled. Even though we'd already memorized most of it, it didn't stop my stomach from flipping. Dahlia was more the social media expert. She scanned all of their accounts from her phone, noting anything new.

"Hey," Dahlia straightened. "Sebastian just checked in at *Shadow & Silk*. They're there. It's happening."

My heart rate doubled. "I'll text the moms."

"Nervous?" Dahlia asked me, her attention still on her screen.

"It's that obvious?"

"No. I was just hoping I wasn't the only one." She managed a shaky laugh, her face paling.

"I'm terrified." I admitted, reaching out to give her shoulder a gentle squeeze.

"Good. Me too." She gave me a half-smile, then looked back at her phone. "At least Sebastian is dumb enough to live-stream every second. We'll have a running feed for the moms."

"Thank god for brainless jocks," I muttered, though it offered little comfort.

"Not brainless, just arrogant."

An email notification popped up from someone named Kelly on Mom's laptop.

Auchter Lineage Archive

"Auchter? Isn't that our Scottish side of the family?"

Dahlia paused, thinking. "Yeah. Why?"

"Looks like my mom was doing some ancestry stuff." I clicked on the document.

My best ancestral-research notes yet.
Potatoes, black pudding, toothpaste (peppermint)

I blinked. "Um, it's a grocery list?" I turned the screen toward Dahlia, who laughed. Another ding popped up with a new email. Also from the same Kelly person.

AARGH! I've sent you my shopping list AGAIN. Forgive me, Cat. Here are the right documents.

Dahlia leaned in closer as I clicked on the PDF attachment. Old parchment scans filled the screen. Birth records from Aberdeenshire, references to an Ivy Auchter, of the old faith.

"Do you remember Great-Nonna's stories?" Dahlia murmured.

"Abuelo Diego's mom? Sure."

"She said her ancestors healed with herbs, whispered to the earth. She called them *Brujas*."

"Great-Nonna is an Ortega. Auchter is from Grandma Bloom."

"Have they ever told you what happened to Grandma Bloom? When I've asked, my mom goes deaf. She has never even talked about their mom," Dahlia looked at me curiously.

"Not really. All my mom said was that she left them when they were really little. She doesn't remember her." I scrolled farther.

"Oh, shit. This Kelly person thinks the Auchters were *witches*."

"Seriously?"

I turned the laptop toward her so she could read the email.

"Dominant bloodline of the Awoken," she read out loud.

A hush fell over us, broken only by the ocean outside.

"The other morning on the beach." My throat went dry. "Do you think..."

"I was just thinking the same thing," Dahlia said, her words barely a whisper.

Her phone dinged again. She swiped up.

"Sebastian's live at *Shadow & Silk.*"

She turned her phone so I could see the feed. The four of them, two girls and a tray of neon shots on the table. "They're doing it again."

My breath caught. "This is it." I grabbed my phone, thumbs flying.

FORTY-TWO

Cataleya

WE TAILED THEM DOWN the coastal road until the headlights swept over a flickering sign. *South Shore Inn*. The weak neon light cast a sickly glow, like a warning. Beyond it, the sagging building hunched in the dark. Half the windows were boarded up, the other half dark, vacant. The lot sat empty except for a truck on blocks, rusted, its tires gone, abandoned before the motel ever was. This wasn't a place for travelers. It was a place for things that wanted to stay hidden.

The SUV pulled into a space near the back. The boys bypassed the office, no one at the window, no light. When they reached the room, one of them pulled out a key already in their possession.

"It's always the same room," I murmured.

I glanced over at Salvia. Her eyes were dark with more than anger, lips pressed into a fine line that trembled just enough to show the turmoil beneath. Gone was the sister I knew, the curator who coaxed beauty from canvas.

I swallowed, reaching over to lay my hand on her shoulder. She didn't flinch. Her fingers dug into the handle until her knuckles blanched.

"Sal, talk to me."

Her gaze tore away from the SUV, her jaw tight, her shoulders squared, and the rage that had been simmering beneath every protective smile in recent days boiled over, igniting something irrevocable.

Jared and Sebastian dragged one girl inside and left the other in the SUV.

Sal reached for the door handle. "I'm going in."

I clamped onto her wrist. "*No.* We call the cops and catch them *in* the act."

Sal's eyes were wild with fury. "They're in there right now. Don't you get it?"

"I *do*," I said, my voice breaking. "That's why we have to get it right. We get one shot."

She sank back into her seat, her body visibly shaking. She pulled out her phone, hit record, zooming in on plate numbers, faces, everything we could get.

Then Jared walked back out. Alone. He slid into the SUV.

"Shit. *Shit!*" I said as the SUV pulled away. "Where the hell are they going?"

"I'm going in. We've got to get something. I don't care if I have to do this every fucking night until I get them all."

"I can't... I can't watch him doing it, Sal. I swear to god—"

"Breathe," she said, her voice cracking. "It'll be quick."

She was right. We'd need all the proof we could get to bring them down.

"And if they see us?"

"We make damn sure they don't."

Staying in the shadows, we made our way up to the room. I kept watch while Salvia tried to focus the camera through the tiny fissure in the curtain.

"Can you see anything?" I whispered as quietly as I could.

Her breath was strangely even, calm. "Yeah. I can see the girl passed out on the bed. I don't think anything has happened yet. *Shit.*"

"What?" I turned to face her, trying to see what she was seeing on her phone. She was focused on a back door propped open with a shoe.

A shadow fell across the wall. Before we could look up, Sebastian's arm arced. An ice bucket crashed into Salvia's temple, sending her head into the brick. Her body buckled.

"Salvia!" I screamed, lunging.

He was faster.

He wrenched my arm, twisting it behind me, the joint screaming. I fought. Claws, teeth, anything. But he was bigger.

A fist drove into my cheek. Copper flooded my mouth. He hit me again.

A high ringing muffled my hearing as the edges blurred to static, and the world folded into nothing.

FORTY-THREE

Jenna

IT WAS SUPPOSED TO be observation only. That's what Mom had promised when she and Sal left for the club.

Watch. Listen. Gather information.

However, as more time ticked by, an increasing sense of dread that the plan had inevitably fallen apart took hold.

All night we'd been digital spies, sending steady streams of updates. Screenshots of posts, captions the guys thought were clever, and time-stamped stories that told us exactly where they were and what they were doing. It was our way of contributing, of fighting back without getting to be there physically. When I opened the *Find My* app to check on the moms, my stomach dropped.

"They're leaving," I choked out.

Dahlia was instantly at my shoulder. On the map, the tiny dot that was Mom's phone moved away from the club, sliding along the highway. Not back toward the beach house, but in the opposite direction.

Her hand clutched mine. "Where are they going?"

We zoomed in, following the slow crawl of the dot until it stopped. A name filled the screen.

South Shore Inn.

My pulse stuttered. Wrong. All wrong.

"That's not good at all." Dahlia shook her head hard.

From his corner, Bramble unwound himself, a shadow detaching from the gloom. His tail, usually a proud banner, was now a slunk question mark. Head bowed, he padded to my side, sensing the apprehension in our voices.

"They're in trouble," Dahlia breathed, her eyes wide with fear.

We looked at each other, no words needed. There was only one person to call.

Abuelo Diego.

It should've been strange, choosing him before anyone else. But it would take too long to catch my dad or Uncle Z up on everything. Besides, Diego had always been more than just a grandfather who showed up on holidays. His stories always carried truths, warnings we hadn't understood until now. I was sure that if anyone would know what to do, it was him.

My hands shook as I pulled up his contact. He answered on the second ring, as if he'd been waiting.

"Jenna?"

"Abuelo," I gasped, words tumbling too fast. "Dahlia's here too. We need your help. The guys left the club. Our moms followed them. Their location on the app stopped at the South Shore Inn. Something's wrong."

"Slow down, *Mija*. What guys and what club? And why are my daughters following them?" His voice was steady, but I could hear the intensity in it.

Swallowing hard, I forced the words out. "They're the ones who..." I stopped and glanced at Dahlia. That promise had been broken back at the hospital. Still, it wasn't mine to tell.

"They drugged us," Dahlia said, her voice trembling but steady. "Me and Jenna. That's why I was in the hospital. I wasn't just sick. It was because of them."

"Now Mom and Tía Sal are after them." I squeezed my eyes shut, tears stinging.

For a long moment, there was only the guttural sound of fury on the other end. When he finally spoke, his words were tempered steel.

"I need you to tell me *exactly* where they are."

"South Shore Inn off Highway 78," Dahlia blurted.

Another silence, more ominous than the first. Then Diego's voice, sharp and final. "I know it. You did good by calling me. Now stay put. I'll find them."

The line went dead, but his promise hung in my head. Dahlia's hand stayed clamped around mine, a silent anchor in the storm.

If anyone could reach them, if anyone understood the darkness that lurked beneath the surface, it was him.

Forty-Four

Cataleya

"S HIT. YOU'VE GOT SOME spunk, lady. I think I broke a finger on that pretty face of yours," Sebastian scoffed, shaking out his hand. "It's okay. I've played with broken bones before."

Blood tasted on my tongue, stung my eye. I blinked through the burn, trying to orient myself. The stale air reeked of mildew and stale cigarettes. He'd dragged us inside. The girl lay sprawled across the bed, unmoving. Salvia was in a heap in the corner, her hair matted, her limbs twisted. When I saw her chest rise, the vise on my lungs loosened.

None of this was supposed to happen. We were only supposed to *watch*. Gather evidence. Stay invisible.

And now we'd blown everything.

If I could just keep him talking. Anything to buy time, to think.

I spat a mouthful of blood at his feet. "Quit bitching. My sister hits harder than you."

"Feisty. I like it."

My stomach churned. His grin oozed the same sick confidence Jared had. I steadied my voice. "Were you the one who touched my daughter?"

He barked a laugh. "Is that what this sad little sting is about? We got a piece of your daughter?"

We.

He looked confused. He didn't even know which girl I meant. Too many to remember.

Whatever fear I'd had evaporated, leaving only heat and clarity.

"You left bruises on her. What else did you do?" My voice shook, not from fear this time. "Did you touch her the way Jared touched Dahlia?"

That got his attention.

"You don't need to be talking about things that aren't your business."

"My daughter and my niece are *definitely* my business."

He shrugged. "I know that Dahlia chick. Lucky for her, Jared's obsessed. Kept her for himself. Pretty little thing. She would have made us a nice bonus. The other one must have been your kid. Yeah, she was feisty, too. Had to hold her ass down so Jared could finish up with Caramel deLite. I'm still bummed I didn't get a taste of Miss Feisty. You can give her my number. We can catch up where we left off."

The last tether of restraint inside me snapped. "I'm going to take you all down, you piece of shit."

He laughed. "You won't be able to touch shit, lady. We've got a good thing going here. You think it's just us? It's a perfect Ring. Unending and impenetrable."

"Fucking cowards," I hissed. "What kind of pussy needs to knock out women to get sex? What's the matter? Can't get it up? You're a bit young for that."

He struck me hard enough to spin my vision. Metallic warmth filled my mouth. Sal groaned. Moved.

Not yet, I thought. Keep him focused on me.

I forced a laugh. "That wasn't a no. You should probably lay off the 'roids. You know those make your dick small, right? Or smaller."

He lunged, grabbing my shoulders, slamming me against the wall. The impact jarred my skull.

"Fuck you, bitch. You don't know shit. I do just fine. The ones we don't have to hand over, I got enough for all of them. Got enough for you, too. I'll take you right now."

Salvia groaned as she pulled herself up, her face pale with exertion and blood dripping from her temple.

"She can watch."

He slammed me against the wall again. My vision spun. I doubled over, sucking in oxygen. Then, his hand closed around my throat.

The world constricted to that single point of contact.

The moment his skin met mine, everything flooded in.

A current jolted through me. My vision split into images.

Flashes.

Darkness.

Sebastian holding Jenna down. Dahlia, unconscious, tears sliding down her cheeks. Two others watching.

Laughter. Voices.

No DNA.

The sickening stench of booze, cigarettes, and pot.

His memories were pouring into me. *Their* night. Their cruelty. His glee.

I saw it all. More than I ever wanted to.

Lines around my vision shimmered, vibrating with Awakening, ancient and furious. A violent wave of rage flooded to the surface, my entire body quaking with it.

My hands fell from my neck, curling into fists at my sides, no longer trying to pry his fingers away. The air zapped around us. The walls seemed to hum, edges vibrating with furious light.

Every cell in my body lit up with Awakening.

I wasn't gasping anymore.

I was *pulling*.

His energy, his breath, his pulse, his very marrow, rushed into me. It hit like a wave of heat radiating at the base of my spine, a current of fire laced with lightning twisting, searing through muscle and bone until every nerve burned with light.

I drank it in.

He choked, fighting for air, his knees buckling as his life bled into mine. The power surged, intoxicating, a tidal wave of strength that made me dizzy with its promise. My breath quickened, not from pain but exhilaration, each second propelling me further.

The room dissolved into color and vibration. For the first time since the Awakening transformed me, I wasn't breaking or frayed.

I was *whole*.

"Cataleya!"

Sal's voice sliced through the haze.

She was on the floor, blood streaking down her temple, one trembling hand reaching for me.

And then she was with me.

Her panic pulsed through my veins, mixing with mine, her anguish flooding into me like smoke. I could *feel* her seeing what I saw. Our girls' terror, their helplessness. The connection between us burned, impossible, yet there.

Her pain hit like recoil as our energies tangled, spiraling out of control.

The hunger screamed louder. The wanting roared inside me like wildfire, licking at the edges of restraint. It felt *good*. Too good. If I looked down at him, if I let myself linger in that rage-fueled high, I wouldn't stop.

I'd *choose* not to. I'd drown them both just to finish him and call it retribution.

I tore my hands free.

The connection shattered.

Air rushed back in a violent gasp. I stumbled backward as he collapsed, skin gray and eyes hollow. A shadow of what he'd been moments before.

My hands trembled with the aftershock of what I'd done, the remnants of his essence shimmering on my skin, a visceral reminder of the energy I'd taken.

It terrified me how badly I'd wanted to pull it all, every ounce he had, shriveling him into a mummified corpse. I stared at my hands, capable of so much more than I'd ever imagined. I should have been twisted with horror and shame over what those hands had just done.

An unsettling thrill unfurled instead. Beneath the tremor lay a deeper craving, a dangerous allure that whispered promises of strength and control, tempting me to embrace the hunger I had unleashed.

For one terrible, glorious second, I understood.

I stared down at the man writhing at my feet, fighting an urge so strong to finish him.

With a savage cry, Salvia ripped the bulky, outdated phone from the side table and hurled it into the mirror. Glass exploded in a cascade of jagged silver shards.

She didn't hesitate.

Grabbing a sharp wedge, she turned and drove it straight into Sebastian's chest.

She pulled it from him, then plunged it in again. And again. Until the blazing wrath faded from her eyes.

He slumped against the wall. Blood pooled beneath him in a thick, tarry puddle, his vacant stare fixed on nothing.

Salvia stood over him, chest heaving, her skin spattered with crimson speckles, a wild aura pulsing around her, ferocious and menacing.

"Sal," my voice rasped, barely a whisper.

She didn't look up.

The silence that followed was eerie. Even the flickering fluorescent light went out. Only our ragged breathing filled the room.

I forced myself to move. "Sal, we have to go."

Nothing.

Her eyes were glassy, still trapped in what she'd seen. What *we* had seen.

I grabbed her shoulders. "Salvia! Come back."

A blink. Then another. Then, her gaze dropped to the blood on her hands. Her arms shook.

"I killed him," she whispered.

"I know."

"He's dead."

I nodded slowly. I reached for her, but she jerked away.

"All this time you could do *that*," she spat, her venom renewed. "And you did *nothing*?"

"Sal—"

"You could've ended him, and you didn't. I had to do it. Always me. I'm the one who does the hard things."

"I didn't know I *could* do that. I didn't mean to. It just happened."

Sal scoffed bitterly. "Of course you didn't *mean* to. Because it wasn't *your* daughter."

Her words stabbed, hitting places I didn't know were still bleeding.

"Don't." My voice lashed out in a harsh whisper. "You know that's not true."

She turned away, staring out the window. "I don't see anyone," she murmured.

She looked back, her eyes softer. "I'm sorry. That was... God, that was cruel." She saw me then.

"Oh, Cat." Her expression crumpled. "Your face—" She rushed over to me, her hand cupping my cheek.

I wiped the blood from my nose with my forearm.

"I'll heal," I lied.

"You always say that," she said with a weak smile.

I assessed her cut, bleeding hands. "Your hands."

"They'll heal," she parroted.

We sank to the floor together, surrounded by the copper tang of blood and the musty stink of mold and old smoke. Our clothes were ruined, our breaths uneven. The girl on the bed still hadn't stirred.

"What are we going to do with her?" I asked.

"Hopefully nothing. She should stay out for a while. Right?"

Neither of us sounded convinced.

Somewhere down the street, music blared.

"We should be freaking out. Why aren't we freaking out?" Sal muttered beside me.

"Because we don't have time to. We have to think."

Reality hardened around us. The body, the blood, the ruin.

"We need to clean this up."

"Clean up? And how are we going to do that?"

I pulled out my phone, my fingers still shaking. "We're going to call Papi."

She gaped. "What? You've lost your damn mind. You must have a concussion."

"I'm serious. He'll know what to do."

"This must be your all-powerful witchiness thing again, because how the hell could Papi possibly..."

"Papi," I said when he answered. "We need your help."

A pause. Then, "I'm almost there."

"What? How did you..."

"The girls called me. Which room?"

I told him the room number.

Another pause. "I'll be there in five." He ended the call.

Sal turned to me, her voice sharp now. "I can't believe you did that."

"What else were we going to do? Besides, the girls had already called him."

Finding out *why* they'd decided to call *him* would have to wait until later. After. "He's the only one who knows what to do."

"What, you think he's some kind of fixer?"

"No," I said quietly. "I think he's done this before."

FORTY-FIVE

Cataleya

FOUR MINUTES LATER, DIEGO Ortega—our father, and right now our savior—stepped into the room without knocking.

He didn't so much as blink at the body. He took in the scene with the same unreadable expression he'd worn when we were kids and had done something unforgivable.

Except this time, we *had.*

Diego crouched, turning the corpse over with the careful eye of a mechanic inspecting a ruined engine.

Salvia and I watched him, stunned at the ease he carried as if it were nothing. To feel comfort in a room full of ruin should have been impossible. But there was no time for shock.

"Why do I have a feeling this isn't your first rodeo?" I asked.

He glanced up. "You go first."

The three of us stood in a silent stare-down, none of us willing to answer.

"We need to get moving." Diego was the first to speak, keeping his ambiguity intact.

He was right. Dawn would break in hours. Not knowing how long the girl would stay unconscious, and never having cleaned up a crime scene or disposed of a body before, I wasn't exactly sure how long it might take.

Diego moved toward us. He looked at my battered face, then touched Salvia's temple.

"Did you make him pay first?"

"Not as much as he should have," Salvia answered through her teeth.

Diego nodded. "I'm going back to the house for supplies. In the meantime, do exactly what I say, exactly how I say it."

He rattled off precise instructions. How this was our life now was beyond my mental capabilities at the moment.

For the next thirty minutes, we worked in mechanical silence, following his orders until he returned with a black duffel.

"Let's get to work. I have cement mix in the truck for after." He unzipped the bag.

Plastic sheeting. Gloves. Bleach.

Sal blinked. "That's disturbingly specific."

"You asked if I'd done this before." He gave a humorless smirk.

"I don't want to know after all."

"You will soon enough," Diego answered, "because now you're a part of it."

We pulled on the latex gloves, the kind we used in surgery, and suddenly the idea of touching the body was terrifying.

What if the Awakening didn't stop at life? What if it showed something in death, or worse? My pulse hammered in my throat.

"Cat? C'mon. We don't have time for this," Salvia was already easing the body onto a sheet of plastic Diego spread.

"I... I don't know if I want to touch him."

Diego looked at me with a kind of sad knowing, while Salvia regarded me with an unreadable tilt of the head. I hadn't needed to explain further. She'd seen what I'd done.

"He's gone. It should be fine. Right?" Sal's question hung in the stale air.

I forced my hand down. My fingers brushed denim and then the hard curve of a phone in his back pocket.

"Wait." I fished it free.

I braced.

Nothing happened when I touched him. Maybe it was the gloves, maybe it was death. Either way, I let out a soft, trivial sound of relief.

I swiped past the lock screen. Facial recognition. I angled the phone up toward his face. It worked. Salvia looked over my shoulder as my fingers flew over apps, looking for anything useful.

"Bring up the pictures," Salvia clipped.

Dozens of images filled the screen. So many girls in various states of consciousness. Quickly, I swiped out of the photos and found a folder labeled The Ring.

Names. Dates. Code words. There were dollar amounts and initials next to each, cross-referenced with the sickening efficiency of a business.

"This is way more than just a few asshole college guys getting off on date rape," Salvia whispered, breathless.

An incoming notification pinged on his phone.

Unknown: *Payment cleared. New shipment good to go out tomorrow. Keep her quiet.*

Sal snatched the phone, scrolling, eyes widening. "I recognize some of these names. One of them is on the Charleston City Council."

She looked at Sebastian's body again, her rage revived. "Killing him didn't end a damn thing."

The room grew cold. "This just got a lot more dangerous," I said.

The ledger on that phone promised a larger, colder ledger elsewhere. The restitution we wanted still lay too far away, behind a wall of people with money and influence.

The phone chimed again, a string of thumbs-up emojis from a different unknown number.

Diego took the phone from Salvia's grip, thumbed it off, and pocketed it.

"We have to get this done. That is for later." He began talking through how to remove even the most minute trace evidence, how to lift prints, how to remove hair so nothing traceable was left behind. Blood had been spilled here. Evidence would tell a story.

Diego's voice cut through, practical and flat. "We sanitize, we bag, we bury. We burn anything that ties back. After that, you go back to your lives until I tell you otherwise."

We didn't ask questions. We didn't argue. We scrubbed until our arms trembled and the room looked like a sterile stage of ruin.

When it was done, dawn was scraping at the horizon. We stood in the doorway, filthy and drained, some portion of us carved away.

Diego shouldered the duffel, the motion looking more difficult than it should have, as if the bag weighed more than just what was inside. His face had gone pale, a tremor ghosting through his hand.

"I'll handle the rest. Get cleaned up. Don't talk to anyone. Not yet."

Sal's hand found mine in the doorway, squeezing.

"Not *yet*," she echoed.

We retreated silently to the car, and then back to the beach house, the ledger on that phone never leaving my thoughts.

Let them think they're untouchable.

It was only a matter of time before they learned the terrifying truth. The hunted had become the hunter, and punishment would come with teeth and claws.

FORTY-SIX

Cataleya

B Y THE TIME WE reached Salvia's house, the rising sun was already casting long shadows across the sand. The silence between us pressed like stone. Only the soft hum of the refrigerator and the ghost of Diego's industrial-strength bleach still clinging to our skin followed us through the door.

The job was done. The body was gone.

We'd scrubbed the motel room down to the studs. The ones still alive, Jared and whoever else was part of this 'Ring', would make damn sure no police went poking around.

Before leaving, I'd checked the girl's pulse. Strong and steady, breathing evenly. I'd rolled her onto her side, just in case, and called in an anonymous tip once we were clear.

Our first concern was our girls. I found them both asleep in Dahlia's room. Dahlia sprawled on the bed. Jenna curled up on a large lounge chair, both clutching their phones like lifelines. I eased the door shut.

Let them rest. Reality would find them soon enough.

"They're okay," I told Sal as she appeared at the top of the stairs.

"Good." Her gaze lingered on the closed door, distant.

"Hey." I set my hands on her shoulders. "Get some rest. We'll talk later."

She nodded, exhaustion flickering in her eyes before disappearing into her room and closing the door.

I understood.

While my body had taken a beating, Sal had looked straight into a darkness that would never let her go. I'd seen it in her the moment he fell. The question that haunted me was whether I'd wear that same darkness if I hadn't stopped, if I'd been the one who ultimately ended his life.

Downstairs, I aimed for tea, but collapsed on the couch instead. My body screamed, my face throbbed, my soul was in the middle of an excruciating game of tug-of-war between benediction and damnation.

The silence pressed in. My hands wouldn't stop trembling. Every time my eyes closed, I saw him. The way his body dropped, the unnatural slackness of his limbs, the dead weight of him on the floor. I'd thought there would be relief. For a heartbeat, there was. Then the acid of it settled in.

We had taken a life.

Even though it was *his* life, one of the men who drugged and violated girls, a monster who laughed while others bled. That truth didn't silence the part of me that recoiled, the part that whispered,

You can never undo what has been done.

I pressed my palms hard over my eyes, but tears still leaked through. What would Jenna see when she looked at me now? Not the mother who packed her lunches and sat up with her when she was sick. She'd see blood staining my hands.

And Dahlia, sweet, broken Dahlia. If she ever found out, would she flinch, afraid of what I'd done? Of what I could do?

I'd sworn I'd do anything to protect them. And I had. That protection had cost more than I had ever imagined paying.

The house creaked, each sound tangled with the echo of his last rasping breath. My body still hummed with what I'd taken from him, the phantom of his energy. A residue in my veins. Intoxicating and terrifying.

I curled into myself, arms locked tight around my ribs, trying to cage the storm inside. Because beneath the nausea and grief, there was something I couldn't admit aloud.

A part of me wanted more.

And that was the most damning truth of all.

Eventually, the last bit of energy drained away. When Diego said he was stepping out for a quick errand, I only nodded and let exhaustion drag me under into a shallow, splintered sleep.

It took more than a few blinks to clear the blur of darkness and remember where I was, which was still lying on Salvia's couch.

Voices murmured just outside the front door. My father's voice, and another I hadn't heard in weeks. Nick.

"I called you here because Cataleya needs you." Diego was saying, calm but absolute. "And I need you to be a pillar of strength for my daughter and granddaughter. This will be hard for you. So when you break, you do it now. Then we get to work."

"Where is she?"

The door opened. Nick stepped inside. I tried to sit up, pain knifing through my face, my throat, my ribs, until nausea forced me back against the cushions.

His face twisted, grief and fury colliding when he saw my pain and my bruised, swollen face. Two strides and he was beside me, kneeling. His fingertips traced the edge of my bruises, his lips brushed my swollen cheek so softly they barely touched.

"What happened?" Nick's voice was low and vibrating.

When I stayed silent, his gaze dropped to the floor.

"Let me in, Cat. Please." He looked back up, his eyes locking with mine. There was a dark rage in his eyes I'd never seen in him before. "I need to know who did this to you."

I hadn't wanted to involve him, trying to protect him from what I'd gotten myself into. That choice collapsed the moment I saw his pain, so raw, feral.

Everything spilled out of me.

Scotland and the Awakening. The girls and the Ring. I didn't spare him the worst. I told him how I'd drawn the life out of a man with my hands.

I faltered when I got to when Sal ended his life, how Diego had helped us clean the scene and bury the truth. If I told him this, I'd be sentencing him to the same fate as the rest of us. He saw my hesitation and put his hand gently on my cheek.

"All of it. I'm in."

I exhaled, letting the comfort of those words wash over me.

Nick sat through it all, unmoving. His eyes didn't blink. His hands clenched into fists, his knuckles turning white. When I finished, Nick said nothing.

He stood, no shouting, no sound, went outside, the door clicking behind him.

Through the window, I watched him stand beneath the live oak, moss swaying around him. His shoulders heaved, then his fists flew. Once, twice, again. Until bark split and blood slicked his knuckles. Each thud reverberated through my ribs.

Then it was over. He stilled, forehead pressed to the trunk as the tree absorbed his fury. He turned to come back inside, emptied. He came straight to me, bowing down to press his head against my chest. His body shook with silent sobs tearing through him. I wrapped my arms around him, cradling his head.

"I wasn't here," he choked. "I didn't protect you or our daughter. You're my everything, and I failed you both. I know it means nothing, but I'm sorry."

"None of this is your fault. Look at me."

He couldn't. His gaze stayed on the floor, shame carving lines into his face.

"Nick," I lifted his chin until our eyes met. "How could you have known? I didn't tell you."

"I should never have left."

"None of this is your fault," I repeated.

For a long moment he said nothing, then his chest hitched, and he exhaled a fractured breath.

"I've broken everything," he whispered. "I lie awake at night wondering how I ever let you go. How the hell I ever thought space would be the answer. I should've fought for you. I walked away when you needed me most." He dropped to his knees, grabbing my hands, forehead pressed to my legs, his voice splitting.

"I need you like I need air. You are the missing part of me, the reason my heart beats. If I could turn back the clock, I'd undo every silence, every distance. I'd replace them with all the words I should have said. I should have made love to you every night until your body ached for me when I wasn't beside you, which I plan to prove to you immediately. I want all those quiet Sunday mornings with you for the rest of my life. I'm here now, and I swear I'll never walk away again. Please let me fix what I've broken. Come back to me, Cataleya."

It was everything I'd starved for, every word I'd stopped believing I'd ever hear. In his truth, I saw my own failures mirrored back. I slid to my knees and pressed my forehead to his.

"It wasn't just you. I kept you at a distance. I watched you walk away, a decision that tore my soul apart. But those days are over. From this moment forward, there is only *us*."

When I kissed him, the man who was the other half of my soul, the world steadied. It wasn't only a kiss of forgiveness but a re-stitching of something unraveled, a binding tighter, stronger than before.

His fingers slid through my hair, drawing me closer. His kiss so delicate, I barely felt the burn of my lip. He kissed the bruises, the swelling, his lips so light like the wings of a butterfly against my skin. Even through the pain, desire rose, fierce and undeniable, fueled beyond flesh.

"When you're healed," he murmured against my mouth, "I'm not going to be this gentle."

I laughed, then hissed when the sting of my smile burned back. "I'll hold you to that."

He drew back just enough to look at me. The early light brushed across his face, catching the salt track on his cheek. His thumb traced the bruise beneath my eye, then softly across my lip. He gathered me against his chest, chin resting on my head, breathing me in.

"If she hadn't ended him, I would have," he whispered into the silence. "We get them all. Every last one."

I nodded against his heart. "Together."

Nick's arms tightened around me. His warmth pressed along my spine. His breath slid along my hairline, hot and uneven, the sound of someone trying to hold himself back.

"You're shaking," he murmured.

"So are you."

He laughed, low and rough around the edges. When his lips found mine again, the kiss was soft at first, then deepened, the kind that steals the air without meaning to. His hand slid to the back of my neck, fingers threading through my hair, holding me there, the taste of belonging. The promise that we were still here.

The kiss deepened slowly, careful and unhurried, his breath mixing with mine until the world outside the window vanished. Every exhale carried heat that sank beneath my skin. My hands found their way to his chest, where his heart thudded beneath my palms, steady. The tremor that ran through me wasn't from pain this time.

"I don't want to hurt you," he said against my mouth.

"You won't."

The words seemed to undo him. His forehead dropped to mine, his breath trembling. "God, I've missed you."

"Then stop missing me," I said.

He paused, searching my eyes for any flicker of doubt. What he saw there must have been enough. He brushed his lips along my jaw, the corner of my mouth, the tender dip at my throat. His smile curved against my lips before he kissed me again, deeper now. The weight of him pressed me gently into the couch, his movements cautious but hungry, as if he needed to relearn every inch of me without taking a single one for granted.

He stilled, catching my breath with his, both of us suspended on that fragile, burning edge between restraint and release.

"Not too much?" He asked, voice rough.

I shook my head. "Just enough."

He moved with me, fitting together, both new and familiar. It was warmth. It was home. His touch was gentle, learning me again, memorizing each place that still trembled. His lips ran along the bruises and new scars, meeting them all with tenderness as he made love to me.

When we finally dragged ourselves apart, my pulse was still racing, my body alive in a way it hadn't been in too long.

He rested his forehead against mine. "We start over from here."

FORTY-SEVEN

Nick

I DIDN'T REMEMBER THE drive. Didn't remember what radio station was on, or parking the car. All I remembered was the sound of Diego's voice in my ear, edged with an unusual apprehension.

"She needs you."

Not Jenna. Not the girls. Not even your family.

Cataleya.

The woman I'd loved since I was a gawky kid fumbling for her hand under the bleachers. The woman I'd let slip through my fingers, believing time and routine were enough to hold us together. The woman who had always been enchanting to me, even before I knew magic was real.

And now I'd seen her. Bruised. Bloodied. Her eyes clouded with pain and darkness. She told me everything. The kind of truth that pulled you under the riptide and never let you find the surface.

Scotland. Awakenings. The Ring. And what they'd done to our girls. To our daughter.

I came apart.

I hadn't known what true rage was until that moment. The kind that shatters everything from the inside out, that turns hands into weapons. I couldn't let that touch her.

I found myself outside beneath the moss-draped live oak in Salvia's front yard, hitting bark until my knuckles tore. I pounded until the world narrowed to the thud of my fists, and then when the thud slowed, I felt my skin and my heart and my breath return to me.

When I came back in and held her, I was a man who'd almost lost everything.

It all hinged on that moment. Whether she'd forgive me, whether she'd let me back. I would spend my whole life proving I was worth it if she let me.

She reached for me first. Fingers brushing the back of my neck, tentative, sure. The moment her mouth met mine, the world stilled. Even tasting salt and iron, that sweetness underneath was still my wife.

I was careful. Every place I touched was a question. Can I press here? Can I hold her close without making her flinch?

"I don't want to hurt you," I whispered.

"You won't."

Those two words broke me open. I kissed her again, slow and deep, my hand threading into her hair. She leaned into me, and all the guilt, fear, and need I'd been choking on slipped loose.

Her breath caught, her pulse thrumming beneath my fingers. I traced the bruise under her eye, down the line of her jaw, across the jagged marks on her neck. She tilted her head back, trusting. That trust undid me more than anything.

I moved with her, not demanding, just following. Heat rose between us, quiet and sure. Every kiss a promise. Every breath a prayer. When she whispered my name, it didn't sound like pain anymore. It sounded like forgiveness.

We fit together slowly, the kind of closeness that mends instead of breaks. I memorized the feel of her skin beneath my hands, the rise and fall of her breath, the way she looked at me as if I'd never left.

When she trembled, I stilled. When she pulled me closer, I obeyed. We moved with unhurried calm, reacquainting with each other.

Afterward, she stayed tucked against me on the narrow couch, her head beneath my chin, her heartbeat settling against mine. I brushed her hair back and kissed the crown of her head.

"We start over from here," I whispered.

Her reply was a satisfied sigh against my chest.

And I believed her.

Now, in the early morning silence, I lay on the narrow couch with Cat tucked into me, her breath warm against my chest, the scent of blood and bleach clinging to her. Even with all of that, she was my home.

My mind hadn't stopped spinning with what had been done to our girls, or the implication that this was way bigger than any of us could fathom.

Z didn't know any of it yet. He was still in Europe at some gallery showing in Berlin, I think. A career-defining show, the reason Salvia had lied to him. Part of me wished I could delay that moment for him just a little longer. Because when he learned what happened to Dahlia, to Salvia...

He'd burn the world down.

And I was going to help him do it.

Not merely for revenge, but for the retribution our daughters more than deserved. For our wives, the versions of them that would never come back fully intact. For the shadows they'd now have to live with. And for the strength it took them all to survive.

He and I could find the rest of them. We would make them pay. *All* of them.

I looked down at Cataleya. Even in sleep, her brow was pinched, as if her body couldn't let go of what it had endured. My arms tightened around her. I'd never forgive myself for letting her carry this alone. She'd never be alone again.

There was still Jenna. She'd been sleeping in Dahlia's room when I arrived, and now I couldn't stop replaying that image. Jenna curled in an oversized chair, still in the clothes she'd worn god-knows-how-many hours, phone in her hand.

I hadn't wanted to admit that I had known something had been wrong for weeks. She barely answered my texts. Hadn't called me back. Not since the night I left. At first, I thought she was angry with me. Then the silence stretched into absence.

She was like her mother in that way. When she was hurting most, she retreated into herself. That broke me more than anything else. She was hurting in a way I couldn't fix. I hadn't been there. I hadn't even known.

The sun edged through the blinds, golden lines across Cat's cheek. She stirred slightly. I brushed a knuckle gently along her jaw, careful not to touch the bruised parts.

Tomorrow, we would begin.

We would finish what she started.

And bring the rest of them to their knees.

FORTY-EIGHT

Cataleya

NICK HAD FALLEN ASLEEP next to me on the couch. We somehow folded into each other on the narrow berth of the cushions. His arms wrapped around me like a vise I didn't want to escape.

Soft footsteps padded quietly past into the kitchen. The sound pulled me from the haze between sleep and waking. The refrigerator door opened, washing the room in a cold spill of light. I slipped free of Nick's arms and stepped into the kitchen.

"Hey," I said to Sal as she drank straight from the juice container. "Super lady-like."

"Fuck being a lady." Her mouth curved into a half-smile that didn't touch her eyes. She screwed the cap back on and leaned against the counter.

"I see Nick finally came to his senses."

I nodded. Now wasn't the time for that story. The storm was still brewing inside her.

"Cataleya," she said quietly, "I want to learn. The Awakening. How to do what you did."

I hesitated. "Sal, you don't know what it takes from you."

"I don't care."

There was danger in her voice, cutting and alarming. A warning. However, a lifetime with my sister had taught me that trying to stop her was useless.

Our father walked in, going straight to the coffeemaker, not looking at either of us. He pulled down three mugs and started filling them. Salvia watched his back, suspicion still her second nature when it came to him. Now more than ever. She glanced at me and, without a word, turned and left us alone.

Diego put one of the mugs back, filled the two, then slid one of them across the counter toward me, careful not to brush my fingers.

I realized he'd kept his distance from me. Even in that tiny motel room, he'd never been too close to me. Come to think of it, he'd been distant since the party. It was another lash that hurt. The Awakening had already made people wary of me. What I feared most with Jenna. If my own father couldn't bring himself to touch me, what would my daughter think?

"You didn't sleep much, either," I said, pulling my hand back, wrapping my chilled fingers around the ceramic.

"Not since you were born," he muttered.

I blinked at him, unsure if I was supposed to laugh. Or if I ever would again.

He stared into his cup, the steam curling between us like a veil. "I wasn't always there for you and Sal. I thought I was protecting you both," his voice roughened. "There is more I should have told you. I hate that it took watching you girls walk through hell for me to realize it."

The muscles in his jaw worked as if he wanted to say more, but the words couldn't find their way out. Then he set his mug down and busied himself at the stove.

"I'll make breakfast before I leave to take care of the other *things*. You need food to rebuild your strength. Your mother always forgot to after..." He didn't finish. Just turned his back, shoulders heavy.

I let it go. For now.

There would be a time, soon, to have the conversation that was forty years in the making.

FORTY-NINE

Jenna

THE MOMENT SUNLIGHT CAME through the curtains, my mind snapped awake.

Mom and Tía Sal.

Dahlia and I had fallen asleep, and I hadn't heard them come back. I nearly tripped on the last step as I rushed to the downstairs guest room, where Mom had been sleeping since we came to stay here. The bed was untouched. Panic spiked. I ran, then froze in the kitchen doorway.

Mom sat at the island, sipping coffee from a steaming mug.

One side of her face was a ruin of bruises. Her lip split and swollen, her eye bloodshot, red spilling over where the white should have been. She winced as she tucked a strand of hair behind her ear, a gesture so ordinary it broke me. My mother, the same woman who used to scoop me up and spin me around the kitchen until I squealed with laughter, was hurt and centuries older in the space of one night.

My throat clamped shut, eyes stinging. "Mom?" I whispered, my voice cracking. "What happened?"

Her spine stiffened as she set the mug down. "Morning, hon. You're up early."

A second later, Sal stepped in behind her, pressing a hand to her temple where a ragged wound peeked through her pulled-back hair.

I glanced at Sal, who glanced at Mom, neither of them meeting my eyes, both saying nothing. Their silence crushed me.

"Are you okay?" My voice was confused and afraid.

Mom cleared her throat. "We're okay." She pressed a hand to her cheek, lips thinning into a fake smile. "It's nothing. Just a few scratches."

"Tía, what about you? You must have fallen over nothing together."

Sal's eyes snapped to Mom, anger flashing before she buried it.

They moved around me. Mom sipping her coffee, Sal reaching for a box of tea bags from the top shelf. Each gesture so ordinary, so impossible. My world had been anything but ordinary since the night I learned how cruel life could be.

I backed away, my heart thundering. "Fine. Don't tell me anything. I—I'm going out." I grabbed my jacket, Bramble's leash. "Come on, Brams."

They watched me go without stopping me.

Outside, the air bit cold against my cheeks. Storm clouds were gathering overhead, the wind heavy with salt. I tried to shake the images from my head as Bramble infinitely sniffed every piece of anything we passed. My mother's bruised face, Sal's temple, the indifference in their voices. It didn't add up.

Why hide this from me now? We were supposed to be in this together.
Mom had never outright lied to me before. Sal was never one to stay quiet.

I walked faster, boots crushing over damp sand, arms wrapped tight
against the chill both in the wind and in my heart.

Then my phone vibrated. Dahlia. A single link.

I clicked on it.

**BREAKING—"Victim Found Unconscious at South Shore Inn;
Assailant Still at Large."**

The headline blurred. I scrolled.

A woman in her early twenties was found unconscious, with no wallet,
no phone. Witnesses reported a scuffle. The girl told the police that
she and her friend had met a group of men at *Shadow and Silk*. She
remembered nothing after that. Police had yet to locate the men for
questioning.

My chest tightened.

South Shore Inn. Shadow & Silk.

The motel that was the last location on the moms' phones. The same
motel we sent Abuelo Diego to. It couldn't be a coincidence.

I stumbled backward, the wind knocked out of me. Bramble stopped
and whined, looking back.

I lifted my gaze to the dark, angry sky, piecing the truth together. My
blood turned to ice. Mom and Tía had said justice needed proof, but
they'd also said they'd do whatever it took to protect us.

I turned and ran.

By the time I reached the house, my lungs burning, the sun had vanished behind thick gray clouds. I threw the door open, Bramble close at
my heels.

Abuelo Diego stood at the stove, scrambling eggs. Tía Sal sipped from her mug, her temple a deep violet. Mom's cheek was now bandaged. They looked up at me with taut smiles.

"Hey," Mom said, voice steady, eyes wary. "Coffee?"

I closed my eyes, letting the truth settle in. They'd done this to keep us safe, to make sure the men who hurt Dahlia, and all the other girls, couldn't ever do it again.

That safety had come at a price.

I nodded, my voice low. "Coffee sounds great."

The quiet was over. From here on, we were all part of this, ready or not. In the aftermath of whatever they'd done, we finally had a voice.

As I poured hot coffee into a chipped mug, I heard another pair of footsteps come in behind me. I didn't need to turn around to know who it was.

"Morning," Dad murmured, stepping beside Mom.

Mom's tired eyes lifted, caught his. She rose onto her toes and closed the distance between them. He wrapped her in his arms the way he used to before our world fractured, and she leaned into him, chin resting against his chest.

My chest warmed. Relief, disbelief, even joy I hadn't allowed myself in weeks swirled together. I stood watching as they held each other, whispering words I couldn't hear.

Tears wet my eyes. I wanted to cheer, to laugh, to collapse into their embrace. Instead, I lingered at the counter. It was too beautiful, too miraculous to be real. My two broken worlds patched back into one. For the first time in a long while, *family* meant something again.

Dad glanced back at me, his eyes warm behind the weariness.

"Hey, kid," he said, releasing Mom.

I offered him the mug. "Morning, Dad. Welcome home."

"Pancakes?"

I smiled.

"Don't worry, I didn't make them this time."

After the dishes were washed and Abuelo Diego left to do some errands, Mom kissed my temple, gave me a quick hug, and nodded toward Dad. She pulled Sal and Dahlia with her, leaving the two of us alone for the first time since everything.

I hadn't seen him since the day he'd left. The same day as *Shadow &* *Silk*. It was literally the worst day of my life.

He sat at the island, shoulders hunched, staring at his scabbed knuckles. He'd lost some weight, dark circles under his sunken eyes.

My heart stammered as I refilled my mug and sat on the stool beside him. "Mom told you everything, didn't she?"

He swallowed and nodded. "Yes. She did."

"You didn't know before? Not until now?"

His shoulders flinched. "I didn't. When you didn't respond to my texts or calls, I thought you were shutting me out because I left. I never imagined..." His voice shook on the last words.

I closed my eyes, trying to still the guilt screaming inside. "I wanted to call you, I did." My voice trembled. "I should've been watching out for Dahlia. I should've been stronger. I knew Jared, and I still let him get close."

"None of that was on you. It should never have been your burden to bear."

"I just shut down. We both did. I pretended everything was fine. She could have died, Dad." My throat closed.

Those words broke open the anguish that I never really let take me. I covered my face and ugly sobbed.

He pulled me against him, letting me cry. He didn't speak, didn't try to fix it. Just held me.

When the tears finally slowed, I pulled back to look up at him. His own face was wet. He brushed his thumbs along my cheeks, wiping away my tears.

"I'm so sorry I wasn't here when you needed me most."

I pressed my face into his chest. "I'll always need my dad."

"You'll always have me," he promised, his voice breaking. "No matter what. I'm here to protect you and fight alongside you with everything I have."

More tears slipped free. "Thank you for coming back."

He kissed my forehead. "I never should've left. I won't ever again."

We stayed like that for a long time.

When Mom walked back in not long after, tears glistened in her eyes when she saw the two of us holding onto each other. She slipped her hand onto my back and leaned against Dad, his hand settling protectively on her hip.

Whatever came next, we would face it together.

FIFTY

Cataleya

V ENGEANCE WAS NEVER GENTLE.

In the days after the motel, we moved through a haze of dread, an unbearable hush, where every unspoken question pressed down like bricks on our chests. I kept waiting for the inevitable knock on the door, where we would find the police wanting to talk about our whereabouts, or the parents of the boy whose life we'd taken.

And Z was due to be home the next day.

When night came, I lay awake, searching the dark for what came next. Every bruise throbbed as a reminder of what still needed to be done.

Nick, with his relentless focus, had already started hacking Sebastian's phone. We weren't going in blind again.

We stayed at Sal's. One unit, one fortress, until Z returned. Maybe even after. Together, we were stronger. Especially because Sal was fracturing. She'd always been steel. Razor-sharp and unbending.

But under her cool gaze, I saw the hairline fractures. Her responses were clipped monosyllables, and she barely looked at me. Since that night, Sal refused to speak about what happened.

And Zion Eze, the gentle giant who lived for his two girls, still didn't know the whole truth. Only that Dahlia had been sick, nothing more. It wouldn't be easy for him, or us, to tell him everything that's been happening to the two loves of his life, his most precious masterpieces.

Sometimes I caught Salvia standing at the back window, still as stone, staring at the horizon as if the ocean had answers.

She was bracing to become. To Awaken.

Because Jared Allon was still out there. The one who whispered, *she's mine*. The one who drugged and raped my niece, who'd nearly destroyed my daughter. He was still free.

So were too many others.

The headlines remained prominent as the police intensified their search for Sebastian, Jared, and the others following a suspicious fire at *South Shore Inn* the very next night after the girl was discovered there.

That girl, the one we hadn't expected, had become our saving grace. Her story had sent the rest scattering into the shadows. If what we'd uncovered so far was even close to the truth, and God, it was only the surface, they had an entire network shielding them. A system built to protect men like them. A system that erased evidence with fire.

It also meant we'd have to dive deeper into dangerous waters to find them. And somehow do it without drawing the law to our doorstep.

Even in the silence, I felt it. A pressure at the base of my neck, a weight pressing between my shoulder blades. The sensation of being hunted. Somewhere in the shadows, Jared was watching. His rage unbroken.

If he didn't already know Sebastian's fate, he would soon enough.

Let them come. Let them see who they should fear.

The silence became a living thing, prowling through the corners of Sal's house. Even Bramble paced. The girls moved quietly, as if sound alone might crack what was left in us.

I caught Jenna watching me more than once, sensing change but not yet knowing its name. Dahlia stayed close to her, quieter than usual. They were waiting. For an explanation, for a plan.

It was Sal who broke first. She came into the kitchen after dusk, her hair coiled tight.

"We can't keep them in the dark," she said, her voice flat but trembling at the edges. "Not anymore."

I nodded. "I know."

We found the girls on the back deck, wrapped in blankets against the ocean wind. The sky had gone indigo, streaked with dying fire. The sea kept moving, relentless and dark, but even its rhythm couldn't ease the tension in their shoulders.

"Come inside," I said softly. "We need to talk."

They exchanged a look, then followed us into the living room. No one sat. We stood like four corners of a square.

"This isn't easy," I began, forcing my voice to stay steady. "There are things we still don't understand ourselves. But you deserve to know what's happening."

Sal crossed her arms, gaze locked on Dahlia as if trying to send strength to her. "It's about our family. Our blood," she said at last. "About something called the Awakening."

The girls blinked at us, confusion flickering across their faces.

"Does this have to do with someone named Kelly and the Auchter family line?" Jenna asked, recognition dawning.

"How..."

"An email came in while you were at the club. Kelly had sent a bunch of old documents about the Scottish side of the family."

"Kelly has been helping me figure it all out. I didn't know this existed until our trip to Scotland. Until it happened to me. I..." My throat went dry. "It was like the truth of who we are woke up. The women in our family are part of a bloodline that is powerful. They are called the Awoken. You're part of it as well. If you choose to be. But there are so many risks, so much we don't know. The Awakening isn't magic the way stories tell it. It's complicated, and it can cost dearly."

Jenna's brow furrowed, her voice small but clear. "That's why you've been so different."

"Yes," I whispered.

Her seeing it undid me. My eyes stung because she'd noticed. Because they weren't girls anymore. They were young women standing on the edge of their lives.

"It took me time to understand. I'm still learning. But I'm stronger now. More myself than I've ever been."

Sal looked at Dahlia, her steel cracked open just enough to show the flicker underneath. "I haven't Awoken, not yet. But when I do..." she trailed off, jaw set.

Dahlia's voice wavered. "Will it hurt you?"

"I don't know. But if my sister survived it, so will I." A smile cracked when she glanced at me, her defiant side surfacing, if only for a moment.

"What does it mean for *us*?" Jenna asked.

"I don't know, honestly," I admitted. "But whatever it is, it's already in you. In you both. I'd rather the two of you waited until we know more. The Awakening can be dangerous. And you've already been through so much. When the time comes, it should be your choice. Just promise me you'll give us time to make sure it's safe. The history that runs in our family, at least what we know of it, isn't all warm and fuzzy."

Bramble let out a soft whine, curling closer to Jenna's leg as if echoing my words.

The wind rattled the windows, the ocean breathing just beyond. In the flickering lamplight, their faces looked older than they should've, shadowed but unbroken.

And for a heartbeat, I saw it, the elements braided between us. Water and fire, earth and air, waiting, restless, inevitable.

I reached for Jenna's hand. Sal did the same with Dahlia's. "Even though we don't have all the answers yet, we're in this together. All of us."

Jenna and Dahlia looked at each other, an entire conversation passing between them in silence. Dahlia's fingers toyed with the edge of her sleeve, but her eyes gleamed with something I hadn't seen in weeks.

A spark.

FIFTY-ONE

Jenna

Bramble and I had barely stepped through the front door when the sound stopped me.

Music.

Dahlia's voice floated through the house from the deck, carried by the tender notes of her guitar.

She sat curled in one of the overstuffed deck chairs, barefoot, a notebook balanced against her thigh, her hair flying loose in the wind.

She hadn't played, hadn't sung, since *that* night. The melody was soft, unfinished. But it was *hers*. A thread of harmony stitched through pain with the kind of aching beauty only she could find.

I didn't even realize I was crying until a tear hit my wrist.

Bramble nudged the screen impatiently until I let him through. His paws clattered against the boards, and Dahlia glanced up, startled, then smiled. Small, brave, radiant.

I wiped at my cheeks and forced lightness into my tone. "How can you write with the wind blowing your notebook like that?"

"The wind is where I can breathe," she sighed. Her fingers found the strings again, testing another chord.

I crossed the deck and dropped into the chair beside her, Bramble pressing his head against my knee. I said nothing else, not wanting to break the spell. Just the sea, the wind, and the sound of her voice I'd missed so much filled the spaces between us.

Dahlia's hand stilled mid-note. "It's crazy, right? That the moms are... different? I mean, my mom has always burned hot, but now it's like she's ready to ignite. And Tía Cat is like water after a storm. Calm, but dangerous underneath. I can't stop thinking about it."

Her words sent a shiver through me. "If my mom is Water, and Tía Sal is Fire..." The thought swirled in my mind, searching for meaning that I'd been trying to grasp ever since Mom confessed everything about our strange and wonderful heritage, and all the possibilities that came with it.

"You'd be Earth. Always steady and grounded. And I'm definitely Air. Like music." Dahlia lifted her chin, her hair whipping. "What if the Awakening can change everything?"

Part of me wanted exactly that. Change. "If it can, then I want it to mean I'd never be powerless again. That I could do something when it matters most."

Dahlia's hand trembled on the strings, but she quickly steadied it. "I want it to give me back the music that was stolen. Not just the notes, or the songs themselves, but the part of me that made them. I want the nerve it takes to play without the shadow of that night clinging to every chord.

And more than that, I want to be someone who could fight to the death to keep that from ever happening again."

I reached across and took her hand.

Bramble let out a playful bark, pushing his colossal head into our joined hands to steal attention. The tension broke. We laughed. Real, unguarded laughter, a sound that defied the silence of our past.

"You're such an attention hog." I leaned over, rubbing his ears.

As Dahlia started strumming again, her voice gaining strength as she sang, I thought of my mother's transformation.

Since the Awakening stirred in her, she carried herself differently. There was a new strength in her now, a confidence that made her seem taller, more sure. She was still my mom, but she was also more.

Like water that had once been dammed, suddenly free to move as it was meant to, fierce and certain in its flow.

"Maybe the Awakening isn't just about power, but helping us become who we're meant to be. Even after everything tried to take it."

Dahlia smiled, the wind taking her hair in caresses against her skin. "If that's true, then I'm next in line."

I leaned back on the cushion and listened as Dahlia sang a heartbreaking song about love, strength, and refusing to break. She'd stop occasionally, bending over her notebook, pen scratching, guitar strumming softly.

The waves kept time. The wind carried her voice.

And for the first time since everything, a fragile hope grew, a tentative promise that the fractured pieces of our world were mending.

Fifty-Two

Cataleya

P UMPKINS AND TIRED CORN husks clung to verandas along the black ribbon of road. Autumn's festivity cheered the marshlands, where herons stood like statues in the still water, and wood smoke and sea salt seasoned the air. The scents of home, inseparable from my youth. Each mile into the Lowcountry was a deeper descent into memory.

Balmy evenings on the porch. Fireflies sparking like embers. The earthy sweetness after the rain. Familiar. Inescapable. Leading me home.

I needed my father. The lines etched on his face, the steady cadence of his voice, someone who could bear the weight of what we had done. Nick hadn't seen the blood, hadn't scrubbed the stains, hadn't wrapped death with us. Only my father could share that burden.

I found him in the garden by the greenhouse he'd built when we first moved in. A hobby that used to be my mother's. He looked up as I approached him, his hands deep in the soil of a raised bed. No judgment in his eyes. Only disappointment, which hurt worse.

"You girls have crossed a line," he said quietly. "Once crossed, you don't get to go back. I'm not saying you were wrong, but you'll never be the same."

"I know," I whispered. "Papi, I wanted it. To take his life. Make him pay. I don't know if I can control it."

When he stood, I reached for him for our usual cheek kiss hello. Diego stepped back. Just a fraction of movement, but enough for me to notice. He covered it with a sad smile and walked over to the iron garden table, busying himself with slipping off his gloves.

It stung more than I wanted to admit. I tried to be understanding. Maybe the Awakening had built a wall even my father wouldn't cross.

He shook out his hands as though trying to get feeling back into them.

"Your mother said the same thing once," he murmured.

"Mom did?" I turned to him sharply. "You never talk about her."

"Because when I do, I remember what I couldn't save her from."

I searched him. "*Save* her?"

"You should know the truth about your mother," he said finally.

"What truth, Papi?"

"She didn't leave because she stopped loving us. She left because of the Awakening. She saw it coming for you girls. Your mother sacrificed everything to protect you and your sister. And for what?" His voice cracked on the last word.

My chest constricted as the questions came faster than I could hold them. One especially. He'd known about the Awakening?

"What was she trying to protect us from?"

His hands trembled as he reached for my knee. Before he made contact, he withdrew, returning his hands to his lap.

"She tried to fight it once, for your grandmother, Ivy." He paused. "She thought she could purge the darkness. Instead... she killed her."

I gasped. "Mom killed her mother?"

"She didn't mean to. She was only trying to transfer it to save her mother. But it took too much. It always takes too much, as you saw for yourself. I swore I'd protect you from that life, but fate doesn't ask permission, does it? Now, Salvia... I'm afraid she's walking Ivy's path." He looked at me with a desperation I'd never seen before.

"Magic has a price, *Mija*. And it can cost *everything*."

I drove back to Salvia's, my father's words still echoing. There were so many more questions, so much more I wanted to know about our mother. But time wasn't on our side.

My sister would stop at nothing to bring a reckoning Dahlia more than deserved. She'd use everything, including an Awakening that had more power over us than we could've ever imagined.

Salvia was on the beach, cross-legged in the sand, her silhouette carved against the silver waves. Her fingertips traced slow, deliberate patterns in the grit. She didn't look up when I approached.

"I talked to Papi," I said gently. "He told me things about Mom and our grandmother, Ivy."

Still, she said nothing.

"Look, this is important. I know you're angry with me—"

"No," her voice was soft but seething, her eyes never leaving the tide. "I'm not angry. I'm furious. At the men who touched our daughters. At the universe for letting it happen. At the Awakening that showed you everything and changed nothing."

"Sal, I didn't know I could pull his life away," I whispered. "I didn't even know what was happening."

"So you said," she snapped. "You could have killed him. You *should* have."

"It would have killed you too. I'd never hurt you, Salvia. Ever."

Painful silence stretched again.

When she spoke again, her voice trembled with heat. "I want fire that burns away weakness. I want fury. I want *justice*."

"You want revenge."

"Same damn thing." She rose, brushing sand from her palms. "And I know how to get it."

My stomach dropped. "Scotland."

She met my eyes at last. "Whatever you found there, I want it. I won't ask it for guidance. I'll ask it for vengeance."

"Sal, please—"

"You had your chance. You used your magic to see. I'll use mine to burn."

Salvia pushed past me, and for the first time in my life, I knew I wouldn't be able to stop her.

At dawn, my phone buzzed on the nightstand.

Sal: *Please watch over Dahlia for me. I've gone to find the truth. Don't follow me. Not unless you're ready to finish what we've started.*

Her words confirmed the dread that had been building inside me. My sister was slipping away, stepping into a dense fog that took her further from the light. I struggled to type through tears blurring my vision, each word a desperate attempt to pull her back.

Me: *I'm with you. Always.*

I pressed the phone to my chest, whispering into the quiet. "How do I save you, Sal?"

The phone vibrated again. For a heartbeat, I hoped it was her.

Instead, my breath caught.

Unknown: *I know who you are. I saw what you did. Funny how the smell of bleach hangs on. Give Dahlia a kiss for me.*

Then came the photo. Grainy, dark. Salvia and me. Our father between us, dragging something heavy. His truck idling in the background.

My heart stuttered, a shiver scraping down my spine.

We finally had each other again. My daughter, my husband, and the family we'd glued back together. But Jared, and whatever else he was mixed up in, threatened to tear it all down.

I reached for Nick, groping for the anchor of his warmth beside me.

"Hey." Nick smiled, his voice groggy with sleep. As soon as his eyes focused on me, the smile vanished. He bolted upright. "What is it?"

"Jared. It has to be." The phone trembled in my hand when I passed it to him.

He didn't flinch when he saw the picture, but his body went rigid. His hand came to the back of my neck, gently pulling me closer.

"He took this from a distance," Nick growled, studying the picture. "Which means this little shit has been watching you."

"He knows," I said, my voice betraying me with a shake.

"We'll handle it." His voice hardened, his hazel eyes burning.

He pressed a kiss to my forehead and pulled me into his chest, where his arms locked around me with desperate protectiveness.

If only Sal were here. She'd know what to do next. Instead, she was somewhere across the Atlantic, seeking an Awakening that would either save us or damn us beyond repair.

Maybe both.

Nothing, not the law, not blood, not even me, could stand in her way.

She wasn't waiting for a reckoning.

She was becoming it.

Diego Ortega

T HE GARDEN HAD GONE still after Cataleya's car pulled away. The last hum of the engine faded down the road, leaving only the faint rasp of wind through dry palms and the whisper of the sea beyond the marsh.

Diego knelt beside the raised bed, burying his hands in the cool earth.

The soil had always quieted him. Even now, when his daughters carried burdens that couldn't be spoken out loud, it grounded him in a way nothing else could. Beneath his palms, the roots he'd tended all season clung stubbornly to life. Basil, rosemary, sage. The herbs Bloom had always favored, the ones she said kept away the shadows.

Sometimes, when he crushed the leaves between his fingers, he heard his mother's voice alongside Bloom's.

"La tierra siempre escucha," his mother used to tell him. *The earth is always listening.*

As a boy, he'd watched her scatter salt along the window ledges before summer storms, murmuring prayers into the wind so the lightning would pass them by. She'd claimed the herbs were far more important than just cooking.

Diego had spent years pretending he'd forgotten those rituals. But kneeling in the garden, the scent of rosemary heavy in the air, he realized he'd been repeating them all along.

He could see his Bloom here sometimes, in the way the light bent through the greenhouse glass. The garden was where she had thrived, always humming a song with no words.

He closed his eyes and let her come to him. An afternoon so long ago, in their garden behind their Appalachian house. The air was thick with honeysuckle and rain. Bloom's hair damp against his skin as they lay tangled between rows of lavender and foxglove. Her laughter against his throat.

He'd called her *Bruja*.

And she'd smiled before whispering, "Then you're my *Mallachd.*"

He remembered the fireflies hovering above them, the earth cool beneath their bare backs, the way she tasted like honey and cloves. They'd made love in that garden too many times to count. But that night was the night she'd told him about Salvia, most likely conceived in that very spot.

He opened his eyes, scattering the memory like dust in sunlight. Brushing the dirt from his hands against his jeans, he stood, knees stiff, the weight of years heavy in his bones.

Inside, the house breathed with the hush of evening, except for the floorboards that creaked under his steps. Photographs lined the hallway toward his bedroom. His girls when they were small. Bloom in one of his favorite sundresses. He paused there, studying her smile, wondering if she had known then what she was preparing for.

In his room, he sat on the edge of his bed, reached into the back of the nightstand drawer, and pulled out the letter. It was heavy in his hand as he stared again through the window at the rosemary and sage his wife, his Bloom, the love of his life, would have adored.

The letter was soft with age, its creases worn by his constant need to reopen the wound. He unfolded it slowly, careful not to tear the crease. He thought of lighting a white candle for peace and clarity. Instead, he let the sunlight fall across the page and read in silence.

Every word was etched in his heart, yet his eyes always returned to the same line, the one that cut the deepest.

Tell them I left. Let them hate me if it keeps them safe.

Diego's jaw clenched as he folded it carefully, as though shutting the words away might change them.

It never did.

"I'm trying, Bloom," he whispered. "I've tried to protect them. To keep it secret. To keep them innocent. But they're asking questions now, and I don't know how much longer I can lie."

Outside, the wind stirred the garden, carrying the faintest scent of sandalwood and clove, though neither grew there. An omen.

The leaves rustled again, and Diego went still.

The past was digging its way out.

He looked back toward the garden, where the wind moved through the rosemary like a whispering tide.

La tierra siempre escucha.

Maybe it was time to listen.

Diego exhaled, slow and steady. Carmen, his mother, the last who remembered the Old Ways, might be his only hope of leading his girls away from the darkness that would tear away everything they loved and cherished.

Just as it had done to him.

Blood opened the door.
Reckoning decides who survives.

RECKONING

Blood and Fire: Book Two

J. ELLE ROSS

Join the Inner Circle

Inside my **Inner Circle**, I share early access to new releases, ARC opportunities, deleted scenes, and exclusive bonus material.

There are pieces of this world I only share there.

The door stays open for those who choose to step inside the circle.

Join the Inner Circle today and receive an exclusive crossover story where Cataleya Ortega-Reynolds meets Sera Delaney:

https://jellerossbooks.com

Acknowledgements

Every book begins long before the first sentence is written. The *Renascence* series was born in quiet moments, in restless thoughts, and in late nights filled with questions about family, power, grief, womanhood, and what it means to begin again. Bringing this story to life has been both a joy and a reckoning, and I would not have made it here alone.

To my children and grandchildren, you are part of the heartbeat behind everything I write. You remind me every day why stories matter, why legacy matters, and why love always belongs at the center of even the darkest things.

To my husband, thank you for your support, for believing in me, and for standing beside me while I built this world one page at a time.

To my friends, thank you for loving me through the chaos of creativity, through the distracted moments, and the endless questions. Your patience, encouragement, and belief in me have meant more than I can ever fully say.

To my one and only Alpha Reader, Bonnie. You are my inspiration and my cheerleader, not only for every story, but for every step of life.

To the early beta readers, the kind souls who encouraged these stories and my endless "weird" questions along the way. Thank you for seeing something special in these pages and for helping me keep going when the road felt so very long.

To my grandmother, Carmen Helena Sarmiento. The strongest woman I have ever known. The woman who showed me what strength truly looks like. Everything good in me began with you.

A special thank you to the ARC readers and book influencers who volunteer their time to read early and share their thoughts with the world. Thank you for believing in these stories. Your reviews, posts, and encouragement help independent authors like me reach readers we could never find alone. I am deeply grateful for your time, your voices, and your support.

And always, the readers holding this book in your hands. Thank you for taking a chance on the *Renascence* series. Thank you for stepping into this world with me, for meeting these women, and for trusting me to guide you through their grief, their power, their fear, and their becoming. I hope something in these pages stays with you long after you turn the final page.

You've made my wildest dreams come true.

About the Author

J. Elle Ross writes from Southern California, where she lives with her husband, three loyal dogs, an ever-multiplying flock of chickens, and two turkeys who may or may not be on borrowed time. A NICU nurse by night and storyteller by day, when she isn't caring for tiny patients, she can be found wrangling grandchildren and chickens, tending her garden, and filling notebooks with ideas that refuse to stay quiet.

Also by J. Elle Ross

<u>Those Who Know Series:</u>

Someone Who Knows

The One Who Knew: Ella's Story

Those Who Know (Cinematic Chronological Telling)

<u>Renascence Series:</u>

Renascence- Bloodlines: Book One

Reckoning- Blood and Fire: Book Two

Resonance- Balance of Blood: Book Three

Reverence- Blood and Consequence: Book Four

www.ingramcontent.com/pod-product-compliance
Lightning Source LLC
Chambersburg PA
CBHW020139170726
47995CB00003BA/639